DYING for the HIGHLIFE

A DAN RENO NOVEL

DAVE STANTON

LaSalle Davis Books

This book is a work of fiction. Names, characters, places, and incidences are products of the author's imagination or are used fictitiously. Any resemblance to actual events or locales or persons, living or dead, is entirely coincidental.

Cover art by *Steve Whan*

ISBN: 0989603113

ISBN 13: 9780989603119

ALSO BY DAVE STANTON

Stateline

Speed Metal Blues

Dark Ice

Hard Prejudice

FOR MORE INFORMATION, VISIT DAVE STANTON'S WEBSITE:

DanRenoNovels.com

For Austin and Haley

Say you're on a wandering drunk binge. The year you spent on the wagon seems a lifetime ago, a life that ended when you came back to the bottle like a soldier coming home after a long war. You don't remember the day you decided to have a quick taste, just one, and then it would be back to your predictable, sober life. But there's no such thing as "just one," you always knew that, and you stayed drunk from that moment, as if it were the most natural process in the world.

Then you run out of money, taking odd jobs to stay afloat, until one morning you wake up in some unknown town out in the godforsaken Southern California desert. You crawl from your bed and step into the parking lot of the fleabag boardinghouse you call home. And for some reason, as you hike down the empty street to your day labor job, you suddenly take a hard left and walk straight out of town, out onto the ancient, sunbaked sand and rock of the earth's floor. You walk through the sagebrush and thistle, heading east toward the horizon, as if the vastness of the land holds some sort of mystical answer to your life.

Before long you fall to the ground and sleep in a patch of shade. Around noon you wake up, parched, confused, your lips so dry they've split, your hair gritty and hanging in your face. Automatically you trudge back toward the distant buildings that shimmer in the heat, sadly but stubbornly beckoning you back to a life you gave up on for no reason you can remember, and traded in for a bottle of whiskey.

But you're broke again, and you got to eat, so it's back to another day of bust-ass, miserable hangover work, with only the prospect of begging a front for chow and liquor to look forward to. That night, for the hell of it, you buy a two-dollar state lottery ticket, get drunk on a quart of beer and a half pint of cheap bourbon, and dream of an existence so farfetched that you almost cry when the gray light of dawn creeps through the ratty curtains in your room and wakes you from your drunken fantasy.

You walk down the deserted street with your head hanging from your shoulders like a bag of wet sand, and stop at the twenty-four-hour market to spend your last four bits on a cup of coffee. The clerk runs your Lotto stub through the machine, and you're halfway out the glass door before his frantic screams jolt you out of your stupor. You stare at him with bloodshot eyes, a Styrofoam coffee cup shaking in your dirt-caked fingers, the steam rising to your trembling mouth. And you listen to him tell you that you've just become a rich man.

1

THE CONFERENCE RECEPTION ROOM at Caesars was crowded with men in business suits. They milled about, talking in clusters of four or five, juggling beer bottles and little plates piled with meatballs and stuffed mushrooms. Most of them appeared gregarious and energetic, and they all seemed to be talking over one another, as if they were competing to be heard and recognized.

Out of boredom, I summed up the group from behind the bar. Salesmen, probably. Too well dressed to sell cars. Maybe they were in technology, or real estate, or stocks. Whatever their industry, it was obviously male dominated—there wasn't a woman in the room. I sighed, and tried to ignore their loud verbal jousting and artificial enthusiasm. Two men leaned on the bar and ordered drinks, their brows wrinkled, discussing some financial matter. I mixed their cocktails stronger than I should have, silently wishing them shot nerves and drinker's remorse. Then I poured myself a discreet drink, with the expensive scotch. On their tab, of course.

You could feel the atmosphere in the room change when the lady walked in, as if sunlight had cut through a thick fog. The hubbub faded as every head in the room turned in her direction. She had straight, dirty blond hair that fell over her bare shoulders and onto a silky blouse a bit too sheer to contain her breasts in a manner suitable for proper company. Her black skirt was more conservative, but still showed off her slim waist and the sweeping curve of her thighs. But it was her eyes, sparkling like dark diamonds above her high cheekbones, that really caught my attention.

She walked toward the bar, her hips swaying in a tantalizing rhythm. I couldn't help but stare, and she met my gaze with the beginnings of a smile on her sensual lips, or maybe it was a smirk.

The silence was awkward only for an instant, like a record had skipped, then the buzz of voices resumed. But it was obvious the room had a new focal point. Before she reached the bar, a tall, well-built man in a dark blue suit and maroon tie fell in step with her. His eyes were unnaturally green, his hair blond and perfect, and he moved with the confidence of a lady's man in his prime. He escorted her to the bar, his hand touching her elbow.

"Hello," he said, smiling to show off his expensive teeth. "Buy you a drink?"

He snapped his fingers at me without taking his eyes from her.

"Yes, I'd like that," she said, then plucked his hand from her elbow and flicked it away like a used tissue. "As long as I don't have to drink it with you."

"What?" he said.

"I'll make you a deal. If I need a pretty boy to run my errands, I'll give you a call. How's that?"

"Are you serious?" he said.

"I don't have time for fun and games. You want some action, go jump your secretary."

The man walked back toward his associates, who were watching him expectantly. He stuck his hand in his pocket like he was searching for some lost article, and smiled bravely, as if his nuts were in a vice and one false move would tighten the crank.

"Sapphire Martini, dry, three olives," she said. I mixed her drink and smiled.

"That was well done, ma'am. But this is a private party," I said.

"Aren't they all?"

I smiled wider. "Do you always crash company cocktail parties?"

"No," she said, sipping her martini. "I don't make a habit of it. And frankly, I don't have that kind of time to waste."

"I know of no better way to waste time than sitting on a barstool," I said.

"That's very witty."

"Yeah, I spend hours coming up with stuff like that."

"You're Dan Reno, right?"

I winced, as it occurred to me she might be a summons server, or maybe worked for a bill collector.

"Yeah. And it's *Reno*, as in *no problemo*."

"I'll have to remember that," she said, lowering her eyelashes and sipping from her drink. "So, Cody Gibbons gave me your name and told me where to find you. My stepson is missing, and I need to reach him as soon as possible. He was last seen here in South Lake Tahoe. Cody said you do this kind of work, and that you're the best."

"Cody Gibbons is a good buddy of mine, so his opinion's probably biased," I admitted.

"I hope I didn't drive all the way here for nothing."

"From San Jose?" I said. It was where Cody lived and where I used to, a four-hour drive from Lake Tahoe.

"That's right."

I pulled the stops from the three bar sinks and watched the water begin to drain, then looked at the lady. She was nearly beautiful, but up close the hard edge to her eyes was a distraction. So was the small pendant that dangled in her cleavage and touched her well-rounded breasts, which were held in place by the skimpiest of bras.

"My shift's over in half an hour. How about we meet in the casino lounge, over near the sports book?"

"See you there," she said, and she finished her drink and slid off the barstool. I watched her walk away, and I could tell by the way she strutted she knew everyone in the room was watching.

2

I ANNOUNCED LAST CALL and served another quick round, then closed the bar and headed out to the casino. The walkways were clogged with gamblers and the card tables and rows of slots were packed three deep. Waitresses glided through the crowds, balancing full trays of free casino drinks—rum and Cokes that tasted like watered-down caramel, syrupy gin tonics, and Vodka Collins I swore were spiked with cleaning fluid. People who live in Nevada know casino work is a sure thing, but also a dead-end gig. A large casino can generate staggering revenues and profit, but most casino workers are paid minimum wage, earn meager tips, and have to tolerate drunken, surly tourists losing money they can scarcely afford to part with.

The bartending gig at Caesars was something I took after my aspirations for a successful private detective agency in South Lake Tahoe became a sad delusion. The small mortgage on my wood-sided A-frame home now threatened to outstrip my monthly income, and I would be short on this month's payment. Unless I improved my financial situation, I'd have to face the grim prospect of selling out and moving back to the rat race, back to San Jose. So when the strange lady showed up, bearing the prospect of paying detective work, I didn't try too hard to hide my interest. Maybe this was the break I needed, the beginning of good things. I yanked off my clip-on bowtie as I approached the sports bar, and resisted the urge to drop it in a trashcan.

She waited at a table, the highlights in her hair glowing under the dimmed lighting. Three men at the bar had swiveled their seats outward so they could eyeball her more readily. I pulled a rumpled card from my wallet as I approached her. It'd been a while since I'd looked at my own card, and it suddenly seemed very plain and unimpressive. It simply read: *Dan Reno—Private Investigations.* I thought fleetingly if I might somehow improve the card.

"Let's start with your name, ma'am," I said, sitting and grabbing a keno pad to take notes. I wanted to get down to business, but when I looked up I was again struck by her, not only on a visual level, but more by a certain aura she projected. Her presence was no doubt sexual, but there was something beyond that, something classy and sultry but also hard edged and manipulative. I didn't know quite what to make of her. I got the distinct impression she'd be equally at home in a biker bar or at a highbrow party for rich socialites.

"I'm Sheila Majorie." She took my card from my fingers, studied it for a moment, then set it on the table and moved it aside with a red fingernail.

"Mrs. Majorie?"

"Miss," she said, looking at me so directly I felt she was challenging me to look away. I did, and watched her pull a pack of Virginia Slims from her black leather purse.

"Residence in San Jose?"

"Yes. That's where I live."

"Okay. So your son is missing."

"My stepson."

"Right. When was your last contact with him?"

"Oh, about five years ago."

"He's been missing for five years?"

"No, he hasn't been missing that long. Actually, it's only recently I've tried to get a hold of him. But I can't find him. The last I heard, he was here in Tahoe, gambling at Harrah's."

"How long ago was that?"

"Must have been five, six weeks ago."

"All right. His name?"

"Jim Homestead," she said, and her mouth tightened.

"Jimmy Homestead?"

"Yes. People used to call him Jimmy."

"I remember him," I said, then raised my eyebrows. "You're Sheila Homestead?"

She tapped her cigarette in the ashtray and slowly twirled the burning end against the glass rim, until the cherry was barely glowing.

"I used to be Sheila Homestead."

I remembered her too.

• • •

I had known the Homesteads back in high school, fifteen some odd years ago. They were a blue-collar family, not poor but definitely a rung below middle class. Jimmy Homestead and his brother Marty were both popular, seemingly happy kids, but it was general knowledge among my crowd that their father, John, was a heavy drinker and a less than ideal parent. Some years later I heard John Homestead had been conned by his younger brother into a bogus investment scheme, resulting in the Homesteads going bankrupt, and forcing them to sell their house and move into a low-rent apartment. I also recalled a high school rumor that circulated regarding John Homestead's wife, Sheila, a sexy-as-hell brunette who looked far too young to be the maternal parent of the two teenage Homestead boys. She showed up on campus one day, for some reason, smoking and wearing a tight leopard-pattern outfit, showing off a body that made the hottest girls at our school stare in wonder. Soon after that, it was rumored that for a hundred dollars, she would take you to a hotel room, and when you left an hour later, you would understand things about love and sex that would change your life.

Later, while I was going to junior college, I came to know the Homestead brothers a little better. Jimmy was a year older than me, and Marty a year younger, and both were tall, handsome men, with wavy blond hair and intensely blue eyes. During a series of seemingly endless summer keg parties, their popularity among the local teenage girls was admired and envied by the rest of us.

Eventually, Marty Homestead enlisted in the Marines and went off to boot camp, leaving Jimmy behind to entertain the gaggles of local females seeking transitory pleasure before settling into the predictable monotony of adult life awaiting most of them. It was around then I saw that Jimmy had a petty selfish streak and was also a compulsive liar. I overheard him boasting about his sexual conquests and going into detail about the particulars of his various partners. His tone suggested he felt he was an expert on the subject. But he started getting caught in so many lies it was impossible to know if there was any truth to his stories.

It was only on odd occasions I saw Jimmy Homestead after that summer, but over the next couple of years I heard he'd been caught stealing an expensive stereo system from a close friend, and later did thirty days at Elmwood when he couldn't pay the fine for a drunk driving conviction. When he was released from jail, he found the pink slip to his brother's car, sold it, then went into business selling pot, coke, crank—whatever there was demand for in his social circle. The last I heard of him was a few years ago. I was told he couldn't hold a job, had given a teenage girl a venereal disease, and was on the run from a drug dealer he'd burned for an ounce of coke.

• • •

"Why don't you start by telling me what Jimmy's been up to since high school," I said.

"Mostly taking after his father, I suppose."

"Can you be more specific, Miss Homestead?"

"Miss Majorie," she corrected, and her eyes flickered darkly. "I go by my maiden name. Can we get a drink in this damn casino?"

I looked around for a waitress, then went to the bar and brought her back a martini, and a bottle of beer for myself.

She sipped her martini and made a face. "This is terrible."

"It's a casino drink, ma'am. They're made with the cheapest bulk ingredients available. They serve them free to gamblers, who think they're getting a great deal. Drink it quick," I advised. "Don't prolong the agony."

"I got a better idea," she said. "Let's go where we can get a real drink. And if you call me ma'am again, I'll slap you silly. Call me Sheila."

"All right, Sheila," I said, but her name felt odd on my lips. "I know a bar you'll like."

Ten minutes later we pulled up to the Mountain Side Mine restaurant and took a table in the adjoining bar, the old Rosewood Lounge. She had sat quietly in my truck during the short drive up the grade, and she wasn't saying much now, as if she were perhaps reconsidering her agendas. She sipped her drink and gazed out the floor-to-ceiling windows, over the dark silhouettes of the pines, to where the lights of the casinos glittered. Beyond the casinos, the black expanse of Lake Tahoe stretched into the night.

"Nice joint," she said.

"It's a good place to relax," I said. The Rosewood was a venerable, elegant bar. The room was shaded in tones of dull green and rich timber, and the seating was private and shadowy. An antique chandelier cast a smattering of faint gold light over the cocktail tables.

"You were about to give me the background on your stepson," I said.

She turned toward me, and the edge to her eyes softened a bit.

"Jimmy was a kid that could have had anything he wanted," she said. "He had brains, he was charming and good looking, very athletic, and very popular. But at some point—it must have been when he was nineteen or twenty—it became clear to me he wasn't interested in making much of himself."

"That's a pretty young age for a parent to draw that kind of conclusion. Maybe he was still sowing his wild oats."

"Yeah, if sowing his wild oats meant ripping off his friends and dealing drugs. He also refused to get a job or go to college. Then he was arrested for DUI, and later for possession of a controlled substance. After that, he started drifting, moving from one town to another. I think he became a heavy drinker, like his father, and also I suspect he was hooked on drugs."

"Did you or Mr. Homestead try to help him?"

"I thought we should have intervened in his life. But John didn't have any interest."

"Didn't want to bother with his own son?"

"That about sums it up," she said, then her brow creased and she took a long breath. "I made a huge mistake in my life when I was a very young woman. I think I must have been looking for a father figure when I married John Homestead. I was seventeen and he was twenty-eight, and he had two sons from a previous marriage. At the time, I'm sure I thought he was very mature and dashing."

"But you found out otherwise," I said, sipping my bourbon rocks.

"Yes, I did, and then some," she sighed. "He was a violent drunk, and a stupid, gullible man."

"When did you leave him?"

"After ten years, ten really lousy years, I divorced him. I've spent the last twelve years rebuilding my life. It hasn't been easy."

I did the math in my head, trying to figure her age. Almost forty, if she was telling the truth. She didn't look it.

"My ex-husband caused me a lot of grief, both during our marriage and during the divorce. At one point I feared for my safety. But there's something else…" Her lips became a tight line, and she turned toward the windows. I studied her profile, thinking how perfect her features were, and then I saw her eyes were wet.

She dabbed at her nose with a cocktail napkin and didn't look at me when she spoke.

"Before he left home for good, Jimmy raped me."

I looked out the window behind her, into the black sky. I became aware of sounds I hadn't noticed before: the clinking of glasses, muted tones of conversation, piano music, and occasional laughter.

"Did you report it to the police?" I asked.

"No," she whispered.

"Did you tell your husband?"

She wouldn't look at me, and I sat and waited while she stared out over the forest at Lake Tahoe. Her eyes looked as dark and liquid as the surface of the lake.

"I never told anyone. Until now," she said, a network of tiny wrinkles emerging around her eyes. I picked up her martini glass and went to the bar for another round. I took my time, and saw her reapplying her lipstick when I looked in the bar mirror.

When I sat back down across from her, her face was cool and distant.

"It was a terrible time in my life. Do you really need to know any more about it?" she said.

"Not right now."

"Good."

"But I'll need you to tell me as much as you know about Jimmy's recent history. Where he's worked, girlfriends, running buddies, where he's lived."

"Hmph," she said. "He'd spent some time as a house painter—on and off, I suppose, but that was at least ten years back. I heard he's done some restaurant work too—washing dishes, and he's been a cook at times. I don't think he held any restaurant job for very long, though.

"What's the most recent job he's had, that you know of?"

"Well, he was working at a diner down in Barstow. That was within the last six months."

"I thought you said he was here in South Lake a month ago."

"Yes, that's what I heard. But I don't think he lived or worked here. I assume he was passing through."

"Where else has he lived?"

"After he left San Jose, he floated around California. He was in Sacramento years ago, and I heard he lived in LA and Fresno at some point. I also heard he worked at a lumberyard in Redding."

"Why do you think he's moved around so much?"

"Let's put it this way," she said, clicking her fingernails on the table. "I suspect he wore out his welcome pretty quick, wherever he was."

"Why's that?"

She looked at me impatiently, as if I should have known, then she leaned forward.

"Jimmy always felt he was special," she began, her eyes boring into mine. "He figured the world owed him some kind of special, glorious treatment. He was a smart kid, and had talent too, but he never figured out all that is meaningless unless you do something with it. He never applied himself to anything, never worked at anything, but just expected a good life would be his reward. He thought he'd be a professional golfer, or maybe a great musician, or some kind of superstar. The truth is, he'd always been a spoiled, lazy brat, and I don't think he's ever changed."

"Did you love him?" I said.

"He was my stepson."

"I see," I said, although I didn't. I wondered if she felt she was obliged to love him, a stepson who raped her. And then I wondered if she'd ever actually given birth herself.

I rubbed my temple. "Why do you want to find him?"

Sheila Majorie blinked and touched her chin with her finger. Her eyes shifted to the side, and when she looked back at me, I knew I wouldn't believe what she was about to say.

"Despite the past, he's my stepson, and I want to make sure he's okay, that he's not in trouble."

It was such an obvious lie I chuckled. Then I sighed.

"Searching for a missing person isn't cheap, Sheila. But if you've got the means, I'll find Jimmy Homestead, and it doesn't matter to me what your motivation is."

She looked relieved for a moment. Then her eyes became wider and her lower lip dropped.

"What is your fee?" she asked.

"Three hundred a day. Plus expenses. And I'll need two grand up front as a retainer."

"That's...that's a lot of money. I don't have that kind of money now."

"I'm sorry."

"I mean, all you have to do is make a few phone calls, and you can track him down, right?"

"Sometimes it's that easy. But I assume you already tried that."

"Yes, I did," she said, her voice small. "How about we talk about a payment plan, then?"

"I'd consider it if you'd be upfront about your reason for wanting to find Jimmy."

"I...I mean, he's my son. What more reason would I have than that?"

"He's your *step*son. A drunk, a drug addict, who's done nothing but leave a trail of grief in his wake. That's what you said, isn't it? A no-morals loser who raped you, right? And you want to pay an investigator to find him? Seems to me you'd be better off if you never heard from him again."

She became very still, and I could see her expression turn resolute. The contours of her face looked cut from stone.

"I can offer you ten grand total," she said. "Payable once you find him and arrange a face-to-face meeting for me. Nothing up front."

We stared each other down. "You can't afford two grand now, but you'll pay me ten grand once I find him?"

"That's right," she said.

I took the bowtie out of my shirt pocket and studied it, then carefully set it on the table. "How do I know you'll be able to pay me?"

"You're going to have to take my word on that."

"Shit," I muttered. I didn't trust her. But I wanted to because I needed the goddamned money. I knew that was a problem. There's nothing like a chump who wants to believe. That's the human dynamic that keeps con artists and sham companies in business. People throw away millions every year on weight loss remedies, baldness cures, exercise programs that promise the perfect body, and various get-rich-quick schemes. All because they're desperate and want to believe. So why, I asked myself, was I seriously considering Sheila's unlikely offer? I paused for a long moment, until I could answer the question in a way I thought was truthful: *Because I had no better prospects, and not much to lose.* That didn't make me feel particularly good, but at least I was being honest.

"Okay, Sheila," I said. "I'm not quite sure what you're up to, but you sign a contract and we got a deal."

3

HEATHER SANDERSON RUBBED COCONUT oil on her bronze stomach, letting her fingers linger over the smooth muscle beneath the skin. Then she applied the lotion to her shoulders and arms, working it evenly around the straps of her bikini bra. Lying back on the lounge chair, she closed her eyes and breathed deeply. The shadow of the balcony would soon fall over the small porch, and she wanted to enjoy the last available sun. The porch was tiny and afforded maybe two hours of sun a day—even less now that it was September. But she couldn't bring herself to lie out at the apartment complex pool, not among the snot-nosed, noisy brats, and their mothers with their cottage cheese thighs and saggy tits. Last time she tried, a group of middle-aged husbands were at the pool, showing off their fat, hairy bodies and sneaking glances at her, hoping to catch a good enough look so they could fantasize about her the next time they screwed their frumpy wives. It was almost enough to make her sick.

Instead, Heather lay on her chair on the small patio, eyes closed, imagining she was on a white-sand beach somewhere in the tropics, on a private stretch of coast, maybe in Hawaii or Tahiti. It was a favorite fantasy of hers, but it never lasted long because the sounds of cars in the parking lot or the neighbor's loud TV always ruined it for her. But today she was wearing earplugs, and she was pleased with the sensation. It made her feel as if she could be anywhere, as long as she kept her eyes shut.

"I see you're getting a lot done today, as usual," Eric Sanderson said, his voice startling her. He stood with his hands on his hips, blocking the sunlight.

"I love you too, babe," Heather said, resisting the urge to ask him what he was doing home so early.

"And the apartment is still a mess," Eric said. He went back inside, opened the refrigerator, and cracked a beer.

She lifted herself from the chair and followed him in.

"I take it the job interview didn't go well?"

"You might say that. Five minutes into it, the guy tells me I'm not what he's looking for. Can you believe that? I get all dressed up, drive out there, and he tells me that after five fuckin' minutes."

She watched him chug his beer and open another one. Yeah, get drunk, she thought. That'll fix everything.

He sat down and banged his beer bottle on the kitchen table, the loud noise startling her.

"You're gonna need to go back to the strip club."

"Bullshit," she said, heat rising in her face.

Eric scowled and pushed his tongue against his lower lip, the way he always did when he was angry. He was a good-looking man, but goddamn, he was ugly when he did that.

He stood abruptly, and she could see the muscles of his chiseled physique bulge under his white button-down shirt. He yanked his tie off, balled it, and flung it across the room. Heather wanted to move away from him, but she held her ground.

"What do you suggest we do for money, then?" he hissed. Heather kept her expression blank; Eric had gotten hold of some potent steroids recently, and his behavior was getting unpredictable.

"I'm gonna take a shower," she said, and started up the stairs.

"Yeah. Have a good time with your toys," he said.

She locked the bathroom door, peeled off her bikini, and stood on the tub so she could see her figure full length in the mirror over the sink. Looking at herself, at her tanned, naked body, never failed to give her a sense she could have anything she wanted. Her waist was still as slender as it had been when she was a teenager, her hips curved invitingly, and her thighs were smooth and muscular. She checked her breasts, accepting the tiny difference in shape between the two after the implants. It was okay—no one noticed but her, especially after the eye was engaged by her plunging tan line, which ended right above the nipples. She turned, standing on her tiptoes, and looked over her shoulder at her ass; she always thought her ass was the sexiest part of her body. Content, she stepped into the shower. Men would still kill to have her—at thirty-five, she knew she could compete with any woman on the planet.

She adjusted the shower head and let the water caress her body. Droplets formed on her breasts as the water streamed between them, running down over her navel and into her pubic hair. She ran her soapy hands over her tanned skin, taking a familiar pleasure in the feel of her curves. She knew men, shallow as most are, were prone to consider her a bimbo, or worse, a piece of fluff, as her husband had once called her. She let them think what they may. Few of them ever realized she was intelligent. In particular, she loved to read, and not just popular magazines. She also read romance novels, and the San Jose newspaper every morning. Heather didn't know many people who read as much as she did. Eric was certainly no reader—she was pretty sure he'd never read a book in his life.

While she showered, her mind replayed once more the brief newspaper article she had read a week ago, reporting that a San Jose native had won a $43 million lottery. The article stunned her. She knew the man—she had gone to school with him. And the memories were not fond. Jimmy Homestead was someone who had seduced her on a drunken night when she was a teenager. The result was a case of venereal warts, but that wasn't all. Jimmy also slept with her younger sister, whom he infected as well. Then the prick bragged to all his buddies about how he had boned two sisters in the same week. She heard he had made a big deal out of comparing and contrasting their technique in bed.

When she came downstairs, in jeans, sandals, and a sleeveless white shirt, she was focused and calm. Her husband sat on the couch, one foot up on the coffee table, the clicker resting in his palm. She sat on the couch next to him with her legs together and moved her blond hair behind her ears.

"I've got an idea," she said.

"Yeah, me too," Eric said, and fingered open the first button of his slacks. Heather could smell the beer on his breath, and she closed her eyes for a long moment. She figured he'd probably been watching a porno.

"Eric, I've got something I want you to read," she said, producing the neatly folded newspaper article.

"Why?"

"Read it."

Eric's eyes scanned the article lazily. Heather waited, watching his lips move every now and then.

"Jimmy Homestead!" he said finally. "I can't believe that lowlife prick!"

"Yeah, Jimmy Homestead," she said. "He—"

"Oh man, this ain't right," Eric interrupted.

She put her hand on his arm. "Eric, listen to my idea."

4

I WOKE EARLY THE next morning, to a mild hangover and a vague sense of unease. I'd driven Sheila Majorie to my house from the Rosewood Lounge to sign my contract, then offered her a drink and asked her more questions about Jimmy Homestead. She steered the conversation in other directions, and by our third drink she was snuggled next to me on my couch, her legs arranged so her skirt was situated well above her knees. I let my hand drift to the bare skin of her thigh, and she told me to behave myself, in the way women do when they really don't want you to. Regardless, I stood and again asked about Jimmy. Within a minute I was back on the couch, and this time she put my hand on her breast for a moment and whispered, "Be patient," in my ear.

Then she rose, signed the contract, and asked that I drop her off at Caesars. I did so, still with no good idea why she'd offered an inflated fee, payable only after I found her stepson. When I returned home, I had one last vodka and fell into bed, hoping she wouldn't torment me in my dreams.

After brewing a pot of coffee, I logged onto the website I subscribed to, and began searching for information on Jimmy Homestead. The site tapped into databases storing mortgage information, court records, business licenses, and other data sources the US government deemed open to public access. Although far less than 100 percent reliable, it usually allowed me to find basic information on a subject, such as recent addresses, phone numbers, income level, and criminal history.

Within a half hour, I printed all I could find on Jimmy. Not surprisingly, it wasn't much. As Sheila suggested, Jimmy lived mostly off the grid, meaning his public footprint would be less than your typical taxpaying citizen's. Two addresses were listed: one in Fresno and a more recent one in Barstow, CA. There was a brief reference to a DUI conviction. No history of property ownership. No record of having ever married. No data available on education, occupation, or relatives. Besides his address in Barstow, the only thing useful was a listing for his cell phone number.

I sipped my second cup of coffee and stared out the window behind my desk. The sun was well above the steep, tree-lined ridges to the north, the clouds sparse against the blue sky. I took my foot off the desk and dialed Jimmy's number. It didn't ring, but instead connected to a generic voice mail message. I tried three more times with the same result. His phone must have been turned off. Either that, or it was an old number no longer in service.

I called the number every fifteen minutes, between doing a half-hearted job of vacuuming and a solid hour of sit-ups, curls with a ninety-pound bar, and eight sets of bench press. Then I fixed myself a turkey sandwich and brought it out to the deck. A family of deer was grazing in the meadow beyond my yard, enjoying the last of the season's warmth. The sunlight filtered through the pines, the patterns of light shifting here and there in the breeze.

It was a fine, early fall morning in South Lake Tahoe, a day perfect for optimism and new beginnings. How tough could it be to track down a guy like Jimmy Homestead? Ideally, I could locate him without leaving town. But I wouldn't get paid until arranging a meeting with him and Sheila, and that might not be so easy, especially if he didn't want to be found. Although nothing Sheila said gave me reason to believe Jimmy was purposely off the air, I couldn't rule out the possibility. Missing people are almost always hiding. Or dead.

After finishing lunch I drove my pickup truck to the sheriff's complex off Black Bear Road. The air outside was fresh and cool in the shade of the huge old-growth redwoods in the parking lot. In contrast, the police station lobby was stuffy and cramped. I waited for Sheriff Marcus Grier, wondering how he would react to my presence. Not happily, once he learned what I wanted from him. But he owed me.

"Mr. Reno," he said when he walked into the lobby five minutes later, his voice all bass notes. He gripped my hand and smiled, a gold molar flashing against his black skin. Marcus Grier had a way of putting people at ease—he always made me feel as if we'd known each other for longer than we had. He was also the type who remembered names, and I appreciated the fact he pronounced mine correctly.

"Good to see you, Marcus. You're looking fit."

"Hey, thanks for noticing. Lost twelve pounds so far."

I followed him back through the bowels of the structure to his office. Grier was close to six feet, but his body was puffy, like an overfilled inner tube, and it made him look shorter. His sheriff's cap barely covered his jumbo-sized head, and his beige short-sleeve shirt and green-striped pants seemed a size too small. But I'd learned long ago to not underestimate men with comic proportions. A few weeks back, I'd watched Grier wade into a drunken brawl at Zeke's Pit and single-handedly remove half-a-dozen snowboarders who were expending their off-season energies by using the bar as their personal boxing ring. Grier threw them out of the place by the scruff of their necks, as if they were puppies. The rowdiest of the group, a young man with a Mohawk hairdo, threw a wild punch at Grier and found himself slapped into an arm lock and begging for forgiveness.

"How's the private investigations business?" he asked from behind his desk.

"Been slow."

"The demographics aren't in your favor is my opinion," he said. "Half the population up here is transient. Mostly kids, come up here for the winter, work at the resorts or casinos for a ski season or two, then move on and settle somewhere they can find a more permanent job. You also got a high population of Mexican immigrants, here to work the restaurants and other low-wage jobs. If you're relying on lawyers to hire you, we only have a handful in town, that's about it."

"I probably should have considered that before I moved up here, is that what you're saying?"

"Lake Tahoe's a great place to live. The challenge is making a living here."

"Tell me something I don't know."

The phone on his desk rang, and Grier punched a button and it went quiet. "What can I do for you, Dan?"

"I'm working a missing person case. I need to ask a favor."

"What kind?"

I pulled myself up in my seat. "You told me once you had a connection at a credit bureau that could provide credit card transaction records."

I heard his feet shuffle underneath his desk. "That was related to an official police investigation."

"I know."

Grier frowned, then said, "Did you ever hear again from Beverly?" The sympathy in his tone made me uncomfortable. My twenty-two-year-old live-in girlfriend had left me a few months back. Grier was happily married, and he and his wife had thought Beverly was a great gal. So did I, until she ran off with a waiter from a local steakhouse.

"How about it, Marcus?"

"Dan, I'm in your debt. You put your butt on the line, and I might not be here if it wasn't for you. But doing this sort of thing creates issues for me. I'll do it this once, but it will be the last time."

"Fair enough," I said. "The guy's name is Jimmy Homestead."

Grier told me to give him a couple of hours, then we spent a minute chatting about our shared history, a positive subject I suppose, though it damn near killed me, and left a case of frostbite on my toes that sent me reminders every time the temperature dropped below fifty.

I had visited Tahoe for a wedding last winter, while I still lived in San Jose, and was hired to investigate the murder of the groom. A corrupt county sheriff out of Placerville was impeding the case, and in the course of events, he fired Grier. During the investigation, my car was destroyed when I was run off the highway outside of Truckee, then I was handcuffed and nearly drowned. When I finally caught up with the county sheriff, I took a round from his .38 against my Kevlar flak jacket before I hit him with a cross-body tackle. I busted his nose and knocked out one of his teeth, and in my rage I might have killed him, if not for Cody Gibbons arriving and shot-putting him over a truck. The sheriff left town after his crimes were discovered, and was executed in a mob-style hit a month later. Grier was rehired as sheriff, and I came out of it with enough cash for a down payment on an upgraded A-frame cabin a mile off the lake.

I drove from Grier's office out to Highway 50, heading away from the casinos and restaurants that were the anchor of South Lake Tahoe's economy. A few minutes later I pulled into my driveway, the pine needles from the two trees in my front yard crunching under my tires. I kept busy working around the house for the next few hours. When Grier called late in the afternoon, I was replacing a board in my fence that had been mangled by critters, maybe raccoons, or a coyote seeking passage.

"This guy Jimmy Homestead must be swimming in dough," Grier said.

"Huh?"

"Yeah, get this. He bought a Lamborghini at a dealership in Orange County a couple weeks ago. Bought it on his credit card. Total came to a hundred sixty-eight thousand dollars."

"Really?"

"There's more. He rang up thirty thousand dollars in other purchases. Looks like he bought himself a new wardrobe and some jewelry at Nordstrom's in Los Angeles. And look at this, he charged fifty-five hundred at the one of the brothels in Carson City."

"When?"

"A week ago."

"Any hotel charges?"

"He was staying here, at Harrah's, last week. But since they already charged him, it seems he's checked out."

I thanked Grier and said I'd come by to pick up the reports. Then I sat and considered the information. A $168,000 Lamborghini? It was preposterous. Jimmy Homestead was the kind of guy who talked about fancy cars, not owned one. Where could the money have come from? I guess he could have pulled off a major score on a cocaine deal. It didn't seem likely, though; I couldn't imagine Jimmy having the brains or balls for it. Or maybe he'd become a gigolo for a wealthy old lady. That was possible, but seemed farfetched.

I went to my desk, did a Google search on Jimmy Homestead, and got my answer. A brief newspaper article came up, reporting that four weeks ago, Jimmy Homestead had won a California State Lottery prize of $43 million. I was stunned for a moment. "Well, that explains that," I said out loud, sipping coffee and staring out my window. What would a guy like Jimmy Homestead do with all of that money? Based on my recollection of him from fifteen years ago, it was feasible he might blow through it in a couple of years. Sheila Marjorie's account of his life also suggested Jimmy would probably not take a prudent approach to money management. His new car and his other purchases, including over five grand at the bordello, seemed to indicate Jimmy was on a roll. I imagined he was partying up a storm—booze, blow, and expensive hookers.

It now seemed pretty clear how Sheila intended to pay me. Obviously she knew Jimmy had run into a windfall, and she intended to get him to share the wealth. I was curious why she wouldn't tell me about it. Maybe she thought I'd double my rates.

Half an hour later, I returned home with the reports from Grier. I pored over the papers, plotting Jimmy's activity over the last thirty days, searching for some pattern that might reveal his whereabouts. He seemed to be bouncing around California and Nevada like a pinball. I finally set the records aside and took off in my truck, heading east across the border into Nevada, settling in for the forty-five-minute drive over Spooner Pass to Carson City. My destination was the last place the records showed Jimmy had used his credit card: the Tumbleweed Parlor Ranch.

5

IT SHOULD HAVE BEEN a happy day for Mort Homestead. After five years in the state prison at Folsom, his parole was granted. They kicked him free with the clothes on his back, forty-eight dollars cash, and a ride to the bus stop. The guard in the prison van gave him a hard look as Mort stepped out onto the street.

"You think you're something special," the guard said. "You ain't."

"Go back to your job. It's your calling," Mort said, his eyes pale green under his thin eyebrows.

"Good luck out there, asshole," the guard sneered. The van pulled away in a wash of gravel and exhaust.

Mort stood at the bus stop, internalizing the brief exchange, filing it away as fuel for future situations. It was a mental practice he'd learned at a young age, at first to deal with his father, and later as a response to the myriad frustrations of his teen years. Every denial he suffered, every woman who rejected him, every person who didn't cooperate—Mort stored it all, saving it as an energy source for when it was needed.

For his first three weeks in Folsom, each day had been a proving exercise. As a forty-three-year-old white man convicted of investment fraud, he was an obvious target, a white-collar criminal thrust into a jungle of predators. The facility was divided into camps run by the Black Guerrilla Family, the Mexican Mafia, and the Aryan Brotherhood. They ruled via intimidation and swift violence. The penalty for the slightest disrespect was generally a severe beating, if you were lucky, or if not, a gang rape. Of course, the latter also could occur without provocation. Mort was attacked by a group of black inmates his first week, and while defending himself bit off one of his attacker's ears. The next night they came for him again. This time Mort was prepared with a knife he bought from a fellow inmate. He nearly castrated one man and cut off another's thumb.

It didn't take long for the rumors to spread. Mort Homestead was a psychotic loner who was quick with a knife if provoked. Yard wolves sought out younger, easier victims. The gang members kept their distance and watched him warily. Mort didn't fraternize much with the inmates, whom he generally considered a lower life form. But at times it was necessary to reinforce his reputation, and once, during a fight with a drug-crazed Mexican, Mort's cheek was sliced open. He still wore the scar, like a diagonal second mouth.

Mort didn't wait for the bus. Instead, he walked six miles east, pacing steadily toward the foothills, away from Sacramento. Eventually he left the road and hiked into the rolling hills. He strode with a single-minded purpose, and though the midday sun was hot, he did not stop to rest in the shade of the oak trees, even after his feet began to blister in his loafers. Sweat soaked through his shirt, and he stripped it off and let the sun beat down on his shoulders and back. His muscles glistened, taut and corded from hours of mindless prison workouts. He shaded his eyes from the sun and kept walking.

He didn't stop until he reached the base of a large oak on a small rise. He stepped off ten paces north, stopped at the three rocks he had left there, then continued through some scrub into a gully where he'd hidden a shovel. Mort went back to the spot and began digging into the hard, crusty ground. It took over an hour, but finally the shovel hit a small steel box.

Mort pried it from the earth and opened it. The canvas bag was still there, with the $7,000 in cash Mort had stashed before the courts confiscated his bank accounts, cars, and real estate.

A couple of hours later he was on a bus, heading into Sacramento. He got off and walked to the Hilton near the state capitol building.

The clerk at the reception counter was a man of mixed race in his twenties. He looked up as Mort approached and wrinkled his nose.

"A room, please," Mort said.

"Sir, this is a business-class hotel, and we have a dress code."

"I'm aware of that."

The clerk felt Mort's eyes staring into his, and he involuntarily stepped back.

"Yes, then. I'll need to see a credit card to cover incidentals."

"I'll give you a cash deposit."

"Sir, we typically…"

"What's your name?"

"My name?"

"Is there something the matter with your hearing?"

The young man opened his mouth but could only manage a confused sputter.

"You want to leave your name out of it, fine. Here's enough cash to cover the room and a deposit. Get me a key, please."

"Yes, sir," the clerk said, deciding he wanted this man away from the counter as quickly as possible.

Mort took the elevator to his room and went inside. He washed his face over the sink, then lay on the bed. He expected he'd be tired, but after a minute he rose, sat at the desk, and again considered the blend of fate and circumstance now directing his future. He had learned of his nephew winning the lottery while in prison. What strange cosmic alignment would result in a worthless dirtbag becoming vastly wealthy, while a rich executive loses everything and rots in jail? The world was a mysterious place. People suffered undeserved fates all the time.

He picked up the phone and dialed the number for his older brother, John Homestead. Mort was mildly surprised when John picked up.

"Well, I didn't think you'd be home, but I figured I'd try anyway," Mort said. "I thought you'd be working, but looks like I was wrong."

"Who is this? Is it...Mort?"

"That's right, John, it's your long lost brother."

"You calling from Folsom?"

"No, they released me today."

"They did, huh?"

"Yeah. Thanks for staying in touch."

"I find it funny you'd think I would."

"Five years in that shithole, and you couldn't be bothered to pick up the phone?"

"I don't want anything to do with you, Mort. I don't think I can put it more plainly than that."

"We're brothers."

"You know our status," John said. "You going to prison hasn't changed a thing."

"You gonna hold a grudge against me forever?"

"Listen to me. I was stupid to trust you on your swindle. It bankrupted me and screwed up my existence beyond repair. But I've moved on in my life."

"You need to get over yourself," Mort said.

"You got to be kidding."

The phone went quiet, then Mort said, "So, have you talked to Jimmy?"

"Why?" John said.

"I don't know, John, seeing how all you ever did is complain about money, I think it's an obvious question."

"Maybe your time in jail has left you with some wires disconnected."

"No, I'm thinking real clearly."

"Then spell it out, Mort, because I'm ready to hang up."

"The California Super Lotto was forty-three million a month ago."

"Who gives a shit?"

"You're telling me you don't know?"

"About what?"

"The little dipstick hasn't told you, huh? Jimmy won it, John. Forty-three million bucks."

"Yeah, sure he did. You know what, Mort? I'm not as gullible as I used to be. I think this is another one of your scams. I don't believe a damned thing you say."

"Hey, don't take my word for it. Contact the *San Jose Mercury*. They wrote an article about it. You know what's funny, John? Your own son wins forty-three mil and won't even cut his old man in for a few hundred grand. You must feel real special about that. Kind of makes you want to revisit the whole concept of fatherhood, huh?"

"Don't ever call here again," John Homestead said, and hung up.

Mort stood and laughed out loud for a long time, holding his stomach and wiping tears from his eyes. Then he sat back down at the desk and considered his next move.

• • •

After slamming down the phone, John Homestead found and printed the online article, and read it over and over while pacing around his small apartment. His hands were shaking and he couldn't make them stop. Finally he took a long drag from a bottle of gin, and that helped. He sat on his couch, closed his eyes, and tried to meditate, the way his shrink had taught him, but a minute later he was walking from room to room, as if searching for something. Another belt of gin calmed him a bit more, and he started to sort through it all.

Hours passed, and the apartment became dark. John turned off the old Super 8 projector he'd set up on the coffee table and stacked the reels scattered about. It had been many, many years since he'd watched those movies. The images on the old celluloid seemed to be from someone else's life. He could barely even recognize himself—lean and tanned, a confident smile under a full head of blond hair, his sexy second wife next to him—god, what a piece of tail she'd been! And his sons, Marty and Jimmy, throwing the football, opening presents at Christmas, hamming it up for the camera. Christ, had he really lived that life? Had he been happy then? He looked happy, but he couldn't remember how it felt.

He took another swig off the bottle and stared into the darkness. So much he once had, and so much he'd lost. Looking back over his fifty years, it seemed unreal that after all he'd been through, he'd end up with nothing. He once had money and a young, gorgeous wife, and he smiled at the stirring in his groin as he thought of her. But his smile faded quickly, because no woman would have him now—a fat, aging man without a pot to piss in.

And his kids—his two boys, Marty and Jimmy. Poor, innocent Marty, not a hurtful bone in his body. Not real smart, but such a sweet kid. Marty the pleaser, always did his chores without being asked, never a problem in school, just a kid who wanted to make his parents happy. But now he was dead, no-luck Marty, one of the few American casualties in the Gulf War. He'd been a little too anxious to please his commanding officer, and he died by a sniper's bullet in Kuwait. No one else in his battalion was even wounded.

But Jimmy wasn't like that; he was almost the polar opposite of Marty. Smart but lazy, Jimmy always found a way to shirk his responsibilities, never wanted to work, just wanted everything handed to him. Nothing was ever his fault, no, and when the going got tough, Jimmy would be the first to fade. And he had a mean, jealous streak—he was a me-first, screw-everyone-else person. John Homestead shook his head, trying to come to terms with his turmoil of emotions, because he had once been the same way. And now he was alone, in poor health, and nearly destitute. Perhaps it was all his fault. If so, he accepted it. But he couldn't find a rationale to justify the behavior of his son, who had won a $43 million lottery and hadn't called his father.

Finally John turned on a light and went to his bedroom closet. Without fully knowing why, he reached to the high shelf and found the hard plastic case that held his pistol.

6

A LITTLE BEFORE NOON, Tony Sanzini walked out of his mother's house to get the mail. Among the bulk ads and a few bills (all his mother's, since she paid the utilities) was a plain white envelope addressed to him in chicken-scrawl penmanship. There was no return address, but he recognized the handwriting of his old buddy, Peco Gomez, who was serving a ten-year jolt in Soledad. Sanzini sat down at his mother's kitchen table and opened the letter.

Hey Sanzini,

Remember that douchebag Jimmy Homestead who ripped off your stake? I just read in the paper he won a $43 million lotto. Couldn't have happened to a bigger asshole, huh? Anyway, just thought I'd give you a heads up. Might be a good time to go collect that two grand he took you for.

Good luck, amigo.

Sanzini read the letter three times. Then he smashed his fist through the wall. The old sheetrock collapsed in a cloud of dust, leaving a jagged hole.

"Where is he?" Sanzini said. He had a habit of talking out loud when no one was around. Sometimes he engaged in long, animated conversations with himself. He considered this habit indicative of higher intelligence.

Occasionally he would try to use a vocabulary word he picked up from a daytime television show. His latest word was "inevitable." He was still a little vague on the meaning, but he thought it was an impressive word. He pronounced it "enviable."

The situation clearly called for action. So Sanzini put on his black leather chaps and vest, got on his hog, and roared around the corner to Little Otto's, his local hangout. The bar was one of San Jose's dozens of anonymous dives, and it had stayed steadfastly in business decade after decade, immune to economic cycles, development trends, and Northern California's fashionable culture. Sanzini swung the door open, and the noon sunshine flooded the joint, revealing stained and threadbare carpeting, the battered wood facing of the bar, and the backs of the day drinkers. Oakland Raiders posters from long-forgotten seasons were faintly visible through motes that danced in the shaft of unwelcome light from the doorway.

"Close the fuckin' door, Sanzweenie," a voice called out.

"Bite me, Rancour," Sanzini said to Garrett Rancour, taking a seat beside him. "I ain't in the mood for any shit today."

"What's up your ass?" Rancour asked.

Sanzini glared at him as his eyes adjusted to the gloom. Rancour had boasted he could bench press four hundred pounds when he was released from jail six months ago. Though he was only about five foot nine and 170 pounds, there was no question he was unusually strong—he had a sort of unpredictable, wiry energy about him. Still, Sanzini outweighed him by at least fifty pounds and he knew he could kick Rancour's ass if he wanted to. He also knew much of what Rancour said was bullshit, and the claim of benching four hundred was a lie. But Rancour had a crazy light in his eyes, and when he said he feared nothing and didn't care if he died, Sanzini felt there was a good chance that was true. It made him wary of Rancour, and so he tolerated Rancour's smartass attitude, to a point, and let him get away with remarks that from anyone else would result in a Sanzini down-for-the-count right cross.

"Go bother someone else, Rancour," he said.

"Hey, man, lighten up. I'm just catchin' a buzz, having a good time."

"What are you using to pay for your drinks?" Sanzini knew Rancour had quit his warehouse job about a month ago.

"You know me, I'm resourceful."

Sanzini looked around the bar. He recognized most of the people there. At noon on a Tuesday, the crowd was made up of old drunks, two Mexican guys drinking beers and eating their brown-bag lunch at a table, and a couple of teenagers the bartender let drink because they tipped well.

"Resourceful, huh?"

"You got it," Rancour said.

"So, how would a resourceful guy like you go about tracking down someone owed you money?"

"How much money?"

"None of your damn business how much."

"Whatever, then," Rancour said. "Finding somebody ain't hard, if you know how to go about it."

"Yeah, right. And you know how to go about it."

"I'll tell you this—if someone owed me money, I'd find them and they'd pay, quick like."

Sanzini felt a surge of irritation at Rancour's flippant tone. The man had a way of talking down to you, as if he were something better than a low-life parolee. Sanzini wanted to tell him to piss off, and then go sit at the other end of the bar and drink shots of Jack Daniels until he didn't give a shit. But he only had five bucks in his wallet. Besides, Sanzini needed help and wanted to hear what Rancour had to say.

"How would you find them?" Sanzini said.

Rancour paused, and took a slow draw off his beer.

"I'd know who to call."

"Who?"

"I got this buddy. His uncle works for a big security company. My buddy caught him humpin' this young slut who works there, so he can basically get all sorts of information, in return for him keeping his mouth shut."

"Hmph," Sanzini snorted.

"Be skeptical, I don't give a shit." Rancour slid off his barstool and ambled toward the jukebox.

"Wait a minute," Sanzini said. "So this buddy of yours can get the low-down on somebody, make it easy to find them?"

Rancour turned back toward Sanzini. "If it's worth it to him, sure he can. 'Course, I need to be cut in on the deal too, right?"

Sanzini stared back at Rancour and after a moment he said, "Right. Let's call your buddy."

7

JIMMY HOMESTEAD WAS GETTING burnt out on whores. Ever since hitting the big time, he'd been screwing the most beautiful pieces of ass money could buy. He'd spent most of the last three weeks whacked out on top-shelf booze and Colombian flake and humping his brains out. But the hooker he just had delivered to his suite at the Mirage in Vegas had been a total bitch. Jimmy recognized her disposition as soon as she arrived. The surly woman wanted to service him for five minutes and then split with his five hundo. Her attitude was a total turnoff, and Jimmy couldn't get it up, and eventually he had to call security when she demanded to be paid.

Afterward, Jimmy sat at the Mirage's oasis-themed lounge, surrounded by plastic palm trees and artificial waterfalls. He ordered a nine-dollar cocktail and crunched the ice cubes between his molars. His anger over the surly whore had subsided, leaving him in a contemplative mood. The possibilities and potential for his life were limitless. But he was feeling empty. The sensation had been gnawing at him for a couple of days now, especially during the brief interludes when he was relatively sober.

"Hey, man," Jimmy said to the bartender, a short Hispanic man in his fifties. "You mix a good cocktail, man, here you go." Jimmy pushed a five-dollar bill across the bar. The barkeep looked at him with blank eyes and nodded briefly.

"Listen, I'm like looking for investment opportunities. I'm thinking maybe investing in this place, the Mirage. Maybe buying it. You know who I would talk to?"

The bartender glanced up from the glasses he was washing. "I would have no idea."

Jimmy watched the man walk away and felt a quick flash of anger. Didn't the bartender know who he was? Christ, he'd dropped fifty grand at the tables last night and had the Mirage's general manager kissing his ass, offering him a complementary room, practically begging to lick his balls. He was no doubt the richest man in the joint, a genuine VIP. And here he was, dealing with snotty hookers and brain-dead bartenders.

Two women walked into the lounge and sat at a cocktail table. One was about thirty, a dark-haired thing with full breasts and nice legs. The other looked a couple of years older, blond, short, and slinky. She had a tough look to her, like she'd been rode hard and was maybe a drink or two away from being up for another ride. Jimmy felt his crotch react to the thought. It was four in the afternoon, and the unhappy noontime episode with the prostitute had left him unfulfilled.

He turned around fully on his barstool, rested his elbows on the bar, and stared frankly at the ladies. They glanced his way, and he smiled, imagining the image he projected in his black leather pants, alligator cowboy boots, and red silk shirt. The women ordered drinks, and Jimmy told the bartender to put them on his tab. He smoothed back the locks of his shoulder-length blond hair and continued staring, a grin on his face. These broads were hot, and Jimmy was starting to think in terms of a two-on-one. One thing he hadn't done in a long time, and really missed, was going down on a woman. Back in the day, he used to take pride in his ability to bring a woman to a screaming orgasm with his tongue. It was a game of his, and at one point he'd kept a written tally. But he hadn't been able to test his skill recently, because diving on a whore was, of course, out of the question. But these two were turning him on and might be just what the doctor ordered.

Jimmy sauntered over to their table, and the blonde looked up at him.

"Hi there," Jimmy said. "What's up, girls?"

The brunette clicked her nails on her glass. "Thanks for the drinks," she said, but she barely looked at him.

"Yeah, thanks," said the blonde. "We're just taking a break."

"Cool," Jimmy said. "Hey, what do you say? Would you like to take a ride with me in my limo, maybe check out some hot spots?"

"No thanks, we're fine here," said the brunette.

"Sure, why not? The Mirage is as good as it gets," Jimmy said. "Heck, I've got a penthouse suite, and it's pretty intense."

"How nice," the blonde said.

"Yeah, it's a real palace."

"I'm sure it is."

Jimmy looked at the blonde, tried to gaze deep into her and seduce her with his great blue eyes. She looked away and lit a cigarette.

Jimmy pulled up a chair and straddled it backward. "So, where you ladies from?"

The brunette reached out with her left hand and straightened her arm, so her hand lay on the table directly in front of Jimmy. There was a large diamond ring on her middle finger.

"I travel a lot myself," he said. "Europe, Hawaii..." Jimmy tried to think of some more romantic and exotic places, but couldn't come up with anything.

"Well, we're going to go find our husbands," the brunette said.

"Come on," Jimmy said.

The blonde rolled her eyes. "Have a nice life," she said. They both stood and left.

Jimmy watched them walk away and heard them giggling. His smile stayed intact, as if he didn't have a care in the world, until he was struck with the realization they were laughing at him. *Well, fuck you, then.*

An hour later he was packing his bag and contemplating where to head next. He was sick of the Mirage and sick of Vegas in general. The city was full of uppity women. He finished packing and was almost ready to take the elevator downstairs and hit the road in his Lamborghini, when an article in a magazine he was glancing through caught his eye.

The headline read: *Tired of the bar scene? Why not Internet dating?*

Jimmy had never owned a computer. During the years the PC had become a ubiquitous appliance, he'd been in a state of arrested development, moving from town to town, working menial jobs. Though he was familiar with the concept of the World Wide Web, he really didn't understand how it worked. He read the article with interest. It listed a number of Internet dating sites and made some brief references to sites that focused on sex rather than relationships.

After rereading the article, Jimmy called the general manager of the Mirage (he'd given Jimmy his cell phone number, saying if there was anything Jimmy needed—*anything*—just call). Jimmy asked him to send a photographer and an Internet-ready PC to his room.

"Jim, are you planning to stay another night with us?" the manager asked.

"I might."

"Splendid. I'll have your request taken care of immediately."

By early that evening, Jimmy Homestead had his Internet dating profile, including pictures, posted on three popular websites. The photographer had done all the setup work. The only thing Jimmy had to do was pose for the pictures and write his self-description. Here's what he came up with:

HANDSOME, HUNG, AND RICH

Hello girls. If you're looking for a man that has it all, I just might be available. I'm independently wealthy and accept only the best life has to offer. The world's most luxurious hotels are my home, at least until I decide where to buy a mansion. My Lamborghini is rare, my eyes are as blue as the sea, and my hair is the envy of most men my age. I have a fun sense of humor, and am an extremely intelligent and interesting alpha male.

Who I'm looking for—well, let's put it this way—I only date women who are head turners. Sex is a BIG priority in my life. If it's a big priority in yours, you've passed the first test. If you have any doubt about your weight, or appearance in general, no need to respond. Please be in your twenties, or perhaps early thirties, as long as you are truly a knock out. I am a breast and butt man—if you are lacking either, no need to respond. Silicon implants are acceptable. I prefer a neatly manicured woman, if you know what I mean. If you've been an erotic dancer, or a model, that may help your chances. Please bring no baggage, and a heavy appetite for sexual adventure. If you are bi, and have friends, that's a plus.

Feeling confident his love life was poised to take an exciting new turn, Jimmy ordered a six-pack and a pepperoni pizza from room service. *It's good to be me*, he thought, and settled in for dinner before another night at the Mirage's blackjack tables.

8

HER PLAN WAS FULL of holes, and Heather realized it wouldn't do. But she proposed it to Eric anyway, hoping the prospect of a few million bucks might spur a creative process in his brain. Eric was basically a hot-headed loser, but Heather had seen him become plenty focused whenever a shortcut to money presented itself. But so far, Eric had offered nothing of value in conceiving a decent plan to find Jimmy Homestead and extract a chunk of his fortune.

Heather's original plan was meager. It consisted of three elements:

– Find Jimmy Homestead.

– Put a gun to his head and convince him he would be killed if he didn't deliver the cash.

– Get away to the Bahamas with the money.

Eric yelled at Heather and pointed out how stupid and lacking in detail the plan was. He seemed more interested in berating her rather than offering anything constructive. Recently, Eric really seemed to get off on ripping into her. She reacted to his criticism calmly; it was his way of projecting the frustration he felt within himself, she knew. But that didn't make it any less humiliating.

That afternoon, after Eric left for the gym in a huff, one of Heather's old girlfriends from high school called. She was a serial dater and had spotted Jimmy Homestead's Internet dating profile. Heather located it and had a moment of inspiration. The pieces of the puzzle then began to come together very quickly. She thought it through and approached Eric the next day.

"Eric, listen to me," she said. He was in his usual position, reclined on the sofa with his feet on the coffee table. "Here is how we find him; all I have to do is respond to his site and set up a date. Then we can get the money out of him."

Eric arched his eyebrows, apparently surprised she had proposed something with promise. Heather handed him a printed copy of Jimmy's personal profile.

"Christ, what a slime ball," Eric said when he finished reading it. He stared out into space for half a minute, and when he looked back at her, his eyes looked smaller and gleamed with an unusual intensity.

"Okay, here's how we work this," he said. "You respond to his profile and send him some pictures from your talent book—you got digital copies of those, right? The only thing I'm worried about is if he'll recognize you."

"It's been almost twenty years."

Eric shot her a reproachful look, as if he hadn't forgiven her for a one-night stand she had when she was a teenager, before she ever met Eric.

"Well, hopefully he's fried enough brain cells, so let's figure he won't know it's you. I don't think we'll have anything to worry about. I'm sure you don't look anything like you did when you spread your legs for him."

"Well, I had my boobs done."

"You also ain't a teenager anymore."

Heather bit her tongue.

Eric stood and began pacing. "Now, the goal is to get him stripped. Tell him you want to blow him or whatever—just get his clothes off. And that's when I'll burst into the room."

"And then?"

"First I'm gonna slap him around a bit, just to scare him. Then you're going to accuse him of trying to rape you. I'll go into a rage and threaten to kill him for that. Then you'll say, 'Let's call the cops instead.' Once he's in a panic over the mess he's in, we'll offer him an easy way out: pay us three million in cash."

"And what if he says no?"

"Then I'll break his fuckin' arm. He'll cooperate after that, I guarantee it."

"My god," Heather murmured. The prospect of violence stunned her for a second. It represented the point of no return. Moving forward with the plan now meant it was all or nothing: success meant wealth for life, tropical drinks in paradise, total freedom. Failure probably meant jail. This was unlike anything Heather had ever been involved in.

"You think he'll actually give us the money?" she asked.

"One way or another."

Eric's face looked charged with an evil energy, and it scared Heather. She was then overcome by a wave of loss and regret so powerful her knees almost buckled. How had things got to this point? She always thought her beauty would naturally result in a privileged life; a rich, classy husband, interesting, successful friends, material surroundings that spoke of higher culture. But none of that ever happened. Instead, here she was, with her whacked-out, unemployed, steroid-abusing spouse, sitting in a lousy apartment, working on a desperate scheme to steal $3 million.

She blinked and took a deep breath. "Let's do it," she said.

9

HEADING NORTH ON HIGHWAY 50, I crossed over the California-Nevada border, passing the casinos and leaving South Lake Tahoe in my rearview mirror. I followed the highway around the lake, then downshifted and began climbing the pass over Spooner summit, toward Nevada's Great Basin desert.

The pine-choked forest became sparse, replaced by brown hills dotted with sagebrush. I crested the summit and coasted down the grade, until I reached the flats outside Carson City. The late-afternoon sun was falling behind me as I cruised Highway 395 through the center of town, past the old bars, second-rate casinos, fast-food joints, and strip malls. Toward the north end of Carson, 50 reconvened heading east again. From there the highway stretched without interruption for four hundred empty miles across Nevada's high desert and into Utah. Fortunately, I only had to drive eight miles before I saw the low billboard marking the brothel complex Jimmy Homestead visited a week ago.

I followed the potholed road around a few bends and back behind a low rise that hid the neon cathouse signs from the highway. The complex was made up of four single-story, chain-link-fence-enclosed buildings set in a horseshoe. In the middle was a large gravel parking lot. One of the establishments was a strip club; the other three were whorehouses, sanctioned and licensed by the state of Nevada.

I drove around the parking lot and parked in front of Tumbleweeds Ranch, the most upscale of the bordellos. The last time I'd been here was a year ago. I got out of my truck and walked over to a spot a little ways out and kicked at the gravel with my boot. It was here I'd shot an ex-mercenary who tried to send me to the next dimension with a sawed-off twelve-gauge. My shot didn't kill him, though; Cody Gibbons finished the job by blowing his head off from twenty feet with a .44 hollow-point round. I lingered over the spot for a moment, then walked back to where I'd parked.

There were two motorcycles among the dozen or so cars in front of Tumbleweeds. One of the bikes was a customized Harley, the other an old Honda with long, makeshift forks and a sissy bar. I rang the buzzer and waited for the lock on the gate to be released. The sun had sunk behind the desert hills, and the temperature was dropping quickly.

When I entered the parlor the madam was nowhere to be seen, so I waved off the lineup of prostitutes and took a seat at the bar, which was scattered with a handful of men. I ordered a whiskey rocks and let the ice cubes melt while I scanned the velvet couches against the walls. A small group of ladies were talking and laughing, led by a stunning Asian whore I'd met last year, but I couldn't remember her name. Three other women sat alone, separate from the group, seemingly aloof, or maybe just bored.

Two seats from me, a pair of men sat huddled over drinks. The larger of the two was a burly moose of a man; his shoulders were broad and bulged with muscle and his torso was thick as a barrel. He had a flat face with blunt features, framed by curly, reddish-brown mutton-chop sideburns that nearly met at his chin. When he spoke, I could see one of his front teeth was broken off, almost to the gum.

"It ain't my problem you were dumb enough to not bring a coat," he said.

"Gimme a break, it was eighty-five in San Jose," said the other man, a wiry dude with matted-down brown hair. He wore an old pair of jeans and a black T-shirt with sleeves that were too short. Below his shoulder was a scrawled tattoo of a naked female.

"You said you were resourceful," the big one said, with a chuckle that was more like a snort. "I'm sure you'll figure out how to stay warm."

The wiry man's face bunched up in cords of tissue, and his eyes grew flat as pennies.

"You are truly testing my patience, Sanzini," he said. "If we're going to find this dude, you're going to need me. I can't ride at night without a jacket. I'm asking you to loan me the goddamn money to buy one."

"Sure, how about if I buy you a whore too?"

I stifled a yawn. The tone of their conversation was one that could be heard endlessly in dive bars. Next they would start talking about how ruthlessly the local cops enforced drunk-driving laws. Or a recent bad-rap domestic violence charge. Or how thirty days in the city jail ain't really that bad of a gig—hell, it's three hots and a cot. I was trying to tune them out when one said something that made my head turn.

"Our whole reason for being here is the guy won the Lotto, right? Forty-three million, right? After I get my share, I'll pay you back."

"We got to find him first," the one named Sanzini said. He cleared his throat, and then said, "Excuse me," in a loud voice to the bartender, a stocky, balding man who wore his hair in a short pony tail.

"I'm trying to hook up with an old buddy of mine," Sanzini said. "He was here a few nights ago. Blond hair, blue eyes, about six foot, mid-thirties. Does that ring a bell?"

"Lot of guys fit that description come through here," the bartender said from around a toothpick.

"This guy probably was throwing money around like he had it to burn."

"Doesn't sound familiar."

"Blowin' dough like he won the lottery."

The man behind the bar shrugged.

"Who runs this cathouse, then? I need to talk to someone who knows something."

The bartender set down a bottle he was holding and leaned forward. "The madam is in charge. She'll be here later. If you ask her politely, she might be able to help you."

"Good," Sanzini said. The bartender walked away, shaking his head.

"Hey, Tony, when the madam shows up, let me talk to her. I got a way with older broads."

"Huh? Screw you, Rancour. You're just here because you got the connection with the security company. This is my deal. You stay quiet."

"Well, try to use a little charm, then."

"Blow yourself."

I left the bar and took a seat at a vacant couch, near where the group of prostitutes had congregated. After a minute the Asian woman I'd met before turned to me. She had an exotic aura to her, and I seemed to remember she'd told me she specialized in unusual positions.

"Meow," she said.

"Excuse me?"

"What's the matter, don't you understand pussy?" she said, and the ladies around her all laughed like crazy.

"So," she said, taking a seat on the arm of the sofa, "you wanna party?"

She wore a sheer turquoise gown, and the slit had fallen open, revealing her thigh all the way to her waist. Her legs were long and slinky, and the nipples on her small breasts were extended and pointy against a thin layer of silk that left little to the imagination. She parted her lips and eyed me with a sly expression that looked practiced.

I had met her during the investigation that resulted in the shooting in the parking lot. I had also been responsible for the death of her best friend's fiancé, but I didn't think she was aware of that fact.

"You're so beautiful I doubt I could afford you," I said. It was the same line I used with all prostitutes.

"We take credit cards," she said, her eyes sparkling.

"Mine's maxed out," I said, but she put her warm hand in mine and sat next to me on the sofa, then her mouth was next to my ear. "I guarantee you won't leave disappointed," she said. The beginning of the full-court press.

"You mind if we talk a little first?" I said, confident she didn't remember me. Prostitutes who spend any length of time in the trade learn to forget the men they meet very quickly.

"Whatever you want," she purred.

"Last week a blond dude came through here. About my age, maybe a little shorter. A decent looking fellow, probably drunk or on drugs."

"Maybe you're talking about Lotto-boy," she said with a laugh. "Kind of handsome, ripped half out of his mind, went to the VIP room with three of us."

"Lotto-boy?"

"Yeah. Guy claimed he won a forty-million-dollar lottery."

I pulled the picture Sheila Majorie had given me from my front pocket. "This him?"

She studied the photo briefly. "Yeah, that's the man. But his hair's longer now, and he looks older."

We sat in silence for a moment, while she snuggled her chest into my ribs and ran her fingers down my forearm. I tried my best to ignore my body's reaction.

"Did he say where he's staying, by any chance?"

"He talked a lot about all his money."

"How about where he's staying?"

"He said he was going to drive his Ferrari down to Vegas."

"You mean his Lamborghini."

"Yeah, right. Then he said he was going to build the most bitchin' mansion money can buy."

"Did he say where?"

"Nope."

I was trying to peel her arms off my shoulders when I saw the man at the bar, Sanzini, approach us.

"What's this about a guy in a Lamborghini?" he said.

"I was having a private conversation with the lady," I said.

He bent down to her. "Tell me about the guy in the Lamborghini."

She looked up at his brutish face and crossed her legs. "You're acting rude," she said. "I don't like rude."

"I asked you a goddamn question," he said, loud enough to get the attention of the bartender.

I walked around the couch and stood facing Sanzini, our faces no more than a foot apart. I noticed his partner at the bar, sitting quietly.

Sanzini stared at me, his eyes twitching in agitation. "Get out of my face," he said, stepping back. I moved toward him, and he shoved me in the chest with both hands.

At that moment, a tall, gangly man emerged from a side room. He came at us, carrying a billy club, the kind with a short handle attached at a ninety-degree angle. A difficult weapon to defend against, assuming your adversary knows how to use it. He also wore a snub nose .38 on his hip. I sat on the back of the sofa and folded my hands in front of me.

The bartender pointed at Sanzini and me with two fingers.

"Maybe next time," I said to the Asian lady, and headed for the door. Sanzini started to say something, but I didn't wait around to hear it.

Outside it was still and dark in the high desert. I waited in my truck, and a minute later Sanzini stumbled out of the whorehouse, his friend trailing behind him. Sanzini held his thigh and limped. The pair made their way to their motorcycles, and I rolled down my window so I could listen to what appeared to be escalating into a shouting match.

"You are one dumb mother, Sanzini. Jesus Christ, ain't no one gonna cooperate with you if you're such an asshole."

"Yeah? Well, fuck you, Rancour! The only dumb thing I did was hook up with you."

The smaller man whom Sanzini called Rancour climbed onto the chopped Honda and crossed his arms against the cold.

I climbed out of my truck. "Why are you looking for a guy in a Lamborghini?" I said to Sanzini.

"Who are you to talk to me?"

"Maybe I know something about where he is."

"Then you best start talking, boy," he growled.

"Tell me his name and why you're looking for him."

"Jimmy Homestead," Sanzini said. "Now tell me where he is, and maybe I won't kick your ass."

I looked over at the man called Rancour, who sat on his bike. He shrugged and smiled.

"See you later," I said and began walking back to my rig. A moment later I heard gravel spitting beneath shoes as Sanzini came after me. I turned in time to see he was limping badly. He must have taken a good shot to the thigh from the billy club. He lunged at me and threw an awkward right cross that I easily sidestepped. Trying to fistfight with a bad leg is usually a losing proposition.

I chopped him across the back of the neck with the meat of my fist and kicked him hard in the ass, hard enough to leave what I knew would be an ugly bruise to go along with the one on his upper leg. The blows sent him sprawling. I continued toward my truck.

But like most low-life dumb-asses, Sanzini wasn't smart enough to know when to quit. He rushed me again, and I turned in time to box him.

We squared off, and when he lost his balance on his hurt leg, I drilled him with two good left jabs to the face. He spit a stream of bloody saliva at my feet and put his head down and tried to tackle me, but I stopped him with a solid right uppercut and felt my knuckles split against his teeth. Busting up my hands on this meathead pissed me off. But I gave him one more chance.

"Go home," I said.

He came at me again.

I ducked his roundhouse and hit him with a straight right to the solar plexus. When he keeled over, I kicked him between the eyes with the toe of my boot. His body flipped back like a fish out of water, and he thudded into the gravel and lay still.

I watched the scene unfold in my rearview mirror as I idled away. Rancour ran over to Sanzini and stripped the leather coat from his body. Then the man with the billy club and the bartender came outside, and Rancour started his Honda and rode after me.

10

AT A HUNDRED MILES per hour, the 1982 Ford LTD was dangerously unstable. The nearly bald tires buzzed loudly against the pavement, the motor knocked and whined, and the chassis jolted at the slightest bump in the road. The man behind the wheel grinned like a maniac, a cigar clamped between his teeth, his mirrored flip-up sunglasses reflecting the sun.

John Homestead hadn't felt this alive in years. He used to go on road trips like this when he was a kid, party trips on the open highway, where roadhouse beers and willing women always seemed just a few miles away. That was when he was young, back when money wasn't a concern, and his natural good looks attracted more women than he knew what to do with.

Maybe those days weren't just a sad memory, he thought, as he popped another couple of diet pills and washed them back with a slug of gin. Join a gym, lose fifty pounds, move out of his dump into a classy condo. Was it possible? Hell, yes. With a couple million to back him up, anything was possible. Fifty wasn't too old to enjoy the good life. He eased up a bit on the gas pedal as he approached the speed traps outside Placerville, while he imagined the details of what his future might hold in store.

Tracking down his son had been easy. As a young man, Jimmy always had an affinity for the Lake Tahoe area, as he loved gambling and whores.

John never quite understood Jimmy's inclination toward prostitutes. Jimmy was always getting laid and had plenty of girlfriends. He certainly didn't have to pay for it. But that was a long time ago.

It took John no longer than fifteen minutes to dial the Tahoe casino hotels and find that Jimmy was staying at Harrah's. Apparently, after all these years, Jimmy's habits hadn't changed. John was quite pleased with his investigative work, but felt his buzz subside as his thoughts returned to the fact that Jimmy had made no effort to contact him after winning the Lotto. He chased the bad vibes away with another swallow of gin and concentrated on thinking positively. But in the back of his mind, he knew the gun in the glove box was there for a reason.

There was a line at the reservation counter when John arrived at Harrah's, so he wandered the casino for a while, working out the kinks in his legs and back from the long drive. He thought a few quick hands of blackjack might help him relax, but he decided otherwise when he saw the minimum at the twenty-one tables was ten bucks a hand. When he turned from the tables, he saw a woman in a fur coat walking away through the crowds. He caught a glimpse of her profile and stood dumbfounded.

Was he losing his mind? No, he wasn't that far gone. It was his ex-wife, Sheila. God, even after all these years she hadn't changed much, she was still a knockout. His eyes weren't playing tricks on him, were they? No, dammit, that was Sheila—you don't see beautiful vixens like her very often. John's mind was fuzzy from the booze and pills, but he was sure it was her. What the hell was *she* doing here?

The obvious slowly dawned on him. It was no coincidence. She must be here with Jimmy. How the hell could that be? Sheila hadn't had any contact with Jimmy after their divorce, at least not that John knew of. When Sheila left him, it was with a flourish of hatred directed not only at John, but at everyone in his family. She had made a clean break, and John thought he would never see her again.

After all this time, he still remembered her wrath. John knew he hadn't been the greatest of husbands, but she wasn't perfect either. Toward the end, he had accused her of sleeping with a younger man. Her response was one he never forgot. She looked him straight in the eye, very calmly, and said, "So?" And then she smiled, a bitchy little grin that cut right through him and made him feel as insignificant as an ant.

Thank god that's over with, he thought, feeling a sense of relief she was out of his life. It didn't matter that she was the greatest lover he'd ever had, a truly unique woman in bed. He still became aroused when he thought of their lovemaking, of her sheer sexual prowess. But eventually he'd realized she used her sexuality to control men. At her core, she knew how badly men wanted her, and how easy it was to get the so-called stronger sex to do whatever she wanted. This was his strongest and most enduring recollection of her. He could almost forgive her for it; imagine how easy life could be with that power. Still, to use people like she did, you had to have a dark place in your heart.

John started after Sheila, but the crowds of gamblers were thick, and he wasn't a nimble man. He soon lost sight of her, and a wave of dizziness overcame him. He sat down heavily on a bench in a quiet hallway. Christ, he was out of shape. He felt a pang of shame when it occurred to him how bad he looked compared to his ex-wife, who seemed as attractive as ever.

After a few minutes his head cleared, and he made his way back to the reservation counter.

"I'm sorry, there's no one named Jimmy Homestead staying here," the clerk said.

"But, he was here yesterday," John said.

"He must have checked out."

"How about Sheila Homestead? I'd like to leave a message for her."

The keyboard clicked briefly.

"No Sheila Homestead on record."

"Try Sheila Majorie."

Click, click, click. "No record of her either."

John walked away slowly and found an empty bar where he could think. He hadn't considered what he'd do if Jimmy wasn't at Harrah's. Nor had he anticipated seeing his ex-wife at the casino. He forced thoughts of her aside for the moment, and concentrated on where Jimmy might be.

His son, with all those millions of dollars. Enough money to buy anything, be anywhere, be anyone. Where would he go? Did the fact he had checked out of Harrah's mean he was leaving the Tahoe area? Or had he just decided on a different hotel? At this moment he could be checking into the fanciest suite at any hotel in the area. Or maybe he was on the road, driving a fancy new car to who knows where. Maybe to an airport.

Christ, this was getting him nowhere, John mused. He needed an angle.

Okay, what about Sheila being here? What a bizarre day it was turning out to be. Drive up to Tahoe to find your son, and find your wicked ex-wife instead. She had to be here because she was with Jimmy, right? But she hadn't stayed at Harrah's, unless…oh god, no. She couldn't have been sharing the same room with Jimmy, could she? A flood of dreaded emotions from a buried place surged to the forefront of his thoughts. John closed his eyes and pressed his temples. You have no way of knowing if it ever happened, he told himself. And it's foolish to contemplate if they are sleeping together now. It's a ridiculous suspicion. Shut it out, think logically.

An hour later, John found himself pacing along a wooded trail that led from the casino to the sandy shores of Lake Tahoe. Fortunately he'd brought his coat, because it had grown dark and cold. How long had he walked? A mile? Three miles? His legs were tired and his back ached. But the walk had served its purpose; his mind was at ease, and he had drawn what he felt were logical conclusions:

1. Sheila likely had already found Jimmy, and had either tapped into his money, or was in the process of doing so.

2. If she hadn't already found him, she was definitely trying to, for the obvious purpose of getting her hands on his money.
3. Sheila's agenda almost certainly would create some conflict with his own.
4. Finding Jimmy quickly was key. Sheila could influence Jimmy against him.
5. Finding Jimmy would require some advanced people-tracking skills, something John lacked.

By the time John hiked back to his car he was exhausted and hungry. He bought a bag of fast food, found a cheap hotel near the California-Nevada state line, and went to bed. Tomorrow would be a taxing day, and he wanted to be well rested.

11

IT WAS ONE IN the morning when Mort finally lay down to sleep in the downtown Sacramento hotel room. He had spent the evening applying his most logical and creative thinking to a plan to seize his nephew's lottery winnings. He didn't quit until he felt satisfied the plan covered every unexpected twist he could imagine. It was meticulous and exhausting work, but it was a process necessary to succeed in business, whether legitimate or otherwise. The primary goal in lawful business was to make an honest profit. The end game in an illegal enterprise was to steal and not get caught. The latter required especially concise, rational planning, because denial of personal freedom was the penalty for failure. Mort's previous enterprise ended disastrously when he ignored certain fundamentals. This time, Mort planned painstakingly. He did not intend to return to prison.

His plan was broken down into three primary elements:

1. Locate and secure Jimmy Homestead.
2. Extract and secure funds.
3. Get away safely.

As an experienced criminal, Mort realized the challenges he was facing. Finding Jimmy would be the easiest part, he assumed. Arranging the transfer of millions into his hands would be considerably more difficult. Vanishing with the money would be equally tricky. To manage these phases,

Mort broke down each into three analytical subsets: strategy, methodology, and tactics.

The strategy to locate Jimmy was simple. First, check building permits and real estate transactions. It was likely Jimmy would spend part of his fortune on a fancy home. The method to access this data required a trip to the city library, or city hall if necessary, to check public records. The tactical execution of this was slightly challenging because Mort's goal was to maintain total anonymity. Any activity creating a trail back to him must be avoided. But finding Jimmy would require talking to people, and that meant there would be links that could result in Mort being identified.

The next morning Mort walked two miles to a theatrical outfitting shop running early Halloween ads in the newspaper. In a cash transaction, he bought a tweed cap, a professional-quality reddish-gray beard complete with bushy eyebrow kit, and an apparatus that attached to his torso with suspenders, giving him the appearance of a man with a bulky midsection and a large rear end. He then took the city transit bus to a discount store, where he found a pair of yellow-tinted, wire-rimmed spectacles that obscured his greenish eyes. Next, a pair of pants, a belt, and a button-down shirt to fit his new physique. As a finishing touch, he found a used pipe reeking of tobacco at a thrift shop.

Thus attired, Mort spent the afternoon at the library and city hall, searching real estate records for Jimmy Homestead. But the fruits of his labor were elusive, and he returned to his hotel that evening empty-handed. Evidently, Jimmy had not moved forward with any real estate plans in California. Mort accepted the situation with even-keeled stoicism. His criminal plan was not one born out of laziness and aversion to work. Setbacks were to be dealt with intellectually and rationally. Lack of patience was a habit of failed criminals.

Mort checked out of his hotel the following morning and took the first Greyhound bus to Reno. The hundred-and-twenty-mile trip took four hot, gritty hours. By sundown Mort had finished checking the Nevada State real estate records. There was no record of Jimmy Homestead. Deep in his gut, he felt a flicker of irritation. He swallowed the emotion and concentrated on thinking logically. Anger was counterproductive—until it could be applied as a means to an end.

That evening Mort decided to begin executing a second strategy to locate his target. The real estate idea would be scuttled—it wasn't feasible to search every state for Jimmy Homestead. He had assumed Jimmy would buy a home in California, but he could have selected any state—Hawaii, Florida, it was impossible to predict. So it was time for plan B.

Now staying at a sprawling, inexpensive chain hotel in Reno, Mort began calling private investigation and security firms. It didn't take him long to find what he was looking for. He got the response he needed on his third call.

"Yes, I'm looking for an old friend who I haven't been able to reach. I don't think it's called for to hire an investigative service, but I'm wondering if you can provide reports of some kind, perhaps listing residences, phone numbers, or any other data that might help me locate this person."

"Yeah, we can do that. We have a basic report we run that includes address history, phone number, date of birth, that sort of thing. You can go to our website and order it with your credit card. The report costs fifty bucks."

"That sounds like it would be helpful. But unfortunately, I don't have access to a PC. Would it be possible for you to run the report, and then I could come pick it up?"

The voice on the other end hesitated. "Sure, that'll work. Just ask for Joe."

Mort woke early the following morning and meticulously applied his beard, working with the glue and blending lotion until he was confident it would pass a face-to-face encounter.

At nine o'clock sharp, a portly, bearded man smoking a pipe arrived at the offices of American Security in Reno. A few minutes later, Mort was seated across from Joe, a fleshy, dark-haired fellow in his thirties. Mort paid him with two twenties and a ten, and noticed Joe quickly slid the cash into his desk drawer.

As Mort suspected, the background report on Jimmy Homestead was not updated recently enough to reflect anything Jimmy may have done since winning the lottery.

"Do you have any other reports, showing more recent activity?" Mort said.

Joe picked at the corner of his mouth. "Recent activity," he said.

"That's right."

"Well, we could triangulate his cell phone. We have a GPS system that can pinpoint his location to fifty feet. The fee for that is two hundred fifty. But we can't just provide that service to anyone. You need certain clearances."

"I see," Mort said. He had begun slipping into a Southern drawl while in costume. He counted $400 from the roll of bills in his pocket. "Is this clearance enough?"

Joe's eyes shifted back and forth. He took the money, and it disappeared into his desk. "Come back at two," he said.

12

What a joke, Jimmy thought. What a bone-smoking joke. All anybody can talk about is the Internet, yeah, check this website, check that website, yeah, yeah, you can find anything. What a bunch of bullshit. Jimmy was at the bar at the Mirage, trying to drink away a grinding coke-and-booze hangover. The last three days had been a blur of casino gambling, liquor of every variety, and a snowstorm of cocaine. It was too much, even for Jimmy.

Within the first twenty-four hours of posting his personal ad, he had received three responses. Two were from Russian women who Jimmy learned were part of a mail-order-bride scam. The third was from a dumpy-looking, dark-haired woman from Sacramento, who sent him a simple six-word greeting: "You sound like a real asshole."

Jimmy blew a gasket when he read that e-mail. What kind of rude, ugly bitch would send a message like that? He was deeply offended a woman so beneath him had actually reached out and made contact. He felt soiled by it. And he was also perplexed and outraged that no quality babes had responded. It was freaking ridiculous.

So he spent three days drinking and snorting away his frustration. And now he was paying the price. He had danced, and it was time to pay the fiddler. It was the worst hangover he could remember, and he'd had plenty.

The midweek crowds at the Mirage were light, and Jimmy spent the afternoon sipping slow, medicinal Bloody Marys, trying to feel human again. Eventually, he went back to his room and passed out for a while, and when he woke he drank a strong Irish coffee, and finally his head started to clear. He searched around for his cell phone, which he'd lost at some point, and found it, dead, buried in his suitcase. It didn't matter, no one ever called him anyway.

He made his way to the bar again and was irritated to find it was now crowded, and the only open seat was next to two men who were laughing and having an animated conversation.

"Man, I'm telling you," said a red-haired guy with blotchy skin and hunched shoulders. "The women down there have a completely different attitude. It's a different culture. In the US, women have it made, right? They expect you to open doors for them, buy jewelry, kiss their ass, and if you're lucky, maybe you get laid every now and them. But it's totally different down there."

The other man was a short, bearded fellow wearing thick-rimmed glasses. "So what are Costa Rican women like?" he asked.

"They're incredible, I'm telling you! Costa Rica has more beautiful women than any other country in the world. And Costa Rican women—they call them Ticas—treat men totally different. It's like the man is dominant, and the woman's role is to please. They cook, they clean, they ask you if you want your back rubbed, or if you'd like to pound their poontang. And they love us gringos!"

"It sounds almost too good to be true."

"I've been there, man! I know! I found this twenty-three-year-old who was a perfect ten. I mean just incredible. And nice as can be. We hung out for three days; it was insane! Dude, when I left to come back to the US, she was totally bummed. And she only wanted, like, eighty bucks a day."

"She was really a ten?"

"Hell, yes! Costa Rica is swarming with women like her. Prostitution is legal there, and it's totally casual. The whores down there love it!"

Jimmy caught enough of the conversation to raise his interest. He turned toward the men and managed a meager smile. "Where are you guys talking about?"

"Huh?" said the red-haired man, looking at Jimmy's horribly bloodshot eyes.

"I overheard you talking." Jimmy's nerves were shot and his voice was shaky.

"Hey, you feeling okay?"

"I've had a few long nights, it's no big deal."

The red-haired man laughed. "I'm Larry," he said and stuck out his hand. "My friends call me Fast Larry."

Jimmy gave his hand a weak shake.

"We were talking about Costa Rica," Larry said.

"That's in Europe, right?"

"Europe?" Larry said, one eyebrow raised quizzically. "No, it's in Central America, down near the Panama Canal."

"Yeah, that's right," Jimmy said, and he was tempted to spin a tale about how he'd been to a lot of countries, but he didn't have the energy.

"It's about a five-hour flight from here," Larry said. "Costa Rica is a tropical paradise. Lush rain forests, stellar deep sea fishing, great food, and it's all dirt cheap."

"Well, the money's not an issue for me," Jimmy said. "But I wouldn't mind checking out a new scene." As the words came out of his mouth, Jimmy had an odd realization he was speaking the pure truth, a somewhat unusual event for him. He was sick of Vegas. He was sick of the murderous weather, which was still a hundred degrees in early October. And he was sick of bitchy, greedy American women, whores or otherwise. An exotic new locale might be just what he needed—especially a tropical paradise with nubile, young Latinas who treated men with the proper respect and admiration.

"Yeah? You got the money and the time, you ought to go, man," Larry said.

"Tell me more about this place."

An hour and a number of cocktails later, Larry was in Jimmy's suite, prompted by Jimmy's offer of a few lines of Peruvian flake. Afterward, Jimmy watched Larry pull up a number of websites on Costa Rica. He wouldn't admit it, but Jimmy found the prospect of visiting a foreign country intimidating. What about the language? And what about a passport? Jimmy didn't have one. But when he brought up his concerns, they were quickly dismissed.

"Dude, everybody speaks English. And anybody can get a passport," Larry told him.

There was something about Larry that Jimmy found soothing, in a down home sort of way. Larry had big, innocent, light-colored eyes, and eyebrows that seemed perpetually raised in laughter or exclamation. His smile was constant and seemed natural, and he had a casual, optimistic aura about him, as if he were immune to typical annoyances. Although Jimmy had only known him for a very short time, he felt Larry was harmless and trustworthy.

As he listened to Larry excitedly prattle on about Costa Rica (everything there was "the best") it struck Jimmy that since winning the lottery he had not contacted anyone he knew—no friends, no family, no one. Instead, he'd spent his time just drifting from place to place, Southern California, Tahoe, Vegas, and mingling with strangers, people who had no idea who he was. There was no question he was a very sociable person, and actually he'd met a lot of people recently, although when he thought about it, they were mostly whores and drunks. Well, what the hell, he was on a roll, living it up, and the truth was, he didn't feel compelled to contact anyone from his past life. Why should he? They'd probably just be looking for a handout, and he didn't owe anybody a thing, not a goddamned thing.

But in the back of his mind he felt a gnawing concern, like a sense of unfinished business. Should he feel any obligation to take care of people who used to be close to him, like his immediate family? No, hell no. Not his father, a man Jimmy thought of as more an acquaintance than a parent. What real guidance and support had his dad ever provided? What real love? John Homestead always put himself first, before his children. Not that this made him such a bad guy, but he hadn't sacrificed much for his son, certainly not enough for Jimmy to feel obliged to reach out and share his wealth. Still, Jimmy felt a tiny edge of guilt when he thought about his father.

As far as his friends, there were so many Jimmy had known over the years that trying to define who might be worthy of a handout made his head spin. The majority of people who came to mind were from San Jose, back in the days before he started drifting. He hadn't talked to most of them for over a decade. He thought back to the different faces, to his old partying buddies, different women he'd bedded, AA contacts, and his dead brother Marty. Sitting in his suite at the Mirage, watching Larry work the computer, the truth slowly dawned on Jimmy: he no longer had any real friends. It wasn't as if he couldn't have friends if he wanted—he'd always been popular. But somehow, over the course of time, it just seemed more natural to keep people at arm's length. People were just too damned sensitive, always judging and blaming him, as if he were actually responsible for the difficulties typically present in his life.

Every time something went seriously wrong for Jimmy, he saw it as the result of people creating bad situations for him. Of course, everything was always his fault in the eyes of the world, and then it was the plumber's motto—shit rolls downhill—with Jimmy at the bottom. As a result, he developed a tendency to stay light on his feet and move on quickly. He was used to changes in locale and environment, which were usually pleasant at first, until people started giving him shit again. And then it would be, "Adios, assholes," and onto a new town.

This pattern had prevented him from ever being anywhere long enough to develop true friends, the type who would be there through thick and thin. A repressed emotion that had been churning for some time finally propelled itself plainly into the forefront of Jimmy's conscience. With a sinking of his stomach, Jimmy realized he was sad, and it was because he was friendless and lonely.

And so, forty-eight hours later, Jimmy found himself with his new buddy and tour guide, Larry, waiting for an American Airlines plane to depart from Las Vegas to San Jose, Costa Rica. All it cost him was the expense of a rush passport and his and Larry's airfare, hotel, and party budget.

13

Tony Sanzini was not a happy camper after the events of the previous evening. Being left sprawled unconscious in front of the Tumbleweeds Ranch brothel wasn't his idea of a positive outcome to his initial effort at finding Jimmy Homestead. To make matters worse, the bouncer at the whorehouse called the cops and reported a drunk and disorderly customer had been in a fight and was passed out in the parking lot. As a result, Tony spent the night as a guest of the county in a filthy cement room, with only a drain hole in the center for a toilet.

He was released at dawn the following morning, and limped away from the Carson City jailhouse toward the nearest bus stop. His clothes felt damp and soiled, and he reeked badly of a potpourri of stagnant body fluids. At some point during the night, someone had apparently hawked a huge wad of phlegm at his head, and Sanzini had been unsuccessful in completely removing the sticky mess from his hair.

He sat in the back of the bus, amazed at the growing list of fools who had wronged him. He was sure Rancour had taken his prized leather jacket, his own personal colors, and that alone was an offense punishable by broken bones. The bouncer who drilled him with his billy club was also due a severe beating, perhaps an ass-reaming with a broken bottle. And the mysterious man who had punched him out in the parking lot? His face would be rearranged if they ever crossed paths again.

Sanzini consoled himself with these visions of retribution during the morning, as he made his way to a hotel at the south end of town. Fortunately, he had been carrying his wallet in his pants pocket and had a credit card that still had some limit, so he wasn't without means. After cleaning himself up, he took another bus to within a mile of the cathouse, then began walking through the desert back to where his bike was parked. The sun floated like a white balloon above him, and it soon became uncomfortably hot. The terrain he was crossing had looked like sand from a distance, but it was actually hard-packed dirt full of undulations and sharp rocks, making the relative flatness difficult to traverse.

By the time Sanzini neared the Tumbleweeds brothel, he was in bad shape. He had fallen a couple of times during the walk, which he now estimated at two miles rather than one. His bruised thigh would barely support his weight, and he felt every blow from the pounding he had taken the night before. As he staggered toward his bike, soaked in sweat, he began feeling sick to his stomach, and tiny flickers of light danced in front of his eyes. He dropped to a knee and waited for the blood to return to his head. What was he doing out here in the desert? Finding Jimmy and settling the score now seemed no more than a fanciful dream. He didn't know what to do next. He rose and limped to his chopper. With a groan he started it, and slowly rode away, back toward his hotel.

14

RANCOUR HAD FOLLOWED ME on his chopped Honda, through the dark desert and all the way back to Carson City. He kept a respectable distance, but didn't try to hide he was tailing me. I finally stopped in the parking lot of a supermarket and waited for him to pull up. He climbed off his bike and hooked a thumb in his belt loop.

"Hey, man, I got no issue with what happened back there," he said.

"That's good."

"My buddy has a serious attitude problem," he went on, smiling wryly. "And so he attracts trouble like flies on shit, if you know what I mean. No offense intended." He walked toward me and extended his hand. "I didn't get your name," he said.

"I didn't get yours," I replied.

His eyes narrowed, and he lowered his hand. But then he shrugged and smiled again. "Look, it seems like we were in that cathouse for the same reason, and it wasn't to tear off a piece, right?" When I didn't respond, he said, "I'm looking for a guy who owes me money. I don't think he'll have any problem paying, once I find him. I get the idea you're looking for the same dude—Jimmy Homestead."

"I see."

"Hey, man, I got no intentions here other than to collect an old debt, then get back home and back to work. I don't know what your interest is, but maybe we could help each other out here. We both knew he was at that cathouse. We're both looking for him. I'm suggesting maybe we could work together here. I got connections."

"I don't think so," I said.

"Look," Rancour said, his friendly tone receding. "We find him together, we both get what we want. We find him separately, maybe that means you'll never find him."

"Yeah, maybe," I said. "It's been nice, but I got to get back on the road."

"What's your fucking problem, man?"

I climbed into my truck and started the motor. "Good luck to you," I said. When I looked in the rearview mirror, Rancour's arm was rigid, his middle finger extended. He stood that way until I could no longer see him.

• • •

Back at my cabin, I made myself a drink and sat with a foot on my desk. Why would a couple of dirtbags like Rancour and Sanzini be looking for Jimmy Homestead? Maybe they were Jimmy's old friends, hoping for a handout. Or maybe they weren't friends of his at all. Regardless, I thought the potential for them to cause me problems was minimal.

My more immediate concern was that Jimmy seemed to be traveling constantly. In the last month, he'd used his credit card in Orange County, Los Angeles, Reno, Carson City, and South Lake Tahoe. But I had no way to know where he might be today, because the credit card records I had showed activity only for a thirty-day period that ended over a week ago. The prostitute at Tumbleweeds Ranch said he talked about buying a mansion and also mentioned driving to Vegas. It wasn't hard to imagine Jimmy might decide to live it up in Sin City for a few days. I did a web search, and the listings for hotels in Vegas were too numerous to count, but the number shrank considerably when I eliminated all but the most expensive.

I began calling and asking for the room of Jimmy Homestead. On my tenth call, to the Mirage Hotel and Casino, the clerk transferred my call to VIP services.

"Mr. Homestead has checked out, but I'd be happy to take a message. Who may I say is calling?"

"This is Chuck Farley from Exclusive Realty," I said. "If he's checked out, why would you take a message?"

"I have his mobile number. I'll let him know you called."

"I have some property I know he's very interested in."

"I'll relay the message."

"I appreciate it. Actually, I'm hoping to meet with Mr. Homestead as soon as I can. Do you know where he can be reached?"

"Mr. Homestead is traveling out of the country at this time. I'm afraid that's all I can tell you."

"That's unfortunate—he was quite eager to hear from me. Do you know when he'll return?"

"I'm sorry, I don't."

I hung up, thinking Jimmy must have blown a small fortune at the Mirage for their VIP services to take such an interest in him. Regardless, it sounded like he had headed for more exotic destinations. I called his cell number, and it connected immediately to a generic message, as it had every time I'd called it.

I wondered where Jimmy might want to hang out and party outside of the US. Maybe Cabo, or some other vacation spot in Latin America. I briefly considered the prospect of tracking Jimmy outside the country. It could get expensive in a hurry, and even if I found him, it might be difficult getting him back over the border.

But the Jimmy Homestead I used to know was not a worldly type, and I doubted he'd be interested in staying in a foreign country for very long. It also sounded like the Mirage expected him back, and it occurred to me his

Lamborghini was probably waiting in their valet parking—I didn't think he would leave his fancy car in an airport parking lot. Bugging his car with a cellular tracking device shouldn't be too tough. Then I could check on the whereabouts of the car every five minutes if I wanted to.

As I checked the flights to Vegas departing the following morning, I stopped and considered Sheila Majorie—her motivations, in light of Jimmy winning the lottery, and also her ability to pay me. If Sheila couldn't extract money from Jimmy by one means or another, she probably wouldn't be able to pay my fee or expenses. That would most likely mean a return to apartment living in San Jose for me. I let my gut chew on that one for a while before I booked a noon Southwest flight from Reno to Las Vegas.

15

AFTER A GOOD NIGHT'S sleep, a greasy casino breakfast, and a couple of large coffees, John Homestead was ready to face the day's tasks. He'd conceded he could not find Jimmy on his own, and he couldn't just stumble around randomly and hope to get lucky. Jimmy could literally be anywhere on the planet. Without professional help, it could be weeks, months, or possibly years before he could find him. John Homestead therefore decided to enlist the aid of a private detective.

He scoured the Yellow Pages and produced a list of five agencies offering people finding services. He made some calls, then drove to Reno to meet three of the investigators. One had a necktie spotted with food stains, another reeked of liquor, and the third wanted a $5,000 retainer. The remaining two were in South Lake Tahoe. He drove to the strip mall office of the first in Tahoe, and the lights were off, the door locked. John arrived at the final candidate's office tired, disappointed, and impatient.

Within two minutes of meeting Lou Calgaretti, John forgot his frustrations. Calgaretti was a well-groomed, smartly dressed man in his early fifties, and he struck John as a class act. He was also physically imposing; he stood well over six feet, and his upper body was muscular and well proportioned. Despite wearing a suit and a necktie with a floral pattern, Lou Calgaretti left the impression he was a man who wouldn't shy from physical threat. He had large, powerful-looking hands and impressively thick wrists.

"Mr. Homestead, I'm fairly certain finding your son is something that shouldn't take more than a day or so. However, in the event it takes longer, we need to agree on the costs involved."

"Of course," John said, and listened patiently while Calgaretti outlined his fees.

"It all sounds reasonable, except for one small thing—the upfront payment," John said.

Calgaretti raised his eyebrows. "Oh?"

"Yeah," John continued. "You see, I'm going to be honest with you, Lou."

"As opposed to being dishonest?"

"Well, how about as opposed to being less than upfront?"

"All right," Calgaretti said. His closely shaved face wore an impassive expression; his tanned, broad features looked relaxed under his full head of curly, graying hair.

"You see, my son recently won the California lottery. He's not been able to reach me, and I've not been able to reach him. Once we connect, it will be no problem getting you paid."

"No problem? Mr. Homestead, it sounds like you'll be relying on your son to pay me. Correct?"

"Well, yes. Sure he will," John said. "He's my son, for cryin' out loud. We have no issues. We've just been disconnected for a while."

"How long?"

"A few months is all," John lied.

"So, you haven't spoken with him since he won the Lotto?"

"No, not yet."

Calgaretti looked at his watch. From his office on Kingsbury Grade, he could see birds flying among the pines in the late-afternoon sun. He shook his head. "I'm sorry, Mr. Homestead, but I need to ask a question. What if I find your son, and he's not interested in paying me?"

Time to up the ante, John thought. The detective wasn't stupid.

"Well, Lou, how about a deal, then? You put me face to face with my son, in an environment where we can talk, and then you'll be paid, plus five grand on top of your regular fee. But you're going to have to trust me."

"Hmm. No risk, no reward, huh?" Calgaretti said, beginning to smile.

"That's right."

"How much did you say his Lotto winnings were?"

"I didn't," John said, and showed a bit of a smile himself. "He won forty-three million."

"Ahhh," Calgaretti said. "I'm going to take a gamble on you, Mr. Homestead. I'll draw up a contract."

16

When Mort returned to the security agency, he was told Jimmy's cell phone was apparently turned off and could not be traced. The man named Joe kept Mort's $400 and promised he would continue calling until he got through and successfully triangulated the signal.

It wasn't until two days later Joe called Mort with positive results. Jimmy's signal was sourced to the Mirage Casino Hotel in Las Vegas. Mort called the hotel, asked for Jimmy's room, and hung up after the front desk said he would be connected.

Getting to Vegas presented a couple of problems. First, Mort didn't want to book an airplane trip under his own name; it would create a clear link to him. He regretted not getting a fake ID earlier, which was poor planning on his part. He didn't have time now—he needed to be in Vegas without delay. Mort weighed the issues for a few minutes, then decided to buy a cheap car and drive. This would let him avoid the airline records and provided him needed mobility once in Vegas.

Mort also considered that he would be violating his parole by leaving the area without permission. He immediately dismissed this concern; he didn't intend to be in Vegas for more than a few days, and once he found Jimmy, he didn't intend to have further contact with his parole officer.

The bottom line was anticipation and planning. Mort vowed to be patient and resist any tack that might be imprudent. A time would come when risk would need to be taken. But that would be when the money was clearly in his sights.

Early that evening Mort took off in his new ride, a silver Toyota Corolla, paid for in cash. It had well over 100,000 miles on the odometer, but the small Japanese four-door seemed sound, its motor humming pleasantly as Mort headed south on Interstate 5. The heat of the day subsided as the late-summer sun set behind the low mountains, and Mort rolled down the window and settled in for the long drive.

• • •

Five years ago, Mort had visited Las Vegas for technology conventions, stayed in luxury suites, and had a company limo at his service. He dined at restaurants where money was no object, and occasionally threw away a few grand at the card tables just for the fun of it.

This time, he rolled into town around dawn and checked into the Thunderbird Hotel, a seedy rat hole off the Strip that didn't require a credit card or ID. He was glad they had some free sweet rolls in the lobby, even though they looked plastic and flies buzzed around the plate. He'd already put a significant dent in his seven-grand stake, and he needed to conserve in case unexpected expenses arose.

After a few hours' sleep, Mort donned his fat man disguise and drove to the Mirage. The midmorning temperature was already near one hundred degrees, and by the time he walked from the parking lot to the Mirage's air-conditioned foyer, sweat was soaking through his shirt. He spent a half hour walking around the casino, familiarizing himself with its layout, then took the main elevator to the top floor, and back down to the hotel registration counter.

"I have a package to deliver to one of your guests," he told the clerk. Mort held up a brown paper shopping bag that held a shoebox-sized container. "I was supposed to meet him in his penthouse suite, but I need an access key to get to that floor."

"Yes," the clerk said. "You would need that. Would you like me to call the person for you?"

"Please," Mort said. "His name is Jim Homestead."

The keyboard chattered for a few moments. "I'm sorry, we have no one here by that name."

"Try James Homestead."

"No one with the last name Homestead."

"Strange," Mort said. "I just spoke with him yesterday."

The clerk worked the keyboard again. "Here he is—I have a Jim Homestead who checked out this morning."

"Oh, my. It appears I've missed him. I wonder how I can get this package to him."

"You may want to talk to VIP Services. They're down the hall and to the right.

"I see. Thank you."

A slender woman in her fifties with skin that had seen too much sun sat at a desk, talking with two women Mort thought were probably lesbians. They left after a minute, and he stepped forward.

"Excuse me," he said. "I was asked by Jim Homestead to deliver some expensive merchandise. I've driven quite a ways to make this delivery, but I'm told he checked out this morning."

"Yes, that's correct."

"I can't imagine how we could have got our signals crossed. He's already paid for this package. Would you by chance have any idea how I could contact him?"

"Unfortunately, I don't," the woman said. "The only thing I can suggest is to try to reach him here a week from now."

"In a week? Do you know he'll be back then?"

The woman paused. "He left his car with us, so I assume he will."

"Do you think he may return sooner?"

"My understanding is he's traveling out of the country, so I doubt it."

Mort walked away and found a deserted tropical lounge. He sat at a cocktail table, stared past a man-made waterfall, and pressed his fingertips together. Four hundred dollars spent to track Jimmy to Vegas. And now he was gone, supposedly for a week.

But his car was still at the Mirage. What kind might he be driving?

Mort went back out into the heat and found the valet parking garage. Parked in the first spots, and sectioned off from the remainder of the parked cars, were a Rolls Royce, a couple of high-end Mercedes sedans, and a few fancy sports cars. Mort's eyes settled on the last car in the row, a Lamborghini Diablo with dealer plates reading Orange County Exotics.

He drove his Toyota to a drug store and dropped forty dollars on a prepaid cell phone and a pair of scissors. Then he got the number for Orange County Exotics from directory service.

"This is Sergeant Williams from Las Vegas PD," Mort said. "I just pulled over a man in a new, orange Lamborghini, which he claims he owns and purchased from your dealership. I need to confirm he owns this car, since he says he's lost his temporary tags. His name is Jim Homestead."

The salesman on the other line didn't even hesitate. "Yes, sir, that was my sale. He came in about two weeks ago. Slim, six feet or so, blond hair, about thirty-five?"

"Correct."

"That's Jimmy Homestead."

Mort returned to the Mirage and found the valet parking manager, a kid in his early twenties. Mort shook his hand and introduced himself as Bruce Stevens. "I deal in rare art," Mort said. "I've been trying to reach Jim Homestead, the owner of the orange Lamborghini in your lot. He's been somewhat elusive." Mort pulled two hundred-dollar bills from his pocket and neatly cut them in half. "Here's an offer," he said. "You call me when Jim Homestead returns to the Mirage, and I'll bring you the other halves."

"You got a deal," the kid said.

Back at his hotel, Mort stripped off his costume and lay on the bed. It was not the greatest mattress, but it was far more comfortable than what he slept on in prison. Compared to the last five years, spending a week in this roach pit would be nothing. But Mort did not intend to be idle while waiting for the valet manager to call. There had to be something more he could do to be prepared. The shoebox rested next to him. Mort opened it and double-checked the items he had assembled. At least that part of the plan was rock solid.

17

I STARED OUT THE airplane window down on Las Vegas as we descended, amazed at how many new casino hotels were under construction. Huge cranes marked at least a half dozen new high-rise projects on the Strip. When the plane finally touched down, I turned toward the middle-aged couple next to me. "Good luck, folks," I said, hoping it would interrupt their nonstop babble about beating the casinos. No such luck.

I left the terminal, walked into the furnace-like air of the Mohave Desert, and picked up a Ford economy-class compact rental. I turned the AC to high. Heat waves shimmered above the asphalt leading from the airport.

I had just turned from Tropicana onto the Strip and was passing the MGM Grand when my cell rang.

"Dirty Double Crossin' Dan," a familiar voice said. Cody Gibbons.

"What's happening, Cody?"

"I just got a job I think you should know about."

"Oh?"

"Yeah. Tell me if this sounds familiar: a woman who gives whole ZIP codes a hard-on offers ten grand to find her stepson."

I was silent for a second. "You're kidding," I said.

"I never kid about five figures, Dirt. She told me she offered you the same deal, too."

"Sheila Homestead hired you for the same case she hired me?"

"Don't sound so surprised. And it's Sheila Majorie. She told me she thinks it would be a good idea for both of us to work it."

"Why?"

"Well, she wouldn't say exactly, but here's what I think: First, Jimmy Homestead is now one of the richest dudes in the country, and she feels a chunk of that dough is coming her way. Which means twenty grand to find the guy is mice nuts to her."

"That doesn't explain why she would hire an additional investigator."

"She said she spotted her ex-husband in Tahoe. His name is John Homestead. She thinks he's unstable and maybe dangerous. So she felt like she wanted an extra man on her team."

"What, to protect her?"

"Look, she has a bad history with the dude. But the key is, she wants to make sure she finds Jimmy before he does."

I pulled over and found a shady spot beside a building.

"She thinks he's looking for Jimmy, too?"

"Now you're getting it, Dirt."

"Cody, you realize if she can't convince Jimmy to share his money, she has no way to pay either of us."

"Yeah, that occurred to me. But we talked about it, and I agreed to help persuade the little creep, if need be."

"Christ, this just keeps getting better."

"Yeah, well, there's something else you should probably know."

"I can't wait."

"Sheila and me, we kind of, well…"

"Don't tell me."

"I really like her."

"You're sleeping with her?"

"Tell me you could resist her, Dan."

I started laughing. The mental image of six-foot-five, three-hundred-pound Cody Gibbons in a romantic situation was funny to me. But he was a natural womanizer, and since his divorce last year, he had been in more brief relationships than I could count.

"Hey, I got to go. She's coming back," he said.

"You're with her now? In San Jose?"

"No, we're in Vegas."

Ah, shit.

• • •

They were staying at the Nugget, on the far side of the strip toward old downtown Las Vegas. I spotted them standing in the lobby, looking like two different species—Sheila, in heels, a low-cut blouse, and tight jeans showing off her hourglass figure, and Cody, towering over her in a Hawaiian shirt that barely contained his massive shoulders. The young lovers, on vacation in Vegas.

"Well, Sheila," was all I could say.

"Come on, Dirt, let's go to the bar, get a drink, and talk strategy."

"Why do you call him Dirt?" Sheila asked.

"Short for 'Dirty Double Crossin' Dan.' When we were younger he used to pick up on every girl I liked."

"Not true," I said. "That maybe happened once."

"Looks like Cody got you back this time," Sheila said, shooting me a look while hooking her thumb in Cody's back pocket.

We found a lounge off the casino floor and sat at a cocktail table. "I assume you're here because you learned Jimmy's been staying at the Mirage," I said.

"That's right," Cody said.

"How'd you find out?"

"I've got a guy that can track digital footprints. Give him a name, and he can trace their e-mails or Internet usage to an IP address. In this case, the IP address Jimmy used was specific to the Mirage."

"Is that legal?"

Cody shrugged. "Supposedly."

"Well, we missed him," I said. "Jimmy's checked out. I heard he's traveling out of the country—partying down in Mexico would be my guess. I'm betting he left his car at the Mirage. Shouldn't be hard to find—he's driving a Lamborghini. I have a cellular tracking device I want to attach to it. Then once he starts driving, he'll be easy to find."

"Assuming his car is at the Mirage," Cody said.

"Let's go look, then," Sheila said.

"I think you might want to wait here," I said.

"You'll just attract attention," Cody added.

"Or, I could provide a diversion," she said.

Cody and I exchanged glances. "Why not?" I said. We finished our drinks, piled into my rental, and headed toward the Strip.

• • •

We went past the check-in circle in front of the Mirage's main lobby, and followed a road toward the back of the hotel, to the parking garage. Near the garage entrance, in plain view, was a lineup of expensive cars. I'd seen hotels do this, displaying patron's fancy cars to create an image of wealth and opulence. Between a Rolls Royce and a Maserati sedan was an orange Lamborghini with dealer plates. I drove us to an adjacent parking lot, and we began hiking back toward the garage.

"It's got to be his car," I said. "I'll sneak over and attach the tracking unit. Sheila, hang behind me, and if you see an attendant coming, stop him, keep him delayed for a minute."

"I'll go watch the main entrance," Cody said, his hand on Sheila's arm. "If I see a valet guy heading out on foot, I'll ring your cell once."

Cody peeled off toward the front of the hotel while Sheila and I continued toward the garage. "You know, we have no way of knowing when Jimmy will return to Vegas," I said. "It could be tomorrow, a week from now, or a couple weeks."

"If you're worried about your expenses, don't. It will be taken care of. You just make sure you bring Jimmy to me as soon as he gets back in town."

I stopped and turned to her. "Why didn't you tell me he won the Lotto?"

"That's none of your concern," she said and started walking away.

"Yeah, it is." I grabbed her arm. "I know the only way you can pay me is if you get the money from Jimmy. How do you intend to do that?"

She moved closer and looked up into my eyes. "Trust me," she purred.

"Lovely," I said.

I left her on the walking path between the main entrance and the garage and watched a Mercedes pull out, a parking attendant behind the wheel. As soon as he was gone, I darted in and slid behind the Lamborghini. Reaching under the low-slung chassis, I felt around until I found a snug, secure place for the magnetized tracking device. When I walked back out, I saw Sheila talking with one of the valet runners.

Cody and Sheila met me at the rental car a few minutes later. I turned on my GPS transceiver, and it connected with the satellite and identified the Lamborghini on a street map with a flashing red arrow.

"Pretty slick," Cody said.

"The tracker will remain in sleep mode until the car is moved. Then it will alert me on my cell phone, and I can track the car on the GPS. The battery on the tracker should last at least a week."

"Did you intercept the attendant?" Cody said to Sheila.

"Yeah. He asked me if I wanted to go to a party tonight."

"And?"

"I told him I'm having my own private party," she said, and leaned over from the back seat and nuzzled Cody. He winked at me, but I could see his face turning red.

Back at the Nugget, the frisky couple headed straight for their room, and I headed straight for the bar. The Nugget was an older, less glamorous establishment than the new breed of casinos that drew hordes of tourists to Vegas. The bar I sat at was weathered and scarred with cigarette burns, and the red carpet beneath my boots was a blur of whiskey stains. The bartender, a full-figured woman, poured me an honest bourbon rocks and slid a bowl of popcorn and pretzels my direction.

Staying in Vegas for a week or more was not something I had planned, or wanted to do—especially since I wasn't particularly confident I would get paid. If I didn't, whatever expenses I rang up would just put me that much deeper in a hole. Sheila Majorie seemed to think I would hang around town for as long as it took to find Jimmy. She might learn otherwise. But the involvement of Cody Gibbons made things more complicated.

I gunned my drink and ordered another. Since Cody's wife left him, his love life had been a boozy kaleidoscope of closing-time bimbos, broke divorcees, strippers, plus a sordid affair with his ex-boss's wife thrown in for variety. Cody had always run on the ragged boundaries of civilian life, but his divorce, coupled with his losing his job as a San Jose PD detective, was no doubt pushing him closer to the edge. To say his relationship with Sheila Majorie concerned me was probably an understatement.

If Sheila was using Cody somehow, and I was fairly sure she was, it was my intention to prevent Cody from doing anything self-destructive. It was a fool's errand. From our high school days, I'd never seen Cody Gibbons show the slightest restraint in his behavior. He threw his varsity football coach in a Dumpster, proposed to the head cheerleader and moved out of state the day after she declined, and was involved in eight shootings in three years of active police duty. And, he once saved my life by shooting a man to death.

I knew there were dark places in Cody's psychology that drove him to behave as he did, but Cody Gibbons also was the most loyal and steadfast friend a man could have, especially when the going got tough. He had stood by my side during my bleakest hours, when I was drinking heavily after I first killed a man, when I was broke and jobless, and when my marriage ended. And when my life was threatened last winter, he put his own on the line without hesitation, and was nearly killed himself.

• • •

The next morning I had breakfast at the casino, then drove out to a nearby gym and lifted weights for an hour. Noon came and I hadn't heard from Cody, so I headed over to the Mirage for a little recon work. I checked to make sure the orange Lamborghini was still in place, then went into the casino.

I toured the Mirage's bars, showing Jimmy's picture to the bartenders. A couple recognized him, and one, a short Mexican man, remembered him well.

"Sure, that guy. He was here for a few days, I think. He was always drunk, or drugged out. He talked like a big shot, a joker like that. He even said he might buy the Mirage."

"Did he talk much about his plans for the future, like where he might be going?"

"I heard him talking about whores in Costa Rica."

"Anything else you remember him saying?"

"He talked about buying a mansion, mentioned Lake Tahoe."

"Interesting. Thanks, amigo."

"Hey," he said. "Why are you interested in this stupid guy?"

"He might be in trouble."

"One day he tried to talk to these ladies who came by for a drink. He paid for their drinks, but then they left. I think it made him very mad."

"No kidding?"

"I think maybe he should stick with whores."

We laughed, then I left the waterfalls and tropical foliage surrounding the bar and headed out into the heat of the day to kill some time.

It was a bit after six that evening when my cell rang, showing the alert code for my GPS unit. A red arrow appeared, moving down Las Vegas Boulevard. I dialed Cody's cell.

"Drop your cock and grab your socks," I said. "The Lamborghini's on the move."

"Five minutes, in the lobby," he said.

"Bring Sheila," I said, but the line was already dead.

Cody showed up in the lobby alone, drinking a bottle of beer and smoking a cigarette.

"Since when did you start smoking again?"

"Since ten minutes ago," he said, flicking the butt onto the hot pavement. He carried his beer with him into the car.

"Try not to get us pulled over," I said.

He finished the beer and tossed the bottle into the back seat. "Drive," he said.

We followed the GPS through the traffic on the Strip, and after a couple of U-turns, I spotted the Lamborghini pulling into the parking lot of an expensive restaurant. We cut across three lanes of traffic and parked a few spots away.

A man climbed out of the car, walked around to the passenger side, and opened the door for a young blond girl.

"That's not Jimmy Homestead," I said.

Cody reached them first. "This your car, son?" he said. The kid looked barely drinking age.

"Ah, no, actually. I'm borrowing it for the night."

"This car is supposed to be secured in valet parking at the Mirage," I said.

"Oh, uh, really?" he sputtered. His date stared at us open-mouthed.

"Do you work at the Mirage?"

"Yeah," he admitted.

"Goddammit," I said. "Get back in the car. I'm going to follow you back to the Mirage, and you're going to park it. You're lucky I don't call the cops."

Cody shook his head. "Don't you think the owner would notice the mileage?"

"Probably not—he's a drunk."

Five minutes later we watched the kid park the Lamborghini back in its spot at the Mirage, and I started driving us toward the Nugget.

"How about finding a bar, Dirt?" Cody said.

"What's wrong with the Nugget?"

"I could use a change of scenery."

We spotted a small bar on the Strip tucked among the casinos. Somehow the narrow building had survived all the recent development in Las Vegas. I imagined the land the bar sat on would probably make the owner rich if he chose to sell out.

Cody ordered a shot and a beer and lit a cigarette. He scratched his beard and smoothed it down, staring at himself in the bar mirror.

"How is it with Sheila?" I said.

"She's pretty amazing. But I needed a break."

"Cody," I said, trying to choose my words carefully. "A woman like her can make a man, well, irrational. Aren't you curious why she would want two investigators working this case?"

"We talked about it. She just said she thought having us work as a team would result in finding Jimmy quicker. Two heads are better than one."

"I guess it doesn't bother her to pay double the fee."

"I guess not."

Cody swigged his beer and ordered another. Mine was still full.

"So what happens when we find Jimmy? And he tells his stepmom to get lost when she asks for a cut of his Lotto winnings?"

"Christ, Dan, you have a suspicious mind. Let's just do our job, and we'll get paid, okay?"

"Our job is to find Jimmy Homestead, not force him to give money to Sheila. Those are two entirely different things. Do you understand that?"

"Yes, Dirt."

"Don't let her use you."

"What, you mean I couldn't get a classy woman like her unless she was using me?"

"That's not what I meant."

"It sure sounded like it."

I drank my beer and took a cigarette from Cody's pack.

"I just don't want to be sucked into any more than I signed up for," I said.

"Come on. Where's your sense of adventure?"

"Maybe I left it at that stream last year, when we nearly froze to death."

Cody laughed. "That was nothing, and you know it. You're just being paranoid."

He shouted at the bartender to bring me a shot. I stared into the brown liquor and raised it to my lips.

"Now, loosen up, let's have a good time," he said, his big mug shining in the light, his eyes laughing at a joke only he knew.

• • •

When we rolled into the Nugget, it was around midnight. "Damn, I hope Sheila is still awake," Cody said. "I'm horny as a three-peckered billy goat." He lumbered toward the elevator, and I went to the bar for a last drink, to contemplate the folly of men, the power women held over us, and my owned damned weakness.

I only saw Cody once in the next two days, when I ran into him and Sheila in the lobby. "We're going shopping," he told me. "Hold down the fort."

I checked on the Lamborghini twice daily, worked out at the local gym each morning, and read most of a paperback novel about a Louisiana cop who saw ghosts from the civil war. Despite enjoying the book, I was bored shitless, but that's an occupational hazard. Spending hours doing nothing but watching and waiting is a part of investigation work not realistically portrayed on TV or in the movies. It's neither glamorous nor exciting, but it's part of the job. No doubt the waiting was less tedious for Cody, sharing a bed with Sheila.

With too much time on my hands, I spent empty hours at the Nugget's casino bar, nursing slow beers, trying not to think about anything. Of course, the opposite happened. My mind wandered to my past, to the day the phone rang when I was thirteen years old, and a voice told me my father had died. He had walked out of his law offices on a pleasant summer evening, not knowing a man released from prison the week before was waiting for him in the parking lot. I imagine my dad's thoughts as he walked to his car were of legal nuances and arguments, and also of beating the traffic and getting home to have dinner with my mother, my sister, and me. I never knew exactly what transpired in the last minute before he was shot to death. If there was any conversation between him and the man who swore vengeance when my father convicted him three years previous, it went with my dad to his grave.

As a district attorney, Richard Reno was a man of strong and often inflexible principles. He had many friends and inevitably made his share of enemies. He could also be a strict parent, but there was a fun loving and easygoing side to him that I often felt he saved for me. When my mother was sometimes having a bad day, he would sneak me into his car, as if we were perpetrators of a grand scheme. Then we would drive around town running errands, maybe stopping for lunch, or at a place that had pinball machines. Once I remember we even drove forty miles, on a whim, to the Oakland Coliseum to watch the A's play the Red Sox.

There were some rocky times for me after my father's death. On my first day of high school, I fought a bully who chose a smaller friend of mine as his target. In a blind rage, I knocked out two of his teeth and dislocated his shoulder. His parents filed suit against my mother. A year later I did a few days in a juvenile detention center for my part in a gang brawl, after being accused of breaking an older boy's jaw and fracturing another's skull. My mother sent me to a therapist who talked in circles and charged a hundred dollars per appointment and said it might take years before he could resolve my issues. I stopped going after two sessions and joined my high school football and wrestling teams.

My thoughts drifted to later in my life, to the five men who've died by my hand during my career as a private investigator and bounty hunter. I've spent a lot of time regretting those killings, even though every man I shot deserved to die. Recently though, my remorse had lessened. Killing is like anything else, a psychologist friend once told me—with enough repetition, you get used to it. He also told me I was probably subconsciously justifying the killings as vengeance for my father's death. I'm not sure I believed him, but a strange quiet now replaced the guilt I used to feel.

Back in South Lake Tahoe, my home needed some touch-up painting before the weather set in. It was the first and only home I'd ever owned.

The street I lived on was deep in a sparsely built residential tract bordering national forest land. A stream ran within rock throwing distance of my driveway, and when the wind blew through the pines in the front yard, it always sounded like a big storm was on the way, even if the sky was cloudless. In the summer I'd sit and enjoy the breeze and the scent of fresh pine while having coffee on my deck. Every other day after breakfast, I'd throw on a weighted backpack and jog through the meadow behind my house, and up a steep switchback trail into the mountains, a workout I learned from a die-hard deer hunter who was strong enough to haul an eighty-pound carcass from ten miles deep in the forest without stopping to rest.

But though the warm months in Tahoe are beautiful, my strongest affections were always for the winter. When the first snow fell, typically in November, the town would be abuzz with predictions for the upcoming ski season, which many residents relied on for their livelihoods. For me, it meant chopping wood in my shirt sleeves in twenty-degree weather, then warming myself by a roaring fire with a heated snifter of Grand Marnier. Or walking a mile through a snowstorm to the nearest bar, Whiskey Dick's, and beating the elements with stout boots and a good jacket. And it also meant tackling the steeps and mogul fields at Lake Tahoe's ski resorts, especially on powder days when the snow would blast into my face with every turn.

I went to bed that night and dreamt of streets blanketed in snow, icicles hanging from my roof, and wide, unblemished fields of powder, the edges of my skis raising wisps of cold smoke, my breath frozen against the blue skies. But the images were interrupted by my car in a traffic jam, an appointment I was late to, and some vague notion of a job interview in San Jose.

A little before noon the next morning, on my fifth day in Vegas, my cell rang again with the alert code for the tracking device.

18

TO AVOID THE EXPENSE of dining out, Mort had bought groceries and a Styrofoam cooler from the supermarket. He bought the least expensive provisions he could find; he intended to not spend a penny more than necessary until he found Jimmy Homestead. His $7,000 stake was now more than half gone.

After the woman at the Mirage VIP desk said Jimmy was traveling out of the country, Mort called Joe at the security company in Reno and asked if it was possible to get airline flight details. Unfortunately, it was not—due to increased security in the post-9/11 era, the airlines were required to keep all travel records confidential.

Without any specific idea when Jimmy would return for his car, Mort kept a close eye on the Mirage and the Lamborghini. He hung out at the casino in his uncomfortable disguise, watching the reception lobby and the bars, checking the valet parking lot every few hours. He thought there was a good chance the parking lot attendant would call him, but by then it could be too late. If Jimmy drove away before Mort had a chance to follow him, it would be a major setback.

When his mobile phone rang a few minutes before noon, Mort had just arrived at the Mirage and was sitting at a slot machine near the lobby.

"This is Tim at valet parking at the Mirage. The guy you were asking about is here. The one with the Lamborghini. He's asked us to bring his car around."

Mort raced out of the casino and sprinted to the lot where he'd parked his Toyota. He spotted the Lamborghini pulling up to the reception circle, and saw a figure walking toward it. The tires of the Toyota squealed as Mort whipped his car into a tight U-turn and floored the gas toward the road leading to the front of the hotel. He saw the valet attendant watching him, and caught himself. If he did not pay off the attendant, it might give the kid reason to take down his license plate number. He hit the brakes and pulled the two half-hundred-dollar bills from his wallet.

"Thank you, young man," he said, and pulled away slowly. He was now close enough to recognize the man at the car. It was Jimmy, taking his time loading his suitcase.

A minute later the Lamborghini was on Las Vegas Boulevard, with Mort's silver Corolla two cars back. Mort's right hand rested on the cardboard box in the passenger seat. The box held a three-ounce lump of homemade plastic explosive. He had bought the ingredients in Sacramento and mixed the batch in his hotel room. The box also contained a pair of electrodes and a battery-powered remote activator, to serve as a detonation system. Next to these items he had neatly arranged a roll of duct tape, plastic ties, a small bottle of chloroform, and a rolled hand towel he took from his hotel.

As he drove, Mort felt oddly disconnected, a sensation he'd experienced often since his release from prison. Though he was a free man, he still felt the weight of the five years of incarceration, as if his jail term had been burned into his brain. He couldn't shake the feeling that all he'd achieved in the years previous to his arrest had been negated, wiped clean from his record. His past successes now meant nothing. The prison sentence had taken his identity, leaving him destitute and with no potential to reestablish himself in the business world. But Mort had retained one key trait from his past. At the center of his being, he was still relentlessly driven to get what he wanted, what he felt the world owed him. It meant nothing to him if his actions caused others to suffer. It was this singular element in his character he always came back to. All he had been through couldn't strip him of it.

When he was a child, his father, Earl Homestead, worked at the Ford plant in Detroit, and his mother was a barmaid at a local tavern. He was six years old when he overheard his parents arguing late one night, when he should have been asleep. Mort had been sent home from school early that day, after a rock throwing incident on the playground put a boy in the hospital.

"Your kid is turning out to be a real angel," Mort's father yelled. "I should have divorced you and put you out on the street as soon as I knew the little bastard wasn't mine."

"Tell me you've been faithful since we were married. Try to tell me that," his mother said.

"That doesn't matter and you know it. I didn't get pregnant and bring that strange kid into our lives. *You* did."

"He's my son, you son of a bitch. What do you want me to do, abandon him?"

His mother started crying, and Mort plugged his ears and hummed so he would hear no more. A year later, he and his mother moved from Earl Homestead's suburban home to an apartment in a black neighborhood in Detroit. The hot water heater often didn't work, and rats left their droppings on the kitchen counter at night. He slept on a cot next to his mother's bed in the single bedroom, listening through the open window to the ceaseless noise from the street below. A woman plunged to her death from the top of their building shortly after they moved in, her body flashing by the window as Mort ate cereal and watched cartoons on a Sunday morning. On another occasion the man next door shot someone dead, the bang of the pistol there for an instant and gone, followed by silence and screaming and turmoil and then silence again.

He sometimes saw his brother John on holidays, back in the big house where he used to live, but Earl Homestead was always absent on those occasions. John treated Mort with indifference, as if he was oblivious to the fact that Mort lived in poverty while John enjoyed the relative comfort of a middle-class upbringing. Mort refused to visit again after a Christmas party one year when John rode up and down the sidewalk on a new red bicycle, honking a horn attached to chrome handlebars that sparkled in the cold sunlight. Shortly afterward, Mort's mother started coming home at dawn a couple of times a week, reeking of booze and cigarettes, her clothes a mess, her eyes as hollow as the empty pint bottles in her purse.

Mort grew to understand his world was one in which he stood alone. He told himself his parents were strangers, and he internalized his anger and never conceded to the slightest vulnerability. By the time he was ten, adults considered him withdrawn or possibly autistic. But inside the walls of his façade, Mort channeled his rage. He had no doubt the day would come when he would prove to the world he existed on a plane reserved for a special class of people.

Finding escape in his schoolwork, he soon realized his intelligence and ability to focus far exceeded his peers'. He saw no reason to develop relationships with those beneath him, at least not until he needed underlings to serve his greater agenda. He left high school early, without a single friend, when he was declared academically gifted and granted a scholarship to a small university in upstate Michigan. By this time, his determination to become rich and reverse the disadvantages of his childhood drove every facet of his personality. But there was also an underlying motivation behind his desire for financial success, one that he didn't fully understand until he was older—the need for absolute control.

After graduating at the top of his class with a degree in business in three years, he was accepted into the MBA program at Harvard Business School. Two years later he graduated from Harvard with honors, but there were two incidents not reflected in his transcripts.

During his undergrad studies, he attended a fraternity party where he planned to introduce himself to a coed he'd been watching on campus. But she was the object of constant attention from a group of beer-drinking frat brothers and seemed particularly enamored with one in particular, a handsome, blond-haired man. Mort finally approached her when the man left to use the bathroom. She was polite, and her smile made Mort's heart skip, but their brief conversation ended when the man returned. He led her away as if Mort's presence was of no significance, and took her into one of the bedrooms. The events of that evening would have been wholly unremarkable, save for one fact: the blond man was found stabbed to death a week later, his bound and gagged body left in a drainage ditch on the edge of campus.

The second incident involved a tenured professor at Harvard who disagreed with a case study Mort submitted discussing the future impact of the personal computer on the banking industry. The professor felt Mort's view was exaggerated and imprudent, and gave him a failing grade. Mort visited the professor in his office to discuss the matter, but the grade would not be changed. Within a week, a fire consumed the professor's Tudor-style home and burned it to the ground. He barely escaped with his life, resigned his post, and relocated out of state. The younger teacher brought in to replace him thought Mort's paper was brilliant and awarded him an A.

Though the police considered Mort the prime suspect of both crimes, they were unable to produce any evidence, forensic or otherwise, that was strong enough for an arrest. After weeks of interrogation following both episodes, they finally gave up on Mort, who then threatened to sue for harassment. He was told to not leave town, but the day after graduating he drove west, having decided that the thriving technology arena in Northern California was the best place to launch his career.

He made only one diversion as he drove across country toward San Jose. It was midnight when he stopped in a small suburb outside of Detroit. Despite the hour, it was still so humid his clothes began sticking to his body as soon as he left his car. The house where he lived the first eight years of his life looked shabbier than he remembered, the paint peeling and the lawn overgrown. A braided rope that once held a tire dangled from the oak tree in the front yard, its end frayed and rotted with age. He went into the dark house with the key he had kept all those years, and crept silently up the stairs.

The man asleep in the bedroom barely knew what was happening before he was gagged and hogtied. He sat staring in mute horror at the strange man in the room. But now that the moment had come, Mort was surprised to find he was at a loss for words.

"You're really just a loose end I need to clean up," he said finally. He tore the duct tape from Earl Homestead's mouth. "Do you have anything you'd like to say?"

"Who are you?"

"The real question is who I'm not."

"What?"

"I'm not your son, remember? I can still hear you telling that to my mother."

"My god," the man whispered hoarsely, sweat beaded on his forehead. "She died a month ago."

Mort looked at the person lying helpless on the rumpled sheets of the bed. "You can go meet her in hell, then."

"You're out of your mind, no, you can't do this…"

But Mort was already resealing Earl Homestead's mouth, wrapping the duct tape tightly around his head. Then he took a spring-loaded clothespin from his pocket and placed it over his father's nose, locking the nostrils shut. He stayed in the bedroom for a few minutes, watching Earl Homestead's face turn purple and his eyes bulge as he suffocated. When his head fell forward and his body stopped jerking, Mort went downstairs and grabbed some cold cuts and a loaf of bread from the refrigerator, then walked to his car and drove away.

• • •

Mort concentrated on staying a few cars behind the Lamborghini. He suspected Jimmy might be headed to another hotel in town, but was more likely leaving Las Vegas. Mort hoped it was the latter—kidnapping Jimmy would be easier to do in a less crowded environment.

Mort had studied the roadmaps and knew if Jimmy were leaving town he would most likely take Interstate 15 heading west. All other freeways were eastbound into the Mohave, with the nearest destinations being Salt Lake City or Phoenix. Interstate 15 led a hundred miles through the Western Mohave to the junction at Barstow. From there, one could turn south to the Los Angeles area, north on 395 toward Lake Tahoe, or continue west to Highway 5, toward San Jose or San Francisco.

If Jimmy headed east, there was a good chance he'd stop to spend the night in a small town. If he was westbound, he might drive straight through to wherever in California he was headed. The Lamborghini drove to the far end of the strip, toward the airport, and like Mort predicted, took the entrance to 15 West. It was noon and the sun was white in the colorless sky. In a few minutes the glitter of Las Vegas faded and was replaced by the brown emptiness of the desert.

The Toyota buzzed along at seventy-five, a couple hundred yards behind the Lamborghini. Mort ate a sandwich and drank a bottle of water as he drove, wondering if Jimmy would stop for lunch. Half an hour later they crossed the border into California. The road was nearly deserted, and Mort relaxed and turned on the radio. All was going as planned. But then, near the exit for Wheaton Springs, a black Corvette blasted by Mort at well over a hundred miles per hour.

Within a few seconds, the Corvette passed the Lamborghini. Mort heard the roar of the twelve-cylinder Italian motor as Jimmy jammed open the throttles in pursuit. Exhaust spewed from its pipes, and the sleek orange car launched forward. In less than ten seconds, Mort could no longer see either car.

Mort floored the Toyota, but the straight-four engine was built for economy, not performance. The speedometer flirted with ninety-five, but after a few miles the motor started to miss, and the temp gauge moved into the red zone. He backed down to eighty-five and turned off the AC, straining his eyes in hope that the Lamborghini had slowed and would become visible. The minutes ticked by with no sighting. Ten miles ahead lay the town of Baker, but after that there was nothing but highway for fifty miles to Barstow. If he didn't see Jimmy by the time he reached the turnoff for Baker, Mort needed to decide whether to stop and look for him in Baker, or continue to Barstow.

Neither choice was good. Suppose Jimmy didn't stop and continued to Barstow? If so, and Mort stopped to look for him in Baker, Jimmy would end up too far ahead for Mort to ever catch him. But if Mort continued to Barstow, and Jimmy had in fact stopped in Baker for food or gas, it was doubtful Jimmy would stop in Barstow; he'd probably just stay on the freeway and keep going.

Mort was pouring sweat in his disguise. It was at least a hundred outside, but every time he turned the air conditioning on, the engine started overheating. So he left it off and kept his speed at eighty-five. The black interior of the car was like an oven, even with the windows open.

He reached the exit for Baker without seeing the Lamborghini. He drove past the exit and continued for forty minutes, until he reached a tiny city called Yermo, about five miles outside of Barstow. A truck stop near the off-ramp was built on a rise in the terrain. Mort found a parking spot with a clear view of the freeway, and waited. He removed the apparatus that gave him the appearance of a fat man and tossed it in the backseat, never taking his eyes from the freeway.

Baker was a nothing town, a speck in the desert. Mort concluded that if Jimmy stopped there, it would be for food and gas only, which shouldn't take long. He decided to wait for exactly thirteen minutes. If Jimmy didn't come along by then, he would be well ahead, already to Barstow, where he would likely stop, for at least a short time.

Mort walked to a bit of shade under a sign and watched for the Lamborghini. Then he moved back to the car and started the motor. The thirteen minutes passed. With a brief curse, Mort hit the gas and got back on the freeway.

Mort now assumed Jimmy most likely drove straight through to Barstow. The driving time from Vegas to Barstow was over two hours. Jimmy would likely stop there, to use a restroom if nothing else.

Mort drove into the center of Barstow and started checking the parking lots of every restaurant, bar, and gas station he came across, driving in an increasingly wide circle. It was still very hot, but the sun had fallen and rested low above the horizon and glared directly in Mort's eyes. Once twilight came, the air cooled quickly. He continued searching until it was full dark.

When Mort checked into a hotel, his jaw was sore, and he realized he'd been clenching his teeth for hours. He had not anticipated losing Jimmy Homestead, especially when Jimmy didn't even know he was being followed.

Why had he stopped and waited along the freeway for Jimmy? Why hadn't he just driven straight to Barstow? The odds of finding Jimmy would have been better if he had. Instead, he waited and evidently gave Jimmy time to gas up and get food and leave for who knows where.

It was a judgment call on his part, and a bad one, he now conceded. He had failed to react effectively to an unforeseen circumstance. He had not analyzed the situation correctly, and that was because he was not prepared. He should have predicted Jimmy might drive the Lamborghini at a high rate of speed across the open desert. That potential simply did not occur to him, and as a result, he had not only lost Jimmy, but also wasted time and a significant portion of his limited financial resources. It was poor planning on his part, and it was unforgivable. Now he needed to come up with a new plan, and he could not afford to fail again.

Mort sat on the bed, his eyes squeezed shut, every joint in his body flexed like a compressed coil. In his head he heard a sound like a phonograph needle screeching across a record, and before he could stop himself, he leapt up and punched three holes in the wall, his fist pumping at lightning speed, his eyes dark and the skin on his face stretched so tight it felt like the seams would split.

19

CODY AND SHEILA HAD just sat down for lunch at a Mexican restaurant when I called.

"Get your food to go. I'll be there in five minutes," I said. "Order me a burrito, too."

Ten minutes later we were heading west on 15 in my Ford rental. Cody sat up front, manning the GPS. "He's at least ten miles ahead of us," he said.

"It doesn't matter. We'll know when and where he stops."

We settled in and drove in silence for a time, until we crossed the border into California. "What's the plan when we find him, Sheila?" I said.

"I'll want to sit down and talk with him in a place where we can have a private conversation. A cocktail lounge would be perfect, as long as it's not too small. I'll want you and Cody to be visible to Jimmy while we're talking. Not close enough to listen, but close enough so Jimmy can feel your presence."

"How do you plan on convincing him to share his money with you, if you don't mind me asking?"

"You let me handle that."

"Hey," Cody said, staring at the GPS. "He's farther ahead of us now. Looks like about twenty miles."

"He's probably speeding. There's nothing but open road ahead. Let's hope he doesn't kill himself."

"You won't lose him, right?"

"No way," I said. "He's got to stop sometime."

Sheila had a California map opened on her lap in the back seat. "The next town is Baker," she said.

But Jimmy didn't stop in Baker. He continued west on 15, and continued to gain ground on us. We ate while we drove, maintaining an even seventy-five miles per hour, slicing through an empty, sun-blasted landscape that was colorless except for the faded brown of the earth's floor.

Half an hour later, the red arrow on the GPS stopped moving. The Lamborghini had stopped in Barstow. We were twenty-five miles away.

"If we're lucky, he stopped for lunch and a few drinks," Cody said.

But we were still ten miles outside of town when the arrow started moving again.

"Damn him," Sheila said.

"He's got onto 58 west now," Cody said.

The map crinkled behind me. "But that leads nowhere!" Sheila said.

"It leads to 395. He's heading to Tahoe." I checked my gas gauge.

"Oh, right," Sheila said. "But there's not much along the way—a couple little towns, Red Mountain, Atolia..."

"Those are ghost towns—I don't think anyone still lives there," I said. "All right, here's what we'll do. We'll make a quick stop in Barstow, fill the tank, then get back on the road. South Lake Tahoe is almost five hundred miles away. He'll need gas again and probably food. There are more towns further north. Hopefully he'll stop long enough for us to catch up."

We took the exit for Barstow, and I filled the tank while Cody and Sheila headed into the mini-mart. When they came out, Cody had a twelve-pack of Budweiser tucked under his arm. "Might as well enjoy the ride," he said, gesturing north toward the high desert.

And so we hit the road again, driving hard through the sparse terrain. Sheila put her headphones on and stretched out in the back seat. Cody and I cracked beers. I rolled down the window to check the midafternoon temperature and was greeted by a gritty blast of hot air. "Christ, it's got to be a hundred and ten out there," Cody said.

"Beats freezing to death, though," I said.

"Your toes still feel it?"

"Sometimes."

"We got those sons of bitches, Dirt. Every one of them." Cody opened another beer and held it up. "Here's to every asshole that gets what's coming to him."

An hour later, we shot past the exit for Ridgecrest, a town of about twenty thousand bordering a military weapons testing area. The mountains of the Sequoia National Forest became visible on our left. To the right the land stretched without interruption across the bleak landscape toward Death Valley.

"The son of a bitch is still gaining on us," Cody said.

"Well, this is a perfect road to go for a speed run. I'd say he has a slight horsepower advantage." I cranked the Ford up to eighty. "If we push it, this heap will overheat."

We plodded along for another forty-five minutes, doing our best to make time, heading north along the eastern rim of California. The Sierra Nevada mountain range now flanked us, and I could see the peak of Mount Whitney, the highest point in the continental US, up ahead. We were driving along a section of 395 where the high desert butted up against alpine peaks created by eons of fault block activity, resulting in the southern Sierras.

"He's stopped," Cody said. "In Lone Pine."

Sheila took off her headphones. "Where?"

"I never heard of it. Let's just hope he stays there long enough for us to catch him."

20

JIMMY WAS STILL ON a high from his whirlwind tour of Costa Rica. He hadn't been sure what to expect, but the experience had been everything Larry promised. The women were wild and friendly, and the culture pulsated with a decadent Latin rhythm Jimmy found to his liking. And besides the party life, Larry arranged a deep-sea fishing expedition on a luxury yacht, and Jimmy caught the biggest fish of the day, a six-foot sailfish.

The previous night, before he flew back on the early flight in the morning, had been an all-timer. He'd brought half a dozen whores to his suite at the El Presidente, and one of them sold him an eight-ball of high-grade Colombian blow, fresh from the border. Jimmy cut lines on a large mirror he removed from the wall, they cranked the music up high, and the girls stripped except for their high heels. The hookers were trying to teach Jimmy and Larry to dance the samba, until finally the party dissolved into a raucous orgy, with couplings of every variety ensuing, girl on girl, two girls on one guy, even oral with no condoms, and on and on until Jimmy's member was raw, and poor Larry lay passed out face down and bare-assed in the corner. Jimmy left him that way when he jumped into a limo at four-thirty in the morning and barely made his flight.

He slept in his first-class seat the entire trip and actually felt pretty good when he landed in Vegas. He took a cab straight from the airport to the Mirage, threw his suitcase into the tiny trunk in the Lamborghini's front section, and drove away. He knew the ass-kissing manager at the Mirage was hoping he'd stay around and drop some more dough at the tables, but Jimmy had other ideas.

While the women in Costa Rica had been great, none could speak much English, so they couldn't appreciate Jimmy's wry sense of humor or insightful comments. Jimmy rubbed at his lips as he drove and felt a pang of panic when he remembered where his mouth had been. Oh well, even if he came down with a raging case of the cankers, his money could surely buy a remedy. Truthfully though, Jimmy thought he'd really reached the point where the constant whoring was no longer exciting. After years of not having a real relationship with a woman, Jimmy felt he might be up for a little genuine female companionship—maybe a woman he could enjoy hanging with, someone he could talk to, and maybe even someone who cared about him.

As Jimmy drove out of Las Vegas, he thought about all the great things he could offer a woman. He considered that maybe it was time to slow down—he knew he couldn't continue to party like this forever. Having a cool, sexy babe by his side might lend some stability to his life. The living-out-of-a-hotel routine was getting old. He began to seriously contemplate his next step: the purchase of a mansion. What better way to attract a woman than to impress her with his home?

Some dickweed in a Corvette blew by Jimmy as he headed west, and Jimmy downshifted and stabbed the throttle. The five-hundred-horsepower engine roared to life, and the Lamborghini accelerated like it was shot from a cannon. Jimmy blew by the Corvette at 150, and reached 170 before he backed off. He had a huge grin plastered on his face. What a rush! His Lamborghini was the baddest car on the road, and he was headed to Tahoe, where the beauty of the alpine lake, plus the abundance of night life, made it the perfect place to live. He had checked out some real-estate magazines, and there were plenty of palatial homes to choose from.

Jimmy stopped in Barstow to fill his tank. He was thinking of fast food, but the remnant of last night's blow was whispering his name from the bindle he'd stashed in his pack of Marlboros. So Jimmy put off eating and instead powdered his nose, then hit the gas and hightailed out to 395, north toward Lake Tahoe.

21

DESPITE CODY AND SHEILA urging me to peg the throttle, I resisted pushing the Ford's small motor to its breaking point. "It's the only car we got," I said. They grumbled briefly and fell silent. It took thirty-five minutes to reach the exit for Lone Pine, which was located at the base of Mount Whitney. I drove across a bridge over a small river and onto the main drag, where crumbling stucco structures with old wood façades were interspersed with newer, remodeled stores and restaurants. Most of the stores on the street offered fishing, camping, and mountaineering gear. The buildings were all dwarfed by a massive pine and fir covered ridge that rose behind the town. It wasn't long before we spotted Jimmy's car.

It was parked in front of Miner's Bar & Grill, a beat-up, aging joint with a wood-post fence out front, as if they expected a pack of cowboys might ride up at any moment and hitch their horses. We parked, but before we could get out, Sheila said, "Now, listen. After I talk to him awhile, I'll get up and go to the ladies room. Then you two go sit with him. Tell him you're not patient men, and he better cooperate."

"You mean, scare him a little," I said.

"That's right. Just make it quick. The less said the better. Just make your point and let him be. If he asks questions, don't answer."

Sheila led us into the building. It was a larger room than I expected and my eyes took a moment to adjust to the dim lighting. The air was dusty, and the murmur of voices from the day drinkers was barely discernible. At the far end of the bar sat a man with shoulder-length blond hair, a dark shirt with some fancy embroidery, and lizard-skin boots.

Cody and I followed as Sheila approached him. "Hello, Jimmy," she said. He turned to her and blinked a couple times. Then his mouth fell open and his eyes widened. Cody and I leaned on the bar and watched them. "It's been a long time," Sheila said.

Jimmy stammered something unintelligible, then managed a weak smile. "What brings you out here, Sheila?" Trying to sound cool, like he wasn't surprised.

"Let's go sit, and I'll tell you."

They moved to a far table, and Cody and I took a table about fifteen feet away. Jimmy was facing us, and we stared him down as Sheila spoke quietly. When Jimmy responded, he furrowed his brow and kept turning his hands up, then his eyes went round and he sucked his cheeks in. After ten minutes Sheila left the table and headed to the ladies room.

We walked over and sat across from Jimmy.

"Who are you?" he asked.

"We're bad news for you, that's who," Cody said.

"This has got to be some kind of joke, right?" Jimmy said, and raised his highball to his lips, but I slapped the glass out of his hand. It thudded against the wooden floorboards, and I could hear the chatter at the bar grow quiet. "I ain't laughing," I said.

"Whoa," Jimmy said.

"I hope you have the right answers for Sheila," Cody said.

"Hey, I'm just—"

"But maybe you'll have to learn the hard way."

Jimmy swallowed, out of words for the moment.

"Don't be an asshole all your life," I said, as Sheila came back to the table.

They talked a few minutes more while we went to the bar to assure the bartender everything was cool. We waited there until Sheila and Jimmy stood and walked toward the front door.

"I'm going to ride with Jimmy," Sheila said, once we were standing on the sidewalk in front of the bar. "We'll continue north to Lake Tahoe." I squinted into the midafternoon sun and watched Jimmy hand his keys to his stepmom.

"Just a nice, pleasant drive," Cody said to Jimmy. "We'll be right behind you."

Sheila climbed behind the wheel of the Lamborghini. Jimmy gave me a curious look, then got into the passenger seat. It had been fifteen years since he'd seen me last. I'd recognized him—did he recognize me, or had too much booze killed his memory?

Sheila kept the Lamborghini under eighty for the next hour, as we drove along the desert floor under the shadow of granite walls veined with moss and gnarled branches. We passed the exit for Bishop, climbed into the Sierras, and drove past the entrance to Mammoth Mountain Ski Resort. South Lake Tahoe lay three hours ahead.

"Did Sheila give you much background on Jimmy?" I asked Cody, as we tailed the Lamborghini along the increasingly curvy road.

"Enough to know he's a real loser."

"You think he's a bad person?"

"He ain't a good person, Dirt."

"Does that give her the right to extort his money?"

"Extort?"

I looked at Cody. "Yeah. That's what she's doing, right?"

"Watch the road, would you?" he said, as a big rig came around a corner. "Extortion means she would specifically threaten him. As in, 'Give me the money or I'll break your legs.'"

"So having us rattle him a bit is no issue."

"Not the way I see it."

"Do you know what her game is, Cody?"

"Her game? What are you talking about?"

"She's got to have some angle to convince him to share his winnings. Do you really think Sheila planned on Jimmy handing over a chunk of money just for the asking?"

Cody didn't reply. I glanced over and saw a flicker of uncertainty on his face.

"She said there's some people from his past he wants nothing to do with," Cody said, lighting a cigarette and exhaling the smoke quickly. "She felt her knowledge of, or access to, these people would motivate him."

"Who are these people?"

"That's all she told me. She wasn't specific."

We drove on and dropped into a forested valley where the road was straight and flat. I didn't think Cody was hiding anything from me, and I couldn't really blame him for his lack of insight into Sheila's plans. I remembered the first night I'd met her. We ended up at my cabin to sign my contract, and she had me panting like a stray dog in heat. And when I dropped her off, most of my questions were still unanswered. But that didn't mean I would continue to let her draw me into her scheme without knowing what I was in for.

Regardless of my suspicions about Sheila, I was happy Cody was enjoying her sensual charms. At least one of us was. He seemed much happier than I'd seen him since his divorce.

I lit one of Cody's smokes, and he handed me a fresh beer. "What the hell, old buddy," I said.

"That's more like it, Dirt. Whatever happens, happens. I doubt we'll run into anything we can't handle."

We settled in and enjoyed the last couple hours of the drive, reminiscing about old times, times we were drunk, women we'd bedded, and even men we had killed.

22

GARRETT RANCOUR ROLLED OUT of bed and brewed a cup of coffee in the little percolator in his room at the Motel 6 on the edge of Carson City. Rancour enjoyed staying at the hotel. It was a nice change from the dingy room in San Jose he'd rented after being released from county lockup. He appreciated getting a break from his whacked-out roommates, who weren't much of an upgrade from the jailbirds Rancour had bunked with during his fifteen month jolt. He appreciated the solitude of the hotel and the freedom it gave him from the constant presence of idiots.

Speaking of idiots, he wondered where Sanzini was. A wide grin split Rancour's face as he recalled the events of the previous night. Sanzini had gotten his ass kicked twice, first by the bouncer in the cathouse, and then he'd taken a royal pounding by the hard-case dude out in the parking lot. He had behaved like a moron, and got just what he deserved, including the loss of his coat.

Rancour considered what Sanzini would do next. Without Rancour's help, Sanzini would be clueless as to the whereabouts of Jimmy Homestead. Having taken a serious beating and minus his leather jacket, he would probably plant his dumb ass on his Harley and ride home to his mother's house to lick his wounds. What else could he do?

With Sanzini out of the way, Rancour could plot his own course of action. What a perfect victim Jimmy Homestead was. Sanzini had said Homestead was a waste case, and Rancour had overheard the whore saying he'd been ripped out of his mind. So a guy who likes to party and get laid has a pot of money fall into his lap. Well, a fool and his money are soon partying. Isn't that the old saying? No, a fool and his money are soon *parted.* That's what was on the horizon for Jimmy Homestead.

Rancour stuck his wallet, which was down to eighty bucks, in his back pocket and put on Sanzini's jacket. The morning air was brisk and smelled of diesel. He kick-started his chopped Honda, revved the motor, and wheeled out of the lot toward the center of town. The first chore was to come up with some slab. To get by until he could rob Homestead, he figured he needed at least a grand.

The ideal target would be a place of business with plenty of cash on hand, no security cameras or guards, and minimal traffic. Chain stores typically had well developed anti-theft systems, so Rancour ruled them out. He was looking for a ma-and-pa-style hardware store or restaurant, or maybe even a bar.

If he couldn't find a suitable mark, he might consider boosting a car, which was a much easier operation. The problem was converting the car into money. In San Jose, it would be no problem—he knew a couple of chop shops that would pay cash and have the car stripped down to the frame in an hour. But he had no such connections in Carson City.

Rancour began contemplating riding back to San Jose and stealing a car or two. He could then return to the Tahoe area with plenty of dough and track down Homestead without having to sweat going broke. But returning to San Jose might delay or distract him from what he was starting to believe could be something really big. How much money might Homestead have on him at any time? How much cash might he keep at his house? Twenty grand? Fifty grand? More?

He spent the better part of the morning driving around Carson City, casing businesses. By noon he had migrated away from the main boulevard to an industrial area, where he turned behind a row of warehouses built along a dry creek bed. On the other side of the creek, an empty field stretched about a quarter mile to a solitary white building standing on the edge of a road. A scattering of cars surrounded the building.

Rancour rode away from the warehouses and made his way to the white structure. It was an Italian restaurant, the parking lot half full with the Thursday lunch crowd. Across the road, there was perhaps another quarter mile of open field leading to a residential neighborhood.

Rancour parked at the restaurant. As he approached the entrance a group of businessmen walked out, past a sign near the front door listing hours as 11:00 A.M. to 11:00 P.M. daily. He went into the place, where it was dark and ritzy in an old-fashioned way, like maybe it was a hangout for wealthy retirees. Rancour became immediately aware his clothes would draw attention to him. He approached a counter where pies and cakes were displayed. Behind a cash register on the counter sat a short, fat woman with a mustache an adolescent boy might be proud of. A waitress, middle-aged and wearing her hair in a bun, walked to the counter and handed the fat woman a slip of paper and some twenty-dollar bills.

"Could I look at a menu?" Rancour asked the waitress. She handed him one and hurried away toward the dining room.

Rancour left quickly. He drove down a small street in the direction of some cookie-cutter houses, parked under a tree, and checked out the menu. The dinner entrees were expensive, and there were over a hundred different wines listed.

He rode off and familiarized himself with the street layout surrounding the restaurant, then went back to the warehouses and timed how long it would take him to get to the freeway heading to Reno. He found an on-ramp five minutes away.

After filling his tank, he stopped at a sporting goods store and spent thirty dollars on a pellet gun that resembled a semiautomatic pistol. At a drug store, he bought a pair of flesh-colored pantyhose.

When the sun went down, he saw there was no moon—a good omen. He waited at his hotel room until nine o'clock, then rode back to the restaurant. A small cluster of Joshua trees stood in the field across from the joint, on the opposite side of the highway. Rancour killed his headlight and turned off the road. It was almost pitch black, and he had to ride very slowly. He reached the trees and waited, watching the parking lot grow less crowded. At ten o'clock, he counted twenty cars remaining. Probably ten belonged to employees, he figured.

Rancour pushed his Honda out of the desert scrub and rode to the warehouse complex from where he'd originally spotted the restaurant. The area was dark and deserted. He parked his bike behind a garbage bin, opened the pack secured to the sissy bar, and pulled out the pellet gun and panty hose.

It wasn't quite ten-thirty when he climbed out of the creek bed and walked across the field. There were fewer parked cars now. He pulled the stocking over his face and stuck the pellet gun in the back of his pants. Staying in the shadows, he watched a man and woman walk out from the main entrance and drive away. Then he ran through the flood of lights in the parking lot and burst through the front doors.

The short, fat woman working the cash register earlier in the day was still there. She stared at Rancour, her eyes like black marbles pressed into a ball of dough. No one else was around.

Rancour leaned over the counter and aimed the gun at her ear.

"Open the register and give me the money. Do it now."

She blinked and locked her eyes on him, her face void of emotion.

"Are you fucking deaf?" Rancour hissed. "Give me the money or I'll blow your fat face all over the wall."

"No," she said.

Rancour braced himself with his left hand and swung his legs up and over the counter. The woman was perched on a padded barstool. Rancour shoved the pellet gun into one of her round eyes. "Last chance. Open it."

Her pudgy finger pushed a button and the door to the cash register clicked open. Rancour hit her across the base of the skull with the butt of the gun, and she fell forward. He pushed her back and began stuffing bills into a plastic bag he pulled from his pocket. When the register was empty, he walked out from behind the counter and saw a man coming around the corner. The man wore a black vest and a white shirt. He was six feet, or taller. Flat waist and wide shoulders. Curly dark hair. Maybe thirty. "Face down on the floor," Rancour said, aiming the gun at his chest.

"You bad thief," the man said in a thick accent. But he moved back a step.

Rancour bolted out the door, and a few seconds later he was sprinting across the field, high-stepping over the terrain, ripping the stocking from his head. He heard a shouted curse, looked back, and saw the man was chasing him.

It was almost impossible to see in the middle of the black field. Rancour tripped on a rock and shoulder rolled, driving his knuckles into the dirt, still clenching the plastic bag full of cash. He came up on his feet and ran to the edge of the creek bed and slid to the bottom. He leaned tight against the wall and counted to five, trying to catch his breath.

The pursuer came bounding over the edge, his legs running in the void. He hit the ground and tumbled onto his side with a snort. Rancour ran up and shot him point blank in the face. The gun misfired after two shots. The man reached out and tried to trip him up, but Rancour danced away, then reared back and kicked him flush in the ear with his steel-toed boot. He kicked him once more just to make sure, then scrambled up the other side of the dirt bank and ran to his motorcycle.

He shoved the bills into the zippered compartment of his pack, then pulled off his sweat-soaked gray T-shirt. He wiped down the pellet gun, put it in the plastic bag, tied it shut and threw it in the Dumpster next to his bike. Then he yanked a black shirt over his head, put on Sanzini's coat, and five minutes later was heading north on the freeway, listening as sirens grew dim in the background.

23

SHEILA PUMPED THE CLUTCH and ground the gear shift into third. The Lamborghini jerked ahead. She eased off the gas pedal, then accelerated again.

"Could you take it easy, please?" Jimmy said.

Sheila grimaced and tried to get comfortable in the low, wraparound seat. "Would you light me a cigarette?"

"No smoking in my car," Jimmy said. "Besides, you need to keep both hands on the wheel."

"I'd let you drive, but I think you might just be dumb enough to try to lose those guys."

Jimmy looked at his stepmother. She was just as slinky as he remembered. He even remembered her perfume, and it made him think of sex.

"I'm still trying to make sense of your story," he said.

"It's not a story, Jimmy. It's the truth. And my involvement in this is coming to an end quickly. How it ends for you depends on what you do."

When Sheila appeared at the bar, Jimmy had been paralyzed by a slew of colliding thoughts. He was basically in the middle of nowhere, and out of thin air Sheila walks in, a ghost from fifteen years past. It had been that long since he'd seen her, but he recognized her in an instant. He actually thought for a second she may have been interested in a repeat of their one-nighter, which happened when she was in the process of divorcing his father. But Jimmy was smart enough to realize Sheila seduced him mainly for the purpose of tormenting John Homestead. Christ, it was sordid, even for Jimmy. It would have been bad if it had just been a quick screw, but Sheila had worked the seventeen-year-old Jimmy over for three lustful hours. How can you ever forget something like that?

What would it be like to do her now? She still exuded the same steamy sensuality Jimmy remembered from when he was a teenager. He thought back to that night with her, how she loved it from behind, panting and crying out when she came. He began to get hard. He could probably offer her a few grand and she'd pull over at the nearest hotel.

Sheila glanced over at Jimmy's leering expression. "You need to think about staying alive, not getting laid," she said, like she was reading his mind.

"Tell me again why someone would want to kill me," Jimmy said.

"It started with the ounce of coke you stole."

• • •

It happened three years ago, when Jimmy was passing through the Bay Area. He intended to stay only until he came up with enough scratch to make it to Redding, where he heard a lumberyard was looking to hire a hundred men. He landed in San Jose and spent the night in a park and worked at a temporary agency for a few days, loading trucks. They assigned him a job working with another man, filling a freezer trailer with hundred-pound boxes of beef. The man had arms as thick as Jimmy's legs and threw the heavy boxes around with ease. His name was Tony Sanzini.

"This is a cake walk," Sanzini said. "I could do this all day and not break a sweat." He pointed across the lot to a construction yard where teams of men were framing an office complex. "You see those dudes? I guarantee you, I could kick the ass of any two of them at a time."

When they broke for lunch, Sanzini stood on the shipping dock, talking as he ate. "I'll share something with you because it looks like you could use a little advice. It takes more than strength and fighting skills to get anywhere. Being able to whip ass comes in handy, but brains are more important."

Jimmy was sitting with his legs dangling off the dock. He looked up at Sanzini, opened his mouth, then thought better of it.

"You got something to say?" Sanzini said. "I don't need this job. I do it to stay in shape. I run my own business."

"What kind of business?" Jimmy asked.

"None of your business is what kind." Sanzini sucked on a can of soda, belched loudly, and sat next to Jimmy. "The kind that pays well, and the kind you keep quiet."

They went back to work. By late afternoon the freezer car was full.

"Hey, man. You know how to keep your mouth shut, maybe you won't have to spend the rest of your life workin' for da man."

"You feel like getting a beer?" Jimmy asked.

They headed to the neighborhood lounge around the corner from the house where Sanzini lived with his mother. Sanzini's cell rang, and he walked away to take the call. When he came back to the bar, he told Jimmy he had to split to take care of business.

Jimmy sipped his beer slowly, until Sanzini returned ten minutes later. "Cha-ching," Sanzini said.

The next day at the loading dock, Sanzini and Jimmy were loading freezer cars again. Sanzini carried two of the hundred-pound boxes at a time, one tucked under each arm. "How many guys you know could do that?" he said.

Jimmy shrugged. "Not many."

They worked together for the remainder of the week. Sanzini's boasting was constant and sometimes ridiculous, but Jimmy never questioned him—not even when Sanzini bragged about being connected to a Mexican drug cartel.

"You seem like a decent guy," Sanzini said at quitting time on Friday. "Cash your check, and I'll cut you a wholesale deal on an eight-ball. Cut it into quarters, and you can make a couple hundred bucks.

"I'm in," Jimmy said, and they had a few beers at the bar before going to Sanzini's house.

It was a small house in a neighborhood where most of the front yards were small dirt or weed plots enclosed by waist-high chain link fences. Telephone wires crisscrossed over the street and left looping shadows on the yards. Sanzini led Jimmy into his bedroom, where posters of football players, a model car collection, and a badly worn student desk left Jimmy with the impression Sanzini had lived in this room since he was a child.

Sanzini pulled out an electronic scale and a plastic baggie bulging across the bottom with white powder. He weighed an eighth of an ounce and poured the cocaine into a bindle fashioned from a square of paper cut from a magazine. Jimmy was handing him a roll of twenties when the doorbell rang. Sanzini went to the window and moved the curtain aside.

"Shit," he said. "You wait here. Don't touch anything." He put the baggie in the drawer of his old desk, removed a wad of cash, and locked the drawer. Someone began pounding on the front door. Sanzini shoved the money in his pocket. "Stay quiet," he said, then left the room.

Jimmy peeked out the window. A lowered '67 Impala was parked at the curb. In the passenger seat, a man with a red bandana low on his forehead sat with his arm hanging out the window.

Jimmy could hear bits of conversation coming from the front door. He looked at the bindle in his palm and started to open it, but stopped when he noticed Sanzini had left his keys on the desk. He froze, his eyes staring at the key to the drawer.

The blow in the drawer was worth close to two grand. Jimmy felt his pulse quicken.

The voices grew louder and Jimmy looked out the window and saw Sanzini and a man talking in front of the house. The man was a dark Latino, tall and slender, his brown arms scrolled with blue ink that looked like random graffiti. He was pointing at Sanzini.

Jimmy picked up the keys. His hands were slick with moisture. He fumbled the key into the lock on the drawer, opened it, grabbed the baggie, and eased it into his pocket. He checked the window again, then slid out of the room, down the hallway, and into the kitchen. He pulled open a rickety sliding-glass door, the runners rusty and caked with grime. Then he was outside, sprinting, his chest pounding as he scrambled over the backyard fence into a neighboring yard. After coming out to the street the next block over, he ran a mile as fast as he could. When he stopped to catch his breath, he heard the roar of a large bore motorcycle engine, maybe a block or two away. The sound faded, and he ran two more miles. Within an hour he was on a bus for Redding.

24

JOHN HOMESTEAD WALKED INTO his dreary apartment. The sun had just gone down, and he was dragging after eight hours on his feet. He worked in the paint department of a chain hardware store, and his co-workers were two young men putting themselves through college. They were happy and athletic, playing grab ass and ogling every female who walked by. They seemed oblivious to life's difficulties and disappointments.

John had driven home from Tahoe after Lou Calgaretti conceded that finding Jimmy might take some time. The private eye said Jimmy's phone was turned off, which could mean a number of things, including the possibility Jimmy was traveling out of the country. Lou promised to call as soon as he had something more to go on. John had been home now for almost a week. All he could hope for was Jimmy would show up in the near future.

He mixed a drink and lowered his weary body onto the couch. "Out of the country" sounded both mysterious and…well, privileged. Like it was a place where people from a higher social status went to vacation, a place reserved for people to whom money was not an issue. The lousy punk. All that money, and not a word from him. Apparently vacationing in a foreign country was more important than contacting his father.

John knew he hadn't been the greatest of parents, but he had fed, clothed, and provided shelter for his son. He had made those sacrifices. He had also put up with Jimmy's lying, laziness, and selfishness. In addition, he suspected, though he could never quite admit it happened, that Jimmy and Sheila had…

He shook the thought from his head and made another drink. It didn't matter now—the past was the past. What mattered was finding his son and working out an arrangement for Jimmy to provide for his father monetarily. And if he was unwilling to, John would beat the money out of him with his bare hands if he had to. John clenched his fists and scowled. The time would come for his ungrateful son to act like a decent human being, or else.

The phone rang, a seldom event.

"Hello?"

"Lou Calgaretti here. Your son just checked into Harrah's in South Lake Tahoe, Mr. Homestead. How soon can you be here?"

John hauled himself off the couch, swallowed a couple of diet pills, threw his clothes in a bag, and was on the road in ten minutes. He sat in the thick rush-hour traffic, muttering to himself, trying to find a decent radio station. It was a Thursday night, and the freeways leading out of San Jose were gridlocked. An AM station reported an accident up ahead. John pounded his steering wheel. The Ford LTD crawled forward.

It took four hours to reach Sacramento. He stopped to fill his tank and buy a few high-caffeine energy drinks. His car did not handle well, and driving the next hundred miles through the mountains would require steady concentration. The moon was a thin sliver, the roads ahead unlit and black.

He finally crested Echo Summit and descended into South Lake Tahoe at one in the morning. His eyes were bloodshot, and his hands shook from the mixture of diet pills and caffeine. He badly needed a drink, but first he pulled over and dialed Lou Calgaretti. No answer.

He drove to Harrah's casino, found a bar, and ordered a double gin. His heart was racing, and he thought he might be on the verge of a panic attack. One more double, and he could feel his jittery nerves begin to relax. He sat slumped at the bar, his eyes burning, feeling utterly exhausted. Finally he trudged to the check-in counter and asked for a room.

On his way to the elevator, he stopped at a courtesy phone. He paused for a long moment, then picked it up and asked for the room of Jimmy Homestead.

The phone rang once, twice, ten times before John hung up. He carried his suitcase to his room, where he fell onto the bed and passed out fully dressed.

Maybe if he weren't so tired, John might have instead walked out to the twenty-one tables at Harrah's, where Jimmy was playing a few lazy hands, catching a tequila buzz, and flirting with a cocktail waitress.

25

WE FOLLOWED THE LAMBORGHINI slowly through the dusk, down the main drag of South Lake Tahoe. Heads swiveled to stare as Sheila eased the Italian exotic through the series of lights leading to the casinos at the state line. She pulled into Harrah's and parked the vehicle on the third floor of the parking garage. As soon as I parked, Cody climbed quickly out of our car and opened the door of the Lamborghini for Sheila. Jimmy stepped out and crossed his arms, watching Cody and his stepmother.

"It's too late to handle any banking today, so we'll have to wait until the morning," Sheila said. Jimmy started walking away, and Sheila followed him, with Cody by her side. I brought up the rear, wondering to what degree Jimmy had agreed to the banking Sheila referred to.

We walked up to the registration counter and stood by while Jimmy got a room and left toward the elevators with his bag.

"After all this, you're letting him out of your sight?" I said to Sheila.

"I've got his car keys," she replied.

"He could catch a cab and be at the Reno airport in an hour."

"I don't think he's going anywhere."

"Why wouldn't he?"

"Jimmy has certain motivations to cooperate," she said.

"You sound pretty sure about that."

"All you really need to know is you'll get paid as we agreed, by tomorrow."

"That easy, huh?"

"Ease up, Dirt," Cody said. "You want to join us for dinner?"

"No, I need to go turn in the rental car."

"I'll call you tomorrow then," he said. "Sheila and I are going to check in."

I watched them walk away, Sheila's tight jeans painted on her heart-shaped ass, Cody's hulk towering beside her like a huge, untamed animal that responded only to her commands.

The rental car agency stuck me with a $200 penalty for returning an out-of-state car at a site other than where it was rented. I put it on my charge card and walked the two miles to my house. It was a cool night, and I was tired and glad to be home. After starting a fire in my wood-burning stove, I found a microwave dinner in my nearly empty freezer. The meal was tasteless, but I ate it anyway, while I tried without success to find a TV show that would hold my interest. I finally turned off the television and sat in the silence and darkness.

I harbored no false hope regarding Sheila's promise that by tomorrow I would be paid the ten grand she now legally owed me. Too many factors didn't add up, the most salient being that Jimmy would be somehow motivated to make his money available to her. The fact that she had asked Cody and me to tell Jimmy "he better cooperate" suggested she was running a ruse on him. And if Jimmy didn't buy it, I thought it likely Sheila's next move would involve Cody and me turning up the pressure.

Last winter I had nearly died while hunting down the killer of a lumber tycoon's son. I'd committed a series of crimes during my investigation, including some that could have landed me in California's prison system. I had done so at first because I wanted to collect the bounty offered, and later strictly out of self-preservation. When the case was finally over, I felt I'd probably used up most of the good luck in my cosmic reservoir.

If I needed to help persuade Jimmy Homestead to share his fortune with his stepmom, I could become involved in any number of crimes—conspiracy to commit extortion, for one. I could almost hear the voice of my father, the ex-district attorney, from the grave. "Not all criminals are stupid or greedy, some just find themselves in tough situations and use bad judgment," he once told me. "These are the saddest cases, but they aren't immune from prosecution."

I laid my sleeping bag on the couch and closed my eyes against the flickering glow of heat from my stove. My last thoughts before I fell asleep were of promises of money and steamy sex, but my dreams were fraught with vague accusations, repercussions, a chase that led nowhere, and alluring women beyond my grasp.

• • •

It was an hour before sunrise when I woke. I brewed a pot of coffee and made myself a breakfast of scrambled eggs and toast. The pots and pans and glassware in my cupboards were all new and neatly organized. It was a pleasant reminder that my home had once enjoyed a woman's touch.

I prepared a forty-pound pack and set out when the sky lightened. Two miles past the meadow behind my cabin, I reached the Sierra's western flank. The trail steepened, and I slowed my jog as the dusty fire road narrowed, until I was maneuvering carefully along a rocky gorge. A sheer cliff fell from the edge of the trail, to a creek far below. The path eventually veered from the ledge and to a shallow field where a series of rock formations rose at the base of a pine-studded ridge. I started jogging again, following a path into a forested hillside thick with aspen and fir.

Half an hour later, I reached a waterfall cut into a hundred-foot column of rock. The flow was a mere trickle this late in the season; the stream below babbled faintly and was nearly dry in places. Earlier this summer the snow melt had gushed over the precipice, and the riverbed roared with white water. I sat for a minute and filled my canteen, and took in the view of Lake Tahoe from two thousand feet. The alpine lake was deep blue against the pale morning sky, the surface sparkling when the wind gusted off the peaks.

I checked my watch, then double-timed it back home, running hard down the mountain. I was soaked with sweat when I walked in my door at 9:30. Before heading to the shower, I called Cody's cell. He didn't answer.

By ten I was dressed in my newest jeans, a button-down shirt, and a blue sports coat. I called Cody again, and this time he picked up.

"Anything to report?" I asked.

"No, nothing," he said, his voice distant and distracted. "I'll call you later."

A minute later I was on the road, a freshly shaved and pressed salesman, business card in hand, a smile glued to my face.

I stopped at every attorney's and bail bondsman's office in South Lake Tahoe, introducing myself, chatting with secretaries, sometimes meeting the proprietors, sometimes not. By noon I was finished in South Lake, so I drove around the lake to the north side to peddle my wares in Tahoe City. That took another couple of hours, and then it was an hour drive to Carson City for more of the same. I only covered about a quarter of the listings in Carson by five o'clock.

Sipping a soft drink as I headed back over Spooner pass toward home, I felt pleased with the day's effort. The most solid result was from a lady attorney who seemed interested in hiring me for a divorce case. This would probably involve following some poor sap for a few days and documenting his activities. Sometimes the subject's only objectionable behavior was spending too much time hanging out in bars and not enough time working. But more typically, I would learn the guy had a woman on the side.

In that case my job would involve taking pictures. It was sordid work, but it was a payday.

I got home, cooked myself some grub, and started watching an old Clint Eastwood cowboy movie. Cody hadn't called all day, and I can't say I was surprised. But before Clint had a chance to draw his pistol, my cell rang.

"Dan, things are getting a bit complicated over here," Cody said. "How about dropping by Harrah's, and we'll talk strategy?"

26

FINDING JIMMY HADN'T BEEN easy for Lou Calgaretti. He was unsuccessful in contacting anyone from Jimmy's past who could provide the slightest information. Not that there were many people to choose from—Jimmy's background seemed void of typical relationships. No ex-bosses or co-workers who had anything to say, no wife or kids, and not much in the way of relatives, except for a stepmother who wouldn't return his call, and an uncle in prison.

Lou scoured public databases, searching for evidence of real-estate transactions, and came up empty. With the social security number John had provided, he ran Jimmy's credit report, a utility company trace, and a DMV check. Nothing in these records offered any direction as to his whereabouts.

After calling Jimmy's cell number and failing to connect a dozen times, Lou suspected the phone was either dead or lost. But it was also possible Jimmy was outside the cellular provider's signal range, maybe even outside the country.

Running out of options, Lou called a company that could triangulate a cell phone signal to within fifty feet, as long as the phone was powered on. He asked them to try connecting to Jimmy's line daily until he instructed otherwise. Lou sighed when he hung up. He knew telephone privacy legislation had recently been passed, and it would soon be a felony to sell information related to particular services offered by a phone company. Rather than relying on methods that were both expensive and soon to be illegal, Lou would have preferred using other means. But Jimmy Homestead was not a typical case.

Lou was pleasantly surprised when a week later the company got a hit on Jimmy's number. He was even more pleased when Jimmy's position was pinpointed to a location only a few minutes from Lou's office: the casino floor of Harrah's in South Lake Tahoe. Lou called the hotel desk at Harrah's and confirmed Jimmy was checked in.

He rang John Homestead the evening he learned of Jimmy's bearing, then headed to Harrah's the next morning. The hotel manager, a woman in her late forties, was a good friend of Lou's—actually more than a good friend. They'd had a serious fling a few years back, and still got together every now and again, for dinner, and sometimes a romp in the sack. So it had been relatively easy for Lou to convince her to provide Jimmy's room number.

The jingle of the phone at nine A.M. woke John Homestead out of a dead sleep. The bed at Harrah's was very comfortable, and if not interrupted, he might have slept until noon.

"Lou Calgaretti here, Mr. Homestead. Are you ready to meet with your son?"

John pushed his heavy frame up and dressed as quickly as he could. He rushed downstairs and met Lou in the lobby.

"Just bring me to his room," John said.

"Of course."

"I'll need a little time to talk things over with him. Maybe an hour or two. I'll call as soon as I'm ready to pay you."

"We would hope today, Mr. Homestead."

"Yeah, we would hope."

They took the elevator to the top floor, where Jimmy was staying in a penthouse suite. John knocked on the door. After half a minute, he knocked again.

"Who is it?" The voice was muted, thick with sleep.

"It's John…your father, Jimmy."

The door opened an inch. "You gotta be kiddin' me," Jimmy said.

"It's me, son."

Jimmy opened the door and let John into the suite. Jimmy was wearing boxers and a T-shirt. His long blond hair was a tangle, and there were dark circles under his blue eyes. The unshaven skin on his face looked slack. Wrinkle lines from the sheets creased his cheek.

"I'm sorry to wake you."

"That's all right. Excuse me," Jimmy mumbled. He went into the bathroom, urinated loudly, and brushed his teeth. After splashing water on his face, he paused and looked in the mirror. He looked like shit. But so did his old man. Jimmy smiled at the irony. But his mouth quickly turned downward. Why was his father here? And what would he say to him, to this person he hadn't seen in fifteen years?

John Homestead was standing in the middle of the suite when Jimmy came out of the bathroom. "What brings you to these parts?" Jimmy asked, figuring that was as good a place to start as any.

John sputtered a bit. Now that he'd found Jimmy, he felt confused and uncertain. The years that had passed since they last saw each other made it awkward. John realized at that moment he didn't know the man standing in the room with him.

"I realize I wasn't the best of parents," he said finally.

Jimmy didn't know how to reply to that. He didn't harbor any animosity toward his father; if he once had, it was long forgotten. But he was beginning to feel pretty weird about his old man showing up out of the blue, just the day after his stepmom did.

The room was dark, and John pulled open the heavy drapes, letting light pour into the suite. Jimmy sat on the couch, and John looked at him, his remaining son, now a full-grown man in his thirties. He looked like a stranger, but when Jimmy looked up at him with his blue eyes, John felt his heart sink. Jesus, it was his little boy, the same kid he had played with and bought birthday presents for, back in the days from the Super 8 films, back when both Jimmy and his brother Marty were sweet, playful kids. It seemed a lifetime ago. A huge sense of paternal love and regret overwhelmed John. How could he have allowed his own flesh and blood to simply disappear from his life?

A deep well of emptiness in his chest, John's eyes filled with tears. Jimmy stared at him, puzzled.

"I'm so sorry, Jimmy," John said. He sat on the couch and put his arm around Jimmy's shoulders and hugged his son.

After years of drifting from town to town, and having almost no contact with anyone from his youth, Jimmy was stunned by the affectionate gesture. His adult life had been mostly void of anything resembling compassion. Love was a concept Jimmy thought was probably bullshit, something the masses contrived to convince themselves their daily existence had some special meaning. The closest Jimmy ever came to being in love was when he was with the different women he slept with. But that emotion always faded once the passion of the sex subsided.

Jimmy hugged his father back—he didn't know what else to do. Then he saw tears streaming down John's face, and the strangest damn thing happened. He felt his own eyes well up, and a weight in his stomach rose to his chest. Before he could give it a moment's thought, Jimmy was crying on his dad's shoulder, blubbering incoherently, his warm tears running everywhere.

They held each other for a while, until eventually John stood. Jimmy sat transfixed, amazed at what he was feeling. It felt good to have his father here. The thought of having a family member, someone who actually gave a shit about him, made Jimmy happy. He had repressed so much over the years, and now he thought maybe this was a turning point, maybe he could repair things and be more like a normal person. He dried his eyes and stood to face his dad. His pop had not aged well. He was fat and looked disheveled, a far cry from the fit and debonair figure Jimmy remembered.

"Come on, let's go get some breakfast," Jimmy said.

They went to the coffee shop off the casino floor and talked until their voices grew hoarse. Jimmy spoke of his life on the road, jobs he had worked, battles with the bottle, his various troubles. John told Jimmy how he had never recovered from losing his house after his brother Mort conned him into an ill-fated investment scheme. They talked about the pain of Marty's death, and the pain of being alone in the world. They both felt a guilty pleasure from the release. It was noon when the waitress suggested they either order lunch or pay the check. Jimmy threw down some cash, and they went back to the suite.

They sat in the comfortable living room, Jimmy sprawled on a couch and John in an easy chair. The TV was on, but Jimmy muted the volume.

"Dad, I'm assuming you know about me winning the Lotto."

"Yes, I heard," John said. He noticed Jimmy's eyes narrow a bit.

"Well, I got no problem helping you out," Jimmy said. "It sounds like you could really use it."

John blushed. He was grateful Jimmy was making it easy, but he felt a creeping shame over having to ask for money. It made him feel inferior to his son, who had just admitted spending fifteen years living barely above the ranks of a hobo.

He swallowed, then said, "Thank you, Jimmy. Things have been tough for me." John started to say something else, but Jimmy interrupted him.

"There's another thing you should know," Jimmy said. "Yesterday I was driving here from Vegas in my Lamborghini—you should see it, it'll blow your mind. I stopped at a small town down along 395 to have a drink, and guess who shows up?"

John started at him dumbly.

"Sheila."

• • •

The sound of his ex-wife's name made John freeze. Since the initial shock of seeing her in South Lake Tahoe a week ago, he had shoved all thoughts of her aside. She was an intangible problem he didn't want to address unless he had to.

"She walked up to me at this bar in the middle of nowhere," Jimmy said. "And she had these two big dudes with her, like they were bodyguards or something. I'm sitting there having a drink, and she just walks right on up."

"What—what did she say?"

"Well, we sat at a table, and these guys with her, they sat away, far enough so they couldn't hear us. Then she goes into this story, and I'm still trying to figure out what to believe or not. She tells me a dude I once stole some coke from was dealing for a Mexican drug cartel, and now these badass Mexicans know I won the Lotto. So they tracked Sheila down, and told her to make me this offer: pay two million to settle the score on the rip-off, or they'll come after me personally."

John blinked, trying to organize his thoughts. "Did you really steal some drugs?"

"Yeah. I was pretty down and out at the time. I was working a temporary job and met this dude named Sanzini, who's got the IQ of a rock. I mean, if he was any dumber he'd need to be watered twice a week. He starts bragging about how he's a big-time dealer, and we end up at his house, and I took off with about an ounce of his blow."

"Do you think he was really connected with Mexican cartels?"

"I doubt it. He's not Mexican, and he was just a low street dealer. But I saw him talking to some *cholos* in a lowrider…"

"Huh," John sputtered, and started pacing the floor. "Did Sheila say the Mexicans contacted her directly?"

"Yeah. She said Sanzini brought them to her apartment. They supposedly offered her a chance to save my ass, is how she put it."

"What about the two men with her?"

"She claims they were associates of the Mexicans, hired by them to make sure the money gets back to the cartel safely. While we were at the bar, Sheila went to the bathroom, and then these guys came up to me and said some threatening shit, like I better cooperate, or else."

"My question is, why would the Mexicans go to Sheila?" John said. "If they wanted to find you, why would they need her?"

"She said she got involved to look out for my best interests, to prevent them from hurting or killing me."

"I don't think that makes sense, do you?"

Jimmy considered this before answering. He originally had thought his stepmom might well have a soft spot for him, given their night of passion. But he realized that was probably a vain notion—especially since she was telling him he needed to hand her $2 million in cash.

"She's expecting me to pay her today. She took the keys to my car."

"She did? Where is she?"

"She's staying here, at this hotel."

John's mouth dropped. "Here? Now?"

"That's right."

"You're not considering paying her, are you?"

"Hell, I sure don't want to. I'm sure she's been calling all morning, but I turned my cell off."

"Why not just tell her to hand over your keys and get lost?"

"Okay, but what if these big dudes she's with start hassling me?"

John paused for a moment, and decided the timing was right. "Jimmy, I hired a private eye to find you. He's a very competent guy—a real pro. I think it might be a good idea to get him involved. He can help us find out what Sheila is up to."

"I like that idea," Jimmy said, "as long as you're sure you can trust him."

John nodded, then added, "One other thing. I owe him five grand for his services so far, and..."

"Not a problem, Dad. Five K is nothing. I wipe my ass with that kind of money."

• • •

The fact that Sheila was staying at Harrah's seemed unreal to John, and with each moment he felt increasingly nervous. He shook his head, wondering what would have happened if she had wandered into the restaurant where Jimmy and he had spent the morning. "We need to get out of here, like now, Jimmy," he said.

"I have a spare set of keys for the Lamborghini."

"Maybe just leave it here for now, son. No need to alert Sheila and her friends what's going on. Besides, if she takes your car, you can report it stolen and have her arrested."

They made it to John's LTD without issue and boogied a few miles down the road into California, until they found an expensive lodge at the base of the local ski resort. Jimmy booked them into the hotel's fanciest room, a two-bedroom spread with a view of the lake. They went downstairs and ordered drinks at the nearly vacant bar. John drank his gin, ordered another, and dialed Lou Calgaretti.

"Good afternoon, Mr. Homestead."

"Hi, Lou. I have good news. I'm with my son now, and I can pay you your fee. But I'd like to meet with you to discuss further services."

"Ahh. Such as?"

"It will take some explaining. Can you meet us at the Timberlodge resort?

"I need to finish a few things first, Mr. Homestead. Perhaps we could meet over dinner?"

John checked his watch. It was four o'clock. "Okay, that'll work," he said.

"Perfect. There's an excellent Italian restaurant at the Timberlodge. Their pasta is the best in town."

John and Jimmy waited in the bar, drinking, chatting comfortably, momentarily unconcerned about whatever Sheila was up to. John assured his son that Lou Calgaretti, the tough, ex-cop private eye, would prove more than capable of shutting down her scam. They were pleasantly buzzed when Lou arrived. Jimmy bought him a drink, then they took a table in the back of the restaurant. The dark-paneled walls, dim lighting, and red-and-white checkerboard tablecloths reminded John of an old mobster movie. And Lou Calgaretti, with his black suit, beefy face, and a .38 in a shoulder holster that became visible when he unbuttoned his coat, fit in perfectly.

"Here's the short version, Lou," John said, once the waiter brought wine and bread. "Sheila Majorie, my ex-wife and Jimmy's stepmother, found out Jimmy won the Lotto and tracked him down yesterday. She confronted him in a bar where he had stopped when he was driving here from Vegas. She must have been following him, and she had two rough-looking guys with her. She told Jimmy a man Jimmy had a bad experience with on a drug deal is linked to a Mexican drug cartel, and she was there to collect two million to settle the score. She said she got involved in order to prevent the Mexicans from coming after Jimmy on their own and potentially harming him."

John had expected Lou to react with surprise, or at least some emotion, but Lou barely raised his eyebrows. "That's quite a story," he said.

"Yeah, no kidding," Jimmy said. "And I want to hire you to find out if I'm really in any danger, or if it's just my stepmom trying to rip me off."

"Describe for me your bad experience on this drug deal."

"I stole an ounce of blow from this jackass a couple years back. It was worth about two grand. That's it."

Lou raised his eyes at Jimmy, his expression flat, then a small smile formed on his lips. "Sounds like it was a bad experience for him, but not necessarily for you."

"I guess so," Jimmy said with a shrug.

"And now you're being told you need to pay two million to resolve it?"

"Basically, yeah."

"I think you might need some protection until we get to the bottom of this."

"At least until we know what we're dealing with," John said.

"Here's what I can do for you," Lou said, the diamond studded ring on his finger clinking against his wine glass. "First, I'll investigate this woman's story to find out if there's any evidence to back it up. I'll see what I can find out about the two guys with her. I'll work to learn if she has any connection to anyone linked to a Mexican drug cartel. If so, I'll find out, but it will take some digging. While I'm working on this, I think the most prudent thing would be for you both to become invisible."

"What, you mean go into hiding?" Jimmy said.

"No, not exactly. The main thing is, I don't want you having any more contact with your stepmother. I don't want her to be able to find you. I'd suggest leaving the area."

"Shit, I was ready to start shopping for a house."

Lou sipped from his wine glass. "I think you probably want to wait on that."

"Should we just go stay in a hotel somewhere?" John asked.

"We could always go chill in Mexico," Jimmy added.

Lou shook his head. "I don't think that's necessary. Here's an idea—I know a realtor in Reno who can rent you a vacation home, and she'll let you use a phony name on the paperwork. You'll be untraceable."

The waiter brought plates of pasta and meat and a fresh bottle of red wine.

"Sheila thought I was going to give her the two mil today," Jimmy said, around a mouthful of lasagna. "I turned my cell phone off, but I'm sure she's called."

Lou considered that for a moment. "It's probably not a great idea for you to stay here tonight. You can spend the night at my place. I've got plenty of room."

"You really think we're in danger?" John said.

"Those two guys with her are my concern," Lou said. "If they catch up to you now, it could be a problem."

"You know, I swear I recognized one of those guys," Jimmy said. "But I just can't place him."

"Really? Keep trying to remember. A name would definitely help."

"I want to get my Lamborghini," Jimmy said. "It's still at Harrah's. Sheila took my keys, but I've got a spare pair."

John cleared his throat. "I thought we should leave it there," he said. "And if Sheila takes a spin, have her arrested for stealing it."

"It's a nice thought. But auto theft is almost never prosecuted if the accused has the keys. Tell you what—why don't I go with you to pick it up? Just in case they're watching your car." Lou looked at the pair, who nodded in agreement.

When they left the restaurant, Lou had a check from Jimmy for $20,000, to cover what John owed, with the balance to serve as a retainer. Jimmy turned on his cell before they got in their cars to head to Harrah's.

"She called three times," he said. "Hold on, she left a message." Jimmy listened to Sheila saying she was concerned Jimmy was non-responsive, and that he needed to call her and arrange the funds right away or things could get ugly. Jimmy pressed a button and handed the phone to Lou, who carefully listened to the entire message.

"Well," he said with a smile. "She sounds like quite a piece of work. Don't erase it."

Lou drove his black all-wheel-drive Lexus SUV and followed John's LTD to Harrah's parking garage. They picked up Jimmy's car without incident, then Lou led them up a steep, winding road to his split-level house in a residential development in Nevada. The stands of redwood separating the homes were so thick the neighbors couldn't see each other's houses.

"Nice spread, Lou. You must have done well for yourself," John said, climbing from his car and looking around.

"I got a good pension when I left the force."

John and Jimmy settled into Lou's downstairs quarters, a large room with a pool table, wet bar, big screen TV, and two couches. Lou brought in a tape recorder and began asking questions. He first asked Jimmy to provide detailed descriptions of the two men with Sheila, and then he began probing into the Homestead family history.

He wanted to know about John's relationship with Sheila, how it had started and how it ended. He wanted a chronological account of everywhere Jimmy had been and everyone he'd met since he left his parents' home. He asked about every family member in the Homestead clan. An hour later, when it seemed to John they must have covered every possible piece of relevant information, Lou started all over again, pushing for even more detail.

Only when Lou asked about his relationship with Sheila did Jimmy pause. He saw no reason to confide he'd had sex with her—especially not with his father there.

Finally Lou concluded the interview and left the Homesteads alone. They each took a couch, and within a minute John was snoring. Jimmy lay awake, thinking how bizarre the events of the last thirty-six hours had been. His emotions were in a jumble over the sudden arrival of his parents in his life. He didn't quite know what to make of his old man showing up, but felt comfortable that time would sort it out. As far as Sheila, he now was sure the sleazebag was trying to run a scam on him, but she would be bitch-slapped back into the hole she crawled from, once Lou got done with her. The thought made Jimmy smile. He picked up his cell phone from the coffee table and listened to Sheila's voice mail again. He repressed a giggle and started typing her a text message, and he almost laughed out loud when he was done punching in the letters. The message read, GO FUCK A DUCK. He hit the send button, a huge smile on his face, then put away his phone and fell peacefully asleep.

• • •

When they woke the next morning, Lou brought them coffee. He had showered, shaved, and dressed while they were still sleeping. In fact, he looked like he'd been up for hours.

"I called the realtor in Reno and explained you'll need an anonymous rental. She understands and can set you up. Bring cash—you don't want to use your credit card for this. Here are directions to her office. She'll be waiting for you."

They walked outside into the crisp, shaded morning, and as Jimmy was climbing into his sports car, Lou stopped him. "One more thing—your cell phone. Don't use it and keep it turned off. Since Sheila has your number, she may try to track you by triangulating the signal."

"Can she do that?" Jimmy said.

"Depends how motivated she is. But yes, it can be done."

Jimmy put on his seat belt and fired up the Lamborghini, its twelve-cylinder motor coming alive with an exotic purr. John started his car, the engine clattering like a card stuck in a bicycle's spokes. The two vehicles pulled away, father following son, as if they were attached by an invisible financial umbilical cord. Lou stood watching until they were gone, shaking his head at the sight. Then he walked back inside and went to work.

27

SHEILA AND CODY WERE waiting for me at a table in the main lounge at Harrah's. Sheila sat cross-legged, her skirt hiked high up on her thighs. A cigarette dangled from her fingers, and her half-lidded eyes acknowledged me with practiced indifference. Cody sat across from her, staring off into space. I took a seat and helped myself to one of Sheila's Virginia Slims.

"How's everything, lovebirds?" I said.

Sheila blew out a stream of smoke. "Jimmy has checked out," she said. "And he hasn't taken my calls."

"No shit, huh?"

She ignored my comment. I looked over at Cody, who seemed uncharacteristically sullen. He greeted me with a glance, silent for the moment.

"Is his car still here?"

"It was about an hour ago," Sheila said.

I reached out and slapped Cody on the shoulder. "Come on, let's take a walk. Wait for us here, Sheila."

"What's the matter?" I said, once we were out of her earshot.

"Looks like the honeymoon's over."

"It is, huh?"

"She's really on the rag. There ain't a goddamned thing I can say to snap her out of it."

"Is this because Jimmy blew Dodge?"

"Probably."

"Well, it's no surprise."

"I fucking know that, Dan. I just hate being treated like I got a highly contagious venereal disease."

"What, is she blaming you?"

"She might as well be."

"All right, look," I said as we got off the elevator to the parking garage and spotted the Lamborghini. "The good news is his car is still here. I assume Jimmy has another set of keys. I'm going to replace the tracker with a freshly charged unit, and I can program the GPS alerts to go to your cell number. So if you want, you can wait for him to pick up his car, then go after him."

"What about you?"

"Me? I got to make a living, Cody. As far as I'm concerned, I've delivered my end of the bargain to Sheila, and she owes me ten grand plus expenses. Any more work on my part would be above and beyond our contract. And given that I have no reason to believe she has the means to pay me, I'm not in a mood to burn further calories on this bullshit."

Cody stared at me hard, but then his green eyes softened. "Christ, I feel like a dumb ass," he said.

"Hey, man," I said. "Don't get down on yourself for trying to have a good time." But the remark was disingenuous, and Cody saw right through it.

"Every woman I've been with since my divorce has screwed me over. You see a trend here?"

"I haven't done much better, old buddy."

"I've paid for everything since she hired me. I can't wait to see my credit card bill."

"It's time to cut our losses. This party's over."

When we got to Jimmy's car, Cody said, "Put the damn tracker on it anyway. You never know..."

But Sheila seemed to have already drawn her own conclusions. She was no longer at the lounge when we returned. A few minutes later, she emerged from the elevators with a rollaway suitcase.

"I need to return to San Jose," she said. "I'll be in touch, gentlemen." She walked off toward the exit of the casino.

"Excuse me," I said. "Look for my bill in your mailbox."

"I'll be sure to do that," she said. Cody and I followed her for a few steps, then stopped and watched her leave the building and get into a waiting taxi. We stood there for a moment after the cab drove away.

"Come on, let's go," I said.

"There goes one expensive piece of ass," he said finally, his face screwed into a grimace.

Cody checked out of Harrah's and came to my place to spend the night. He had trimmed his beard and looked somewhat less unruly than usual. We sat at my kitchen table, and he quietly asked for a bottle of whiskey. I wasn't used to seeing Cody subdued, and I wondered if after a lifetime of bucking the odds, he was facing a time of reckoning. But after a couple of shots, the impetuous fire that was both his vice and his virtue returned, glowing in his eyes like high beams on a dark highway.

Cody's best moments were also his worst. The attributes that had made him a great cop also led to his being fired from the force. His intuitions on criminal behavior were uncanny, but were due in part to his own disregard for convention or rules. His parents had considered him incorrigible, and his father had kicked him out of their home when Cody was fourteen. He forged his way on the street, and he never spoke of how he survived. But there was no doubt in my mind that his juvenile brushes with the law did not reveal the true nature and extent of his teenage criminality.

When it came to the opposite sex, Cody's reckless libido and ribald charm attracted the type of women who recognized him as a kindred soul. Females needing to validate their desirability flocked to him. So did wild women who lived on the fringes of society. Stable, mainstream types avoided him like the plague. His first and only wife seemed fairly normal to me, and I can't account for the chemistry that brought them together. Their marriage lasted two years before she handed him the divorce papers and never spoke to him again.

"Here's an angle, Dirt," he said, pouring me a shot. "Let's track down Jimmy, and in return for him paying what Sheila owes us, we come clean with him."

"Come clean with him? About what, Sheila's scam? We don't really know what she's up to. At least I don't."

"Me neither, but it doesn't matter. All we have to do is tell Jimmy she's full of shit and he's got nothing to worry about, and we were just a couple private dicks she hired to find him."

I rolled the shot glass between my fingers, the amber fluid twinkling like a magical elixir. Cody raised his glass and smiled and nodded, as if he had just unlocked a great mystery. I knew better—he was just catching a buzz. But his idea intrigued me, and it reminded me that Cody had not survived living on the edge by accident. His resourcefulness in extracting himself from difficult situations, and righting those situations in his favor always surprised me.

"You don't think Sheila really has anything on Jimmy?"

Cody shrugged. "I doubt it."

I raised my glass and toasted Cody in return. "To our partnership," I said.

28

JOHN WATCHED HIS SON'S Lamborghini as he followed it through Stateline, Nevada. It looked like a futuristic dayglow orange toy that might sprout wings and take flight at any moment. John was a bit concerned that the car was an ultimate attention magnet—not a good thing given their situation, but he resigned himself to not worry about it.

Jimmy stopped at a bank before they headed around the lake toward Reno, and fifteen minutes later walked out with a large envelope stuffed with cash. "Hey, if I lose you heading up Spooner pass, don't worry. I'll stop and wait for you," Jimmy said. John wanted to tell him to not do anything stupid, but settled for, "Just be careful, okay, son?" Jimmy responded with an irreverent smile.

Sure enough, once they turned east at Junction 28, Jimmy downshifted and accelerated as if a green flag had waved. He rounded the first sweeping curve, and John saw no more of him. The grade was moderate as the road climbed out of the forest and into the sparse desert terrain of the Eastern Sierra. It was a crisp morning, and winter would probably come early this year, John thought. The Ford labored in the thin air, heading toward the summit at seven thousand feet. John could smell his motor oil burning, and when he looked in the rearview mirror, he saw a haze of white exhaust smoke. It wouldn't be long before the LTD blew its final gasket and would have to be retired to the scrap heap.

But John had more important things to consider than the condition of his car. So far, he was pleased at finding his son, and quite pleasantly surprised by their quick and comfortable bonding. And now they would be staying together, for at least a week, or maybe longer, with a common goal: to eliminate whatever threat Sheila posed. John felt absolute confidence in Lou Calgaretti, but what about after Sheila was a nonissue? Then would Jimmy be agreeable to give John enough money to retire comfortably? When the time was right, John would talk to Jimmy straight out. No bullshit, just the simple facts: John was getting too old to work and had no money put away for retirement. Jimmy would have to be one cruel SOB to not sympathize with that.

John was doing some financial calculations in his head when he came over the summit and started heading down toward Carson Valley. He steered into a broad right curve, and when the highway straightened, he could see a series of fresh skid marks where the next turn began. The curlicues of rubber were thick and black. He peered through his dirty windshield, a tiny pang of panic growing in his stomach.

When he came around the bend, he saw the orange Lamborghini on the shoulder of the road. The car looked undamaged but was facing the wrong way. John slowed to a stop. Jimmy was not in the car, but then John saw him kneeling near the rear bumper.

"Wow," Jimmy said, standing. "Too much, man. I thought I was headed to the big bar in the sky on that one."

"Jesus Christ, what happened?"

"I must have hit a patch of gravel. I swear I did two 360s."

"Your rim is ruined," John said, looking at Jimmy's flattened rear tire. The wheel was dented and bent out of round.

"I slammed the curb at the turnout back there."

They stood looking at the rim. The damned thing probably would cost two grand to replace, John thought.

"Hey, it could have been worse," Jimmy said. "I could have ended up down there." He pointed beyond the guard rail where the hillside fell away into a sheer canyon.

"You would have been dead," John said, and he wanted to say more but bit his tongue.

"Not me, Pop. Lady Luck is watching over me."

"Just because you're rich doesn't mean you can't die."

"No worries. Can you call a tow truck? I lost my charger and my cell is dead again."

"You're supposed to leave it off anyway. What about a spare tire?"

"I shit-canned it because I needed the trunk space. Oops."

John called an auto repair garage in Carson City and arranged for a tow truck to pick up the Lamborghini. He and Jimmy sat waiting on the heated hood of the LTD. The sun was obscured behind a hazy white sky and didn't emit much warmth. They sat and looked out over sagebrush-covered hills that rose and fell in a series of undulations until the terrain flattened at the floor of the Carson Valley.

"You ever think about your future?" John said. "Say, a year from now?"

Jimmy fired up a Marlboro and leaned back on his elbows. "Haven't really thought that far in advance."

"A man's got to have some direction in life, don't you think?"

Jimmy thought about that for a moment. Besides buying a home and maybe meeting a gal or two to hang with, he hadn't given much consideration to what he would do. Actually, he thought the answer to the question was fairly obvious. Fancy cars, five-star hotels, hot women, vacations to places most people would never see, liquor and blow—pretty much an endless stream of indulgence. The good life.

"Pretty simple, Dad. I just want to enjoy myself. Hell, why not?"

"Well, just don't get too crazy. You can't enjoy all that money if you get hurt."

"Don't worry about me," Jimmy said. "I've survived a lot of shit."

John decided not to say more on the subject. He walked over to the edge of the road to take a leak. With a little stretch of the imagination, he could see Jimmy killing himself, by driving like a lunatic, or maybe even overdosing on drugs. But Jimmy was a grown man, and John didn't think a lecture would be either appropriate or effective.

Then another thing occurred to him. If his son was so stupid and immature he went and got himself killed, well, maybe he deserved his fate. Life was a precious thing, especially so if you were granted enough money to enjoy all the finer things without working. But if a person threw all that away by behaving like an idiot, what do you say to that?

For the first time, John wondered if he would automatically inherit Jimmy's fortune if his son died.

• • •

They drove in John's car, following the tow truck to the garage in Carson City. It would be a few days before a replacement rim would be available, so they left the Lamborghini, picked up a couple of greasy cheeseburgers at a local diner, and headed to Reno in the LTD.

Half an hour later, they went through the arches touting Reno as "The Biggest Little City in the World." Similar to Las Vegas, without its casinos Reno would be an anonymous watering hole in the desolate terrain of Nevada. But even the bright lights of the casinos couldn't save downtown Reno. The city had been built around the old Southern Pacific railroad, and freight trains rumbled through at all hours, blowing their horns and waking outraged hotel guests. Hobos patrolled the sidewalks on the main drag, toothless winos slept in doorways, and even the harsh winter storms couldn't wash away the squalor and desperation that seemed to funnel into the city center from all directions.

The real estate office was in a recently developed uptown location. The agent Lou referred them to, a friendly brunette with a chunky figure, greeted them with a smile. She seemed to understand exactly what was needed before John or Jimmy had a chance to explain. They climbed into her big Mercedes sedan, and she drove them to a neighborhood south of Reno, off Highway 431. A newly built community was nestled in the foothills, and at the highest point, atop a broad plateau, a large tri-level stone and timber estate sat overlooking Reno and the desert beyond.

John and Jimmy followed the agent through the luxuriously furnished four-thousand-square-foot home. The hardwood floors were beautifully stained and lacquered, the carpets plush, the bathrooms and kitchen appointed with the most splendid and expensive fixtures and appliances.

"One of the wonderful attributes of this home is the decking and swimming pool," the agent said, as they followed her out the French doors onto a huge redwood deck with an unobstructed view of Reno. On the level below the deck, a turquoise pool sparkled next to a manicured lawn surrounded by colorful shrubs and foliage.

"A computer executive had this home custom built a year ago, but then he moved to Europe. He's never stayed here—he just rents it out."

Beneath the four bedrooms, on the ground level next to the three-car garage, a gym had been built, complete with a universal weight machine, an exercise bike, and a couple of fitness machines John didn't recognize. Jimmy patted his old man on the back. "Hey, you said you wanted to lose some weight."

Back at the real estate office, John filled out the necessary paperwork while Jimmy walked across the street to a strip mall and drank a beer at a pizza joint. He came back and was puffing on a smoke outside the office when John called him in. Jimmy counted out a month's payment in advance, plus a security and cleaning deposit. It came to twenty grand.

• • •

The next morning they drove off in John's LTD to buy groceries. Jimmy also wanted to buy a computer to check on his Internet dating site. He then suggested to John some new clothes might be in order.

"And your car—well, it's an embarrassment."

"I told you, I haven't been doing well. It's all I can afford."

"We'll have to see what we can do about that," Jimmy said.

By midafternoon they left the mall in Reno and headed toward home. "Let's get a drink somewhere," Jimmy said. "Don't you know—that's the first things you do when you move, scout out the nearest bar." They found a sports bar in a shopping complex near their neighborhood and killed an hour playing video poker and watching college football on TV.

"You know, I could get used to this lifestyle," John said.

"Like I told you, it's all about having a good time," Jimmy said, and signaled the bartender for another round.

They stayed at the bar for an early dinner, and when they got home, John helped Jimmy set up his new notebook PC. It took most of the evening and part of the next morning, but finally Jimmy had Internet access. He logged onto the dating website the guy at the Mirage had arranged for him. Three new women had responded to his ad. The first didn't submit a picture. The second one offered photos of a trashy-looking white chick who looked like she'd been freshly gang-banged by the local biker club. But the third response made Jimmy blink and sit up straight in his chair.

"Hi there. I'm Debbie. You look pretty cute. I hope you feel the same about me. I'm a casual girl, low maintenance. I like to party and get physical. You look like fun. Let me know if you want to hook up. See ya."

The six pictures posted were of a hot blonde in a bikini. Jimmy stared at the photos, blood racing to his crotch. Now, this was more like it! He checked out every picture at length, his eyeballs undressing her. She had an ass that begged for a ten-gun salute and the type of knockers that made his pecker stand up and whistle Dixie. He peered at the photos until his eyes hurt, then typed her a reply:

"Hi Debbie. You look like my kind of gal. Nice bod! I'm renting a mansion outside of Reno for now. It's awesome. Want to come chill out for a couple days?"

He watched the screen for the next ten minutes, hoping she'd reply quickly. When she didn't, he went downstairs to the exercise room where his dad was messing with the equipment.

"Hey, Pop, mind if I borrow your heap for a couple hours?"

"As long as you're not going far. I'm not sure how much life she's got left."

"Maybe we'll get you a new ride later this week, okay?"

"Sound great, Jimmy," John said, grunting as he began peddling the stationary bike.

Jimmy hopped in the LTD and took off toward the cathouses outside of Carson City. The prospect of a date with Debbie, a real woman, not a hooker, made him feel like ten pounds of concrete had been poured into his pants. He was so horny he was almost panting by the time he reached the brothels, where he chose a young blonde with fake boobs and banged her so hard she pushed him away until he agreed to pay double.

29

As Garrett Rancour had surmised, Tony Sanzini had ridden home to his mother's house after the debacle at the Carson City bordello. Before heading to San Jose, Sanzini stopped at a thrift store and bought an inexpensive and rather ridiculous-looking red down jacket, in order to make the 220-mile ride without freezing his ass off. When he got home, his mother chewed him out over the hole he'd punched in the wall and ordered him to repair it or she'd kick him out.

Sanzini called a temporary agency and got a job moving furniture, and was fired after two days when he threatened to beat a co-worker to a pulp. He found another job through a different agency, and three days later, he was told they didn't need him anymore. He got stinko drunk at the dive bar he frequented, and woke up broke and deliriously hungover. When his mind could function again, he locked himself in his room and did some serious thinking on how his life had gone wrong.

In high school, he'd been a genuine big man on campus, a badass who made his own rules. Most of his classmates and teachers afforded him a wide berth in the hallways, if they were smart. Instead of working at some crappy fast-food joint, he made his money dealing pot, buying in pound increments and selling dime bags to his fellow students. He kept his grades up, thanks to a group of nerds who fed him test answers and did his homework on demand. His girlfriend, a horny hippie chick, called him "stud" and had lunch with him daily in the center quad. Sanzini liked to stand there after eating and watch the students and their ongoing social dramas, as if their petty lives were a source of great amusement.

Back then, he use to brag he was a top performer in every important category of life: he could brawl, party, and get laid with the best of them. Equally important, he had top-notch intelligence. Anyone stupid enough to disagree risked a Sanzini haymaker. And he'd never lost a fight.

But when his parents divorced in his senior year, things began to unravel. After his old man left town, rumors circulated he'd been sent to prison and Tony would no doubt follow in his footsteps. Then his girl had a sudden change of heart and dumped him for a preppy athlete who'd been accepted at Stanford. Not long afterward, Sanzini ran his Plymouth Roadrunner low on oil and blew the motor while drag racing a spoiled rich kid whose parents bought him a Corvette.

He hit rock bottom on the last day of school, when he was knocked off his ten-speed and mugged by a pack of jocks. They ripped his jacket and took the pocketful of dime-bags he was carrying, leaving him to walk his damaged bike home as students drove past and jeered.

It became clear to Sanzini in the next ten years that there would be no return to the glory days of his youth. The sole highlight of his adult life was when a Mexican gang granted him a local territory and fronted him an ounce of pure Colombian flake. Sanzini began dealing eight-balls to coke-heads and low-level dealers. He moved about an ounce a week, at a profit of $500. It took only six months to save up and buy his Harley.

Living rent free at his mother's home, cruising the town on his hog with plenty of spending money in his pocket, Sanzini was content. He hooked up with a couple of coke whores who serviced him on a regular basis, hung out at his local bar, and envisioned one day inheriting his mother's house. But that was before Jimmy Homestead blew his dealing career out of existence.

When Homestead ripped him off, Sanzini had just bought his bike, and he owed the Mexicans two grand. They went berserk when Sanzini told them he needed more time to pay. One of the Mexicans, a slim man with a long head and big hands, told Sanzini he had two days to come up with the scratch, or else they would slit his throat. Sanzini begged everyone he knew for money. He even tracked down Jimmy's stepmother, hoping Jimmy might be hiding at her apartment. The woman looked like a porn queen, dressed in a leotard, a cigarette dangling from her fingers. Her half-lidded eyes were lazy and content, like she'd just been plowed big time in the sack. Sanzini never forgot her. She answered his questions nonchalantly, and after telling him she hadn't heard from Jimmy in years, she sent him away. He limped back to his hog with a hard-on that reoccurred every time her image came to mind. She became a mainstay in his nighttime fantasies.

Eventually Sanzini scraped up the cash, using up every favor he could muster. When he paid the Mexicans, they laughed and called him a *pendajo* and a dumbass gringo, then told him to get lost.

• • •

Sitting in his room, Sanzini pulled out his electronic scale. It had been inactive for almost three years. Sanzini had not given up on finding Jimmy Homestead, and in fact felt confident that eventually he'd turn up and then would regret the day he was born. Until then, though, he needed cash, and the temporary job scene wasn't working out. Dealing was easy money, but he would need to reconnect with the Mexicans and get back on the program. Might it be possible? Three years had passed, but Sanzini still had connections. He picked up his address book and was scanning through the names when his doorbell rang. Probably a solicitor, Sanzini thought, a scowl on his face. But he got up and went to the door anyway.

The gorgeous blond woman waiting on the porch made Sanzini's eyes bulge and jaw drop.

"Shelly?"

"Nice try."

"No, Sheila, right?"

"Want to go get a drink, big boy?" she said.

30

THE NEXT MORNING CODY and I were drinking coffee on my deck under a gray sky. The cold wind blowing off Lake Tahoe was spitting tiny needles of rain, and the grass in my yard looked hard and brittle. Cody sat bundled in his huge green parka.

"Let's go inside and cook some more bacon," he said.

"Remember I told you I knew Jimmy Homestead from high school?"

"Yeah, so?"

"Everyone we went to school with came from middle class white suburbia. Some kids had parents better off than others, but for the most part, we were all just middle class, right?"

"Pretty much."

"I know a few guys from back then who ended up with good careers. But I know a lot more who can't even hold a job."

"Not everyone is destined to live the highlife, Dirt."

"Who said anything about the highlife? Look, I'm not trying to judge someone by how much money they make. I'm just saying I'm surprised to see so many guys, the products of hardworking parents, become jobless derelicts. I don't buy that was their destiny."

"You getting philosophical on me again?"

I shook my head. "I look at Jimmy Homestead, and I see someone born into a decent family, with a decent amount of intelligence. But he doesn't make it through high school and lives for almost twenty years as a bum. It's the result of a character defect."

"I thought he was just an alcoholic."

"Maybe, but it's more than that. He was too lazy to work, or maybe thought he was above it. He thought the world owed him something."

"Looks like he was right."

"I don't think so," I said.

When we went inside, my cell phone was beeping with an alert for the GPS. "Son of a bitch," I said, waiting for the satellite to locate the Lamborghini.

"What's up?" Cody said.

"This thing's gone haywire. I'm not sure if it's working right."

"Let me see."

"Hold on. Now it says the car's stopped on Spooner Pass."

"Gimme that thing," Cody said. He stared at it for a second, then tossed it back to me. "What the hell? Damn it, man, let's go."

We jumped into my truck, and I sprayed gravel onto Highway 50 and raced into Nevada, passing the casinos at double the speed limit. Fifteen minutes later the Lamborghini started moving again. "He's heading over the pass, into Carson," I said.

"How far are we behind him?"

"About half an hour."

"How come we didn't get alerted sooner?"

"I don't know. The technology's not always that reliable, I guess."

A few minutes later, the red arrow on the GPS stopped. I pushed my foot to the floor, and we barreled over the summit.

We rolled into Carson City and stopped at an auto shop in the center of town. The Lamborghini was parked out front, its flattened tire folded under a rim that had obviously taken the brunt of a collision. Cody and I walked into the small, dirty lobby, where a man with white hair and spectacles was working behind a computer.

"Is the guy who owns the Lamborghini around?" I said.

"You just missed him," the man said. "He and his father drove off not five minutes ago." He looked up from his screen.

"His father?" Cody said.

"He called him 'Pop.'"

"What were they driving?" I asked.

"A Ford, if it's any of your business." The man was staring at us now, and Cody and I left and walked back to my truck.

"Jimmy Homestead has now officially become a pain in my ass," Cody said.

We stood in the gritty parking lot, kicking at pebbles and looking around at the bleak desert features, as if a clue to Jimmy's whereabouts might magically appear.

"You told me Sheila had seen Jimmy's dad in Tahoe," I said. "And she felt sure he was looking for Jimmy."

"It looks like he found him. She said the guy's a pathetic asshole. Those were her exact words. She thinks he's desperate and probably unstable."

"His name is John, if I remember," I said, thinking back to my original interview with Sheila.

"We find him, we find Jimmy," Cody said.

• • •

As an ex-cop, Lou Calgaretti still had friends on the force, not only in Chicago, but also in Southern California, where his career started. His first assignment as a rookie patrolman had been in Compton, the infamous ghetto near Los Angeles. The Bloods and the Crips ran the show there in the 1980s, when the crack trade was rapidly becoming a huge business. In the process, the ghettos were turned into a war zone. Lou made his name busting black gangsters born into a world where the only hope of exit was through drug money. He attacked the street thugs with an imposing fearlessness that made his more experienced partners doubt his sanity. After three years of battles and a stellar record of arrests, he was shot in the shoulder during a raid. When he recovered, he was promoted to plainclothes, and then assigned to homicide.

The day after Jimmy and his father spent the night, Lou sat in his office and ran all the usual reports on Sheila Majorie. She lived in an apartment in central San Jose that cost $1,345 a month. She owned a ten-year-old white Toyota Camry, and worked as a cosmetologist, with a declared annual income of $49,000.

Lou dialed an old friend from LAPD who owed him a favor, and asked if he could get Sheila's cell phone records for the last thirty days. When Lou got the report, he spent an hour identifying every number through a reverse directory. Not a single Hispanic name was on her call record. He set the records aside and studied the notes from his interview with the Homesteads. The story about Mexican drug dealers coming after Jimmy through Sheila seemed unlikely, almost ridiculous, but Lou had seen crazier shit happen.

He circled Tony Sanzini's name with a red pen. If there was any truth to the story, it would start with him. Within a few minutes, his printer started chugging out information on Sanzini: his employment records, address history, arrest jacket, even a mug shot. Lou picked up one of the pages and studied Sanzini's photo. Small eyes, broad nose, broken teeth, scraggly beard—a textbook caricature of a hard-partying, white-trash loser. "What a prize," he muttered. Sanzini's arrest record confirmed the impression. He had spent time in jail for a number of petty offenses, with one felony conviction, for assault and battery. One of his misdemeanor convictions was for possession of a half gram of cocaine.

The next morning, Lou drove the four hours to San Jose and found Sheila's apartment complex. Her Camry was not in the parking lot. He drove to the hair salon where she was employed but didn't see her car there either. He walked into the salon.

"I'd like to make an appointment with Sheila," he told the teenage girl working behind the counter.

"She's off today, but she's working tomorrow afternoon," the girl said.

Lou left the salon and drove to the address he had for Tony Sanzini. The faded yellow house sat quietly under skies heavy with clouds moving in from the north. There was no landscaping, no shrubs or flowers behind the chain link fence surrounding the yard. From his vantage point parked down the street, Lou would have guessed the house was empty, except a Harley was parked on the walkway next to the dirt and weeds where a front lawn might have once grown. A few raindrops splattered on Lou's windshield. The neighborhood seemed deserted in the midafternoon. It started raining harder, and after a minute, Lou saw Sanzini walk outside and lug open the garage door. It was an old fashioned spring loaded unit that swung outward, and when Lou heard its tired squeak, it made him think of his childhood home in Illinois. Sanzini pushed his motorcycle into the garage.

Two hours later the rain stopped, and Sanzini rolled down the driveway on his Harley, the loud rumble shattering the damp stillness of the day. Lou followed him for a half mile to a bar called the Iron Door. The windowless building stood alone between two strip malls on Bascom Avenue. The parking lot was half full with pickup trucks, choppers, and gas guzzlers. Two bicycles were propped near the front door, where a fat man wearing a dirty T-shirt stood smoking a cigarette.

Lou watched Sanzini walk into the bar, then climbed into the back seat of his Lexus and changed into blue jeans and an old sweatshirt. He fitted a Giants cap over his professionally styled hair and followed Sanzini into the joint. A few heads turned to size him up as his eyes adjusted to the darkness. Even by the low standards of dive bars, the Iron Door was a dump. The furniture was so old and rickety half the patrons stood rather than risk collapsing a chair. Two broken barstools were stacked in a gloomy corner, next to a table with only three legs. The carpet was worn through to the floorboards in many places, and the wood surface of the bar was peeling, water stained, and splintered.

The bartender was a woman probably not thirty, obviously hired to bring some life to this cheerless place. She was dark skinned, perhaps Filipina, and wore a top cut so low her large breasts seemed ready to fall out with the slightest motion.

She greeted Lou with a big smile. "Whatcha drinkin', stranger?"

"How about a draft," Lou said, and when she reached below for a mug her brown nipples were plainly visible.

Down the bar, Sanzini sat drinking a beer.

The day drinkers began to filter out, replaced by a blue collar happy-hour crowd. Sanzini kept to himself, sipping beer and watching television for an hour or so until a stocky Latino man in his twenties walked in. He wore a loose-fitting white T-shirt and a red bandana knotted behind his head and pulled low over his eyebrows. Blue tattoos stitched his skin, beginning at his knuckles and crawling up his arms and out from his collar.

The Latino surveyed the bar, and everyone in the place turned to stare at him. He sauntered to where Sanzini was sitting, and Lou got up and walked by them to the jukebox. When he passed, he saw the tattoos on the Latino's fingers. Four small circles configured in a square on one finger, and on the next, two horizontal lines beneath three vertical ones.

"You Sanzini?" the man sneered, his tone clearly declaring his disdain and disrespect not only for Sanzini, but for everyone in the bar.

"Yeah," Sanzini said.

"Then let's go, homeboy."

Sanzini kick-started his Harley and followed the man's customized purple pickup truck onto the boulevard. Lou fell in a few cars behind and tailed them to the freeway, scribbling the license plate number as he drove. It was dusk, and the rush hour traffic was heavy. The pickup exited on 7th street and headed east, away from downtown. A couple miles later, the neighborhoods turned increasingly darker and poorer, until they entered the Mexican barrios in east San Jose.

In the seventies, the greater San Jose area was mostly orchard land. Traffic was nonexistent, downtown's tallest building was three stories high, and the suburbs were quiet pockets of middle-class Americana. Then, almost overnight, Santa Clara County was transformed into the epicenter of the technology revolution. Within five years the orchards vanished, replaced by office complexes to house the hundreds of computer and electronics companies that flooded the area. Real estate prices skyrocketed, affluent neighborhoods with multimillion-dollar homes became commonplace, and the population exploded as hordes of ambitious professionals rushed in to participate in Silicon Valley's newfound prosperity.

But for the slums of east San Jose, there was no benefit to be had from the technology boom. The barrios existed, much as they always had, as home to people who worked as janitors, yard laborers, or dishwashers. Old, dilapidated, graffiti-covered stucco homes with flat roofs lined the narrow streets, some partially torn down and boarded up, most with iron security bars covering the windows and doorways. Residents parked rusted junkers on their lawns and sat on weathered couches watching the streets from their front porches. Groups of men hung out on the corners, drinking forties, flashing gang signs, and looking for action.

Lou kept his lights off and pulled over down the street from the house where Sanzini parked his motorcycle. He was painfully aware his black Lexus would not do for surveillance in this neighborhood. To make matters worse, Lou knew he looked like a cop, and Mexican immigrants distrusted and hated the police more than anyone, based on their experiences with the mostly corrupt *policia* in Mexico.

The skies were now dark, which afforded Lou a bit of comfort, but it also prevented him from seeing if anything was happening at the house. After a minute he pulled forward, stopped in front of the house, and took down the address and the license plate of a Chevy Impala parked in the driveway. Figures were moving inside a lighted room visible through partially opened drapes. Lou peered at the window, but was startled by a thump that jostled the springs of his car. A face appeared in his rearview mirror. Lou pushed a button and lowered his window.

"You in the wrong part of town, homes," the face said. Red bandana, gold-plated front tooth, thin goatee, black eyes, gang tats on his forehead.

"Did you touch my car?" Lou said.

The *cholo* blinked. "That's right, homes. You got a problem with that?"

Lou opened his door and walked around his Lexus, inspecting it for damage. When he came back to the driver's door, the man was holding a knife. "You had your chance to vamoose, see? Now give me your wallet, *maricón*," he said. Lou stared at the man. He was maybe eighteen years old, his lips curled in a scowl, his body thin, his forearms corded with veins. He held the knife in his fist pointing away from his body, in position for either a backhand or an overhead strike. From his coat pocket, Lou pulled his .38 and flipped open a badge.

"San Jose PD," he said. "Drop the knife, get on your knees, and put your hands behind your head."

"*Tu madre es una puta*," the gangbanger said, but when Lou clicked back the hammer of his revolver, the man let the knife fall to the ground and slowly sank to his knees.

"My mother's a whore?" Lou said. He secured the man's wrists behind his back with plastic restraints. "Your mother raised a *puto*. You can tell her I said that." Then he pulled the punk's bandana down over his eyes and climbed into his Lexus, leaving the gangbanger kneeling on the side of the street. As he drove away, three *cholos* came running up, shouting obscenities and gesturing wildly. One threw a beer bottle at the Lexus, but it fell short. Lou smiled and headed back toward the freeway.

31

AFTER FAILING TO FIND a security outfit in Barstow that would trace Jimmy's cell phone, Mort began calling investigation agencies in Los Angeles. He spent the entire day in Barstow working the phone, trying to find an investigator he thought would likely sell him the service under the table. It had been easy the first time in Reno, but Southern California was proving to be a different story.

The maid knocked on his door once in the morning and again in the afternoon. Each time Mort told her to come back later. He went through every listing in the phonebook until the sun glared in his hotel-room window and he realized it was already late afternoon, and he hadn't eaten all day. He rubbed his eyes and went outside to his Toyota. After sitting in the car for a while, he noticed some people watching him, and he pulled away and began driving around town, vaguely wondering if he might get lucky and see the Lamborghini. But he knew there was no chance of that.

As he drove aimlessly, he found himself thinking of his life as a businessman. He'd once had an impeccable ability to solve problems. He had not gotten rich by accident. Had the years in prison robbed him of that skill? No, he was sure it was still there; he just had to work harder, be more creative.

But it hadn't always been this difficult. Success had come swiftly for Mort after graduating from Harvard and moving to San Jose. His first job was as a financial analyst for a fiber optics company. When they were acquired by a larger corporation three years later, he resigned his post as director of finance, cashed out his considerable stock plan, and spent the next few years working his way up the ladder at a telecommunications firm. Within a couple of years, that company hit tough times, and Mort moved on, landing at a networking company and becoming a vice president. By his mid-thirties, he had accumulated enough money to venture out on his own.

The company Mort founded supplied components in high demand by the exploding personal computing industry. Business boomed, and in five years he amassed a personal fortune of more than $10 million. But competitive forces were taking their toll, as new technologies began rendering his company's products obsolete. In an effort to develop leading-edge technology, he reinvested the millions he had paid himself, but larger corporations with vast resources had moved into his space, and Mort was forced out of business.

The day after he laid off the last of his employees, Mort leaned on the deck rail extending from his custom-built home in the Cupertino foothills, and looked out over the lights of Silicon Valley. The sun was setting behind the Santa Cruz mountains, and wisps of pink and orange clouds stretched across the twilight sky. Most people would have considered it a lovely evening, but Mort barely noticed. He was too busy deciding on the next direction to focus his energies.

The failure of his company illustrated to Mort how difficult it was to control the random issues that could either allow a business to thrive or drive it down the toilet. The series of setbacks that led to his demise were no more predictable or manageable than the bounce of a roulette ball. His next venture would be one not as subject to the fickle winds that dictated success or failure in the business world.

Fortunately for him, the dotcom craze was gathering steam at a furious pace and presented the perfect opportunity. In two months he launched a website selling a wide variety of computing products. Revenue began to roll in, but profits were thin, and the infrastructure required to execute online sales cost more than Mort anticipated. But lack of profitability did not concern him; he responded by dropping prices even lower. Sales increased dramatically, and Mort crafted a prospectus, complete with an accounting statement that falsified every key financial metric.

Dotcom stocks on the NASDAQ were making instant millionaires out of amateur investors everywhere. Mort reached out to everyone he knew and found plenty of individuals eager to invest some of their easy stock market winnings in founder's shares of his pre-IPO offering. Soon he had accumulated $15 million in capital, including $250,000 that his brother John invested after Mort reacquainted with him. John Homestead was amazed and impressed his long-lost brother had a Harvard MBA and was a big time player in the Internet arena. When Mort assured him that his company would go public and deliver a return of many multiples to early investors, John refinanced his home and handed Mort a check.

• • •

Barstow faded in a haze of dust as Mort drove out of the Mohave toward Los Angeles. The next night, after a long, futile day of visiting security agencies, he had dinner at a bar advertising a country-western band. He ordered a hamburger and drank a beer and was ready to leave and spend another solitary night at a cheap hotel when the band kicked into their first song. The singer, a plump, blond girl, had a voice with a pleasing drawl to it, and when the man playing the steel guitar took a solo, the slow, beautifully arranged melody stopped every conversation in the joint. Mort drank another beer and momentarily forgot his frustrations. He realized he was relaxed for the first time since his release from prison. A few beers later, a woman with too much make up and tight clothes meant to show off her figure came on to Mort. She was around thirty, with thick hips and curly, brown hair sprayed in place.

"I like your scar," she said, tracing his cheek with her finger, slurring lazily. She smelled of cigarette smoke.

They went back to his hotel, where she got on her knees and unzipped his pants. He pushed her head away and shoved her onto the bed and held her down with his weight. "Don't be so rough," she whined, struggling as he yanked her jeans down. He forced her legs apart and penetrated her anally, thrusting away until she bled and cried. When he let her up, she grabbed her clothes and cast a terrified look at him before fleeing without saying a word. Mort went to bed and slept more peacefully than he had since being becoming a free man.

It took three more days, but he finally found an investigator who took his $400 bribe. That afternoon Mort learned Jimmy's cell phone was signaling from Harrah's in South Lake Tahoe. Mort filled the Toyota's gas tank and headed out to Interstate 5.

32

HER HANDS MOIST WITH sweat, Heather Sanderson logged on to the dating website and saw that Jimmy had responded to her initial e-mail. Her stomach fluttered and she felt light-headed. He had taken the bait, and now there would be no turning back. But her nerves steadied when she reminded herself that she and Eric were quickly running out of money. If she backed out now, returning to the strip club would be the only answer. That meant spending her evenings doing lap dances for drunken men who reeked of liquor and treated her like a whore.

She had once accepted $500 from a man for an encounter in the VIP suite, or the "BJ room," as the girls called it. The other strippers did it on a regular basis, and Heather needed the money. But when the man took his thing out, the realization that she was on the brink of prostitution made Heather freak. She returned his money and quit the club that night.

Eric had been outraged, of course, as he had just lost his own job. He bitched about their lack of money constantly and pushed her to go back to lap dancing, almost as if he was her pimp. She stopped having sex with him unless he insisted, and daydreamed about finding a good, solid man with whom she could live a normal life. With the right man by her side, she would gladly disappear out of Eric's shitty world—just pack up and leave a note telling him to expect divorce papers in the mail.

She would have left him a month ago if it weren't for her dwindling bank account. Eric still had a month's rent money put away, but that was only part of the reason she was hanging around. Though she hated admitting it to herself, she was scared Eric would go into an insane rage if she tried to leave. He would view her rejection as a blow to his manhood, even if he didn't love her anymore. His ego was so fragile that he saw every setback as an insult to his masculinity, and he'd become increasingly prone to violent outbursts. Heather knew better than to put herself in his line of fire; she really thought he might hurt her. When the time came, though, once she got her hands on Jimmy's money, she planned to begin her life anew. If Eric came after her, she'd just have to deal with it. Hopefully she could make a clean break, and leave him to rot with his steroids and porno movies.

With nervous fingers, she replied to Jimmy's invitation to join him in Reno. She didn't want to appear too eager, so she asked him some questions about his life. When Jimmy turned the subject matter to sex early on, Heather sighed and played along. The slimebag even bragged he was well hung. The mention of his prick made her think of a greasy, wart covered snake. Heather resisted the temptation to tell him to stick it up his ass. Instead, she wrote, "I'm sure I'll be impressed." That really got him going, and he started asking all sorts of bright questions, like what her favorite position was, how often she shaved, whether or not she liked oral, and on and on. She finally signed off late in the afternoon, telling him she'd be in touch tomorrow.

Heather didn't bother asking Eric where he'd been when he came home that evening, six hours after he left for the gym. She could smell the alcohol on him, and he wasn't demanding food, which meant he probably picked up dinner on his own. Of course, he hadn't bothered to bring her anything.

"Jimmy Homestead replied back to me," she said. "He's invited me to visit him at some place he's renting in Reno."

Eric turned away from the TV. "When?"

"Anytime, I suppose. He seems pretty eager."

He stood up. "Go pack our bags, then. Let's drive there tomorrow and get this done."

She hesitated for a long moment, then did as she was told.

33

WHEN LOU WOKE THE next morning at the Best Western in San Jose, he called his old partner from LAPD. Tommy McCoy was a grizzled veteran who had battled alcoholism for years and was nearing retirement. Lou had sent him a bottle of Glenlivet every Christmas until a few years back, when Tommy said his liver was shot and the doctors ordered him to dry out.

They reminisced for a minute about the old times, then Lou asked him to run the plate numbers he had copied the night before.

"What are ya gonna send me for Christmas this year, another freaking fruit basket?" Tommy said.

"Actually, I just got a new shipment of Cubans."

"Christ, you're killin' me. My physician told me to give up the stogies or I'll get mouth cancer. If I even take a couple puffs, my wife smells it on me and kicks my ass. Getting old is a bitch."

"Beats the alternative though, huh?"

"That's debatable. You know what it's like to go through life sober?"

"I assume it's a sobering experience."

"You're a funny man. All right, here's your names—the purple pickup belongs to one Octavio Sanchez, Mexican male, age twenty-two, five-nine, 190. He just spent two years at Elmwood for possession with intent to deal—got popped with a suitcase full of pills. He was also busted for robbery when he was a juvenile. He's linked to 14 Locos in San Jose, a *Nortenos* affiliate."

"He's got the four circles tattooed between his knuckles."

"If he's killed someone, he's never been arrested for it."

"Hmm. All right, how about the Impala?"

"It's registered to Hector Escobar, twenty-seven years of age, six-foot, 170. Now, this young man is quite the citizen. You ready to take notes?"

"Go."

"Escobar was originally with MS-13 in LA. He was a refugee from the civil war in El Salvador and was granted citizenship here when he was fifteen. It says he was a guerilla fighter down there when he was a child. When he was seventeen, he was a suspect in a triple homicide in San Diego that was never solved. Then a year later, he was arrested when a truck crossing the border with twenty keys of heroin was stopped. He wasn't in the truck, but he was dimed as the brains behind it. The charges against him were dropped after two witnesses were murdered. After that he had a falling out with MS-13 and fled north to San Jose."

"Any detail on the falling out?"

"Yeah, they suspected he killed the two women who fingered him, who happened to be wives of two MS-13 gangbangers. Apparently MS-13 wasn't too happy about that."

"That's understandable. What's he been up to in San Jose?"

"He's the *Mero Mero* of 14 Locos. You know how that works—it doesn't mean he's particularly bright, it just means he's the most violent in the gang."

"Kind of unusual for a Southern Cal gangbanger to become the leader of a Nor Cal outfit, isn't it?"

"Sure, the rivalry between the *Nortenos* and the *Surenos* is as intense as ever. Escobar is rumored to have earned his way to the top of 14 Locos by orchestrating the torture and murder of three members of a Vietnamese gang in San Jose."

"Sounds like he's a man of irrepressible charm. What else?"

"San Jose PD nailed him a couple years ago on an aggravated assault charge involving his girlfriend. He did six months in the local clink for that."

"Anything specific about cocaine trafficking on either of them?"

"Let's see—the only mention is the Vietnamese thing. It was apparently a battle over drug-dealing turf. Pot, crystal meth, coke—the usual."

"Thank you, my friend," Lou said. He hung up and turned to his notebook computer and updated the case document he'd been compiling. The connection between Sanzini and Hector Escobar was interesting, but without a link to Sheila Majorie, it was meaningless. He left the hotel and climbed into his SUV. The morning fog was lifting, but the skies were still a pallid white when Lou pulled into the parking lot of Sheila's apartment complex. He spotted Sheila's Toyota this time, and after parking nearby, he walked through the light mist and found her unit, which was on the first floor and plainly visible from the parking lot. He returned to his car, and at 11:30 followed her to the beauty salon where she worked.

Lou watched the salon from his car during her entire eight-hour shift, relieving himself in a plastic jug when necessary. When she left at eight, he followed her home and staked out her apartment until the lights went out at midnight. In the morning he returned and again followed her to work. When her shift was over, he followed her home and waited until her apartment went dark before leaving.

The next two days were identical to the previous two. Sheila Majorie's life consisted of waking up, going to work, and coming home. The most exciting thing she did was stop at the drug store. There was not the slightest indication of anything that tied her to anyone involved in drug dealing.

Though he was using up a lot of favors, Lou again called Tommy McCoy and asked him to pull her police file. It came back clean; not even a parking ticket.

As a last resort, Lou followed her to the beauty salon the next day and walked in when they opened at noon. Sheila was wearing black jeans and a cream-colored sweater that clung to her curves. Her hair was in a bun, her fingernails painted red. Within a minute Lou was seated in a leather barber's chair, and she was assessing his hair.

"Thin out the sides with your number three and take no more than a quarter inch off the top," he said.

She lowered the seat and rested the back of his head in a sink where hot water was running, and began shampooing his hair. "You're very lucky your hair is so full," she said.

"Tell me about it. I'm surprised I'm not bald by now with the grief my kids put me through." Lou stared up at Sheila's bosom as she massaged his scalp.

"Like my daughter. I put her through college, and it cost me a fortune. She just graduated, but instead of going to work, she ran off with her boyfriend."

"You don't like him?" Sheila asked, her palms rubbing his temples.

"I don't know him; that's what bugs me. I've only met him once."

Sheila rinsed his hair, then lifted his head and wrapped it in a towel.

"He's Mexican, and he's covered in tattoos," Lou said. "I don't know if that's supposed to be a fashion statement, or what."

"Tattoos *are* fashionable these days."

"Really? Do you have one?"

"I'll never tell."

"My sister thinks he's in a gang, like the Mexican Mafia," Lou said, his face serious again. "You ever hear of anything so crazy?"

She dried his hair and began clipping. The salon was mostly empty, and they were in a semiprivate nook. Her perfume was vaguely tropical, and when she moved around him, her hip brushed his shoulder.

"The world's a crazy place," she said, and he waited for her to say more, but she had put down her scissors and was looking through her drawer for the right attachment to her electric trimmer.

"Would you be concerned if you were me?" Lou asked.

"I can't really say," she said.

When she was finished, Lou admired her work in the mirror.

"Very nicely done," he said, and handed her an extra ten, their hands touching.

"By the way, do you have plans for dinner tonight?" he asked.

"You're sweet, but sorry, I never date customers."

"That's a shame," Lou said, and walked out of the salon into the bland, overcast day. "A damn shame," he muttered, as he clicked his seat belt and headed toward the freeway leading back to South Lake Tahoe.

34

The Carson City Library occupied a corner a block off the main drag. The faded brick structure was surrounded by maple and ash trees, but fall had come early this year, and the branches overhead were bare and colorless. I stood inside looking out the window at a group of teenagers playing basketball in the adjacent school yard. A shirtless kid with brown skin sank a nice jump shot. It started to rain, but they played on. Eventually Cody waved at me, and I walked back to where he sat behind my laptop.

"Any luck calling Jimmy?" he asked.

I shook my head. "Still goes straight to voice mail."

"I e-mailed my hacker buddy. He'll let me know when Jimmy gets online again, and maybe he can trace the IP address."

"I tried to get John Homestead's cell number," I said. "No luck. You have any friends left at San Jose PD who would call the phone company for us?"

Cody smiled. "Not a chance.

I sighed and sat in the chair next to him.

"I guess we could stake out the repair garage," he said.

"I suppose that's an option."

"Yeah, but why bother? Your device will let us know when the Lamborghini's on the road again. Let's go kill some time."

Which of course meant finding the nearest bar. I looked at my watch. "It's noon somewhere, Dirt," Cody said.

We walked into a nameless joint with a horseshoe-shaped bar and slot machines lining the walls. The early day crowd was rife with missing teeth and wino breath. A dense brume of cigarette smoke hung above the drinkers, like a radioactive cloud. When we sat, a middle-aged woman with a plaid shirt and pigtails shuffled over to me. Her face was weathered beyond her years, her teeth and gums dark when she spoke.

"Stay away from the slots in this dump," she said.

The bartender raised his voice, and she wandered away, muttering a steam of babble about an unjust and piss-poor world. Cody and I drank up and split.

"I've been to funerals that were a better time than that shithole," he said.

"Let's go get some lunch," I said. But before we made it through the next light my cell rang. It was one of the attorneys I had solicited earlier in the week.

"My client's husband is leaving tomorrow on a business trip to Salt Lake City," she said. "She suspects he has some extracurricular activities arranged. As we discussed, the more incriminating the photos, the better."

I pulled over and jotted down the necessary details. Then I snapped my phone shut and hung a U-turn.

"What's up?" Cody said.

"You said you wanted to kill some time. How about putting Jimmy on the back burner for a few days?"

"Why?"

"I got a paying gig. You up for a road trip?"

"Where to, if you don't mind me asking?"

"Utah, for a couple days."

"That's a hell of a road trip. You sure you want to leave town?"

"I need the money."

Cody shrugged. "I guess we can track down Jimmy when we get back."

"Sometimes a little benign neglect is a good thing," I said.

"Or not," Cody replied, "but what do I know?"

• • •

By midafternoon we were heading eastbound on Highway 80. Four hundred miles of high desert lay ahead, the land parched and cold under a pale blue sky banked with faint clouds. Vast fields of sagebrush and dry grass lined the road and stretched as far as the eye could see. The monotony of the flat terrain was occasionally broken by a random pinyon or bristlecone pine, but otherwise the country was featureless.

"Empty territory," I said.

"Empty, and dry too. How far until the next truck stop?" Cody said.

"Lovelock is an hour away. Tell your liver it will get a break until then."

"Damn. We should have picked up beer in Reno."

East of Winnemucca we dropped into a shallow valley and began climbing a short grade. The highway sliced through the rock-strewn pastures, the landscape jagged with treeless bluffs and mesas that jutted from the earth's crust like massive burial mounds. We crossed a short bridge and passed over a gully that fell away into a steep canyon, the walls serrated and strangely uniform, as if carved by a mason to the gods. In the distance, a deeply shadowed ridge rose into the gray clouds along the northern horizon. Cody gave up trying to find a radio station with decent reception and tossed his empty beer can into the backseat.

"Let's stop at Elko for dinner," he said.

"Yeah, my ass is about wore out. Crack me another beer, would you?"

We rolled into Elko in time to see the last of the sunset, the low clouds lit with purple fire, the sky above florescent and twinkling with starlight.

Halfway down the main drag, we stopped at the Pioneer Hotel and Saloon. Inside, the old lounge was crowded with a party of some sort. We elbowed our way to the bar and ordered steaks and whiskey.

"What's the occasion?" I asked the bartender.

"It's our annual arts festival. We get poets, musicians, and painters from all over the place."

A couple of whiskeys later, I felt myself crossing the line from a slight buzz to a pleasant drunk. I struck up a conversation with a pretty black-haired woman in a leather jacket who was trying to order a drink. We talked for a while before I realized Cody was no longer at the bar. I heard a commotion and spotted him at a table with a group of people, telling what was apparently an uproarious story. A buxom redhead wearing a frilly dress clung to his arm. Her eyes had an alcoholic shine and her exaggerated expressions made me think of a circus clown.

"Your friend?" the brunette asked me.

"For as long as I can remember."

"He better watch out for that fire crotch. She's screwed everything with pants in this town."

"My god, do you think I should warn him?"

"Oh, shut up."

Somehow we ended up at a house a few miles outside of town. It was a large, ranch-style spread built on a lot surrounded by nothing but open plains. The interior was done in polished woods, except for a massive stone fireplace that covered an entire wall. Full-length windows looked out over a backyard party, complete with heat lamps, a side of beef, beer kegs, and a hired bartender. Beyond the yard, miles of grazing pasture lay under the moonlit sky.

In my blur of drunkenness, I was perplexed at the bizarre mix of people gathered at the place. A woman about seventy was reading poetry in one room to ten college-aged kids who listened in absolute silence. In another room, a man played the banjo and harmonica and sang about a cattle drive. In the main room, a writer who wrote a book I had read years ago began reading passages from his new novel in front of the roaring fireplace. His audience became distracted when a topless female with a six-foot snake wrapped around her torso walked in the front door. The writer hurried outside to the bar and spent the remainder of the night there.

All the while, folks dressed as if attending a Renaissance fair roamed about, sipping wine and discussing the western art murals that covered the walls. Searching for a bathroom, I opened the door to a bedroom where a half dozen men huddled over a mirror lined with cocaine. Outside, speakers blared ZZ Top, and at least twenty people were dancing on the patio, gyrating and pumping as if they hoped an orgy would break out. I spotted Cody near the roasting pit, holding a knife, cutting huge slices of rare beef and eating with his bare hands. He was wearing a rawhide leather coat with fringes that someone must have given him.

"I guess we're not gonna make it to Salt Lake tonight," I said.

He looked at me in surprise, then grinned, his teeth bloody. "Make it to where?"

• • •

When I woke the next morning, I had no idea where I was. Indoors, fortunately. In bed, in a strange room. And still drunk. I sat up and smelled perfume. Fragments of the night began to dance around in my head, but I wasn't quite sure until the black-haired lady I'd met early in the evening walked in stark naked and parked her shapely ass next to me.

"Coffee, tea, or me?" she said.

"How about a Bloody," I croaked. "Or if that's too much to ask, whiskey will do."

"Take these first," she said, handing me a fistful of pills and a glass of water. "Then take a shower, cowboy, and I'll bring you further medication." I groaned and made my way into the bathroom, and a minute later, her hand reached through the shower curtain and handed me a Bloody Mary, complete with a celery stick.

"You are a rare woman," I said, guzzling half the drink as hot water pounded on my back. I wondered what time it was. The thought was quickly lost when I stepped out of the shower into a soft towel she held. "Don't even think about leaving yet," she said, dropping to her knees. Then she led me to the bed and made me regret my poor memory, but she made damn sure I'd remember the morning. I finally disengaged from her limbs an hour later and found my truck beached on the sidewalk in front of her place. She gave me directions to the house where the party had been held, and promised to visit the next time she came west. The idea brought a happy anticipation to my chest, even made me feel a bit giddy, but maybe that was just the booze.

• • •

Finding Cody, on the other hand, didn't go so smoothly. I knocked on the front door to the ranch house, and when no one answered, I turned the unlocked doorknob and went in. Leftovers were scattered about, asleep on couches, and more were in the bedrooms I peeked into, but Cody was nowhere to be found. Out in the backyard two men smoked and sucked on drinks. I assumed they'd pulled a sunrise show, up all night on cocaine, and were trying to consume enough liquor to come down and pass out. I wandered out to a large barn I hadn't noticed the night before. Frost coated the prairie, and a cold wind had kicked up. I was anxious to get on the road.

Cody lay atop a pile of hay in a corner of the barn, wrapped in a mass of furry blankets, his bearded face serenely asleep. When I tried to wake him, I saw he wasn't alone.

"Come on, get your ass up, Cody," I whispered. "I need to be in Salt Lake." He moaned as he came to, then shushed me and threw his clothes on. Ten minutes later we were in my truck heading down the road.

"The barn?" I said.

"We couldn't find an open bedroom. Christ, she was a nut case. She got a big kick out of doing it in the hay, but afterward she just wouldn't shut up. I was trying to sleep, but she was babbling all sorts of crazy shit, nonstop. It was starting to really piss me off."

"Sounds like you fucked her silly."

We laughed at that as much as our hangovers would allow, then found a diner at the edge of town, where we ate breakfast and drank coffee until our heads cleared. Then we drove back out to the desert, east on 80, through Wendover, Nevada, and across the salt flats into Utah.

• • •

At two P.M. we were in position at the Salt Lake City Airport. The skies were overcast and dull, the city blanketed in gray. To the east, the granite faces of the Wasatch Range, streaked with early snowfall, rose above the valley and merged with the clouds. Cody stayed in my truck, parked outside the rental car parking lot, while I waited in the terminal for the flight from Reno to land. I picked up the subject as he left the security area. He was a short man, dark haired, narrow hips and wide shoulders, his blue pinstriped business suit well-tailored. He strode at a brisk pace, the flaps of his overcoat trailing behind him. We walked along the overpass to the rental car counter, and I returned to my truck. A minute later, the man drove off in a blue Ford Taurus, and Cody and I followed him out of the airport.

We waited for him to finish a three o'clock meeting at a downtown high-rise, then spent an hour outside his hotel, a small, single-story complex north of the city. When he came out of his room he'd lost his tie, and his hair was still wet. He drove away like a man with a purpose.

The bar at the Mexican restaurant was big and crowded, which made for easy surveillance. A much younger woman, wearing a tight red skirt and white blouse, met him at the bar. They ordered drinks, and soon her hand was on his thigh. I snapped a few discrete pictures with my cell. Cody waved down a waitress, and before long, a huge plate of nachos and a pitcher of margaritas arrived at our table.

An hour later I took more pictures of the couple as they parked and walked into his hotel room.

"Too easy," I said.

"Let's go back to the restaurant and get another pitcher. You've got all you need, right?"

"No. I want to wait until she leaves so I can document it."

"What? What if she spends the night?"

"You can get a room. I'll wait here."

Cody was silent for a minute, then he picked up my 35mm camera and started fiddling with it. He clicked off a couple photos of the parking lot.

"What are you doing?"

"How do you turn the flash on?"

"That button. Why?"

"Wait here," he said, then left my truck and walked to the hotel office.

"What now?" I muttered. I peered toward the office, and had started out of the truck when I saw him come out the door. He waved me off and went down the walkway to the couple's room. I stood outside my truck and watched him insert a key in the door and go inside. A scream and shouted curses ensued, and a few seconds later Cody was running toward me, a huge, irreverent grin on his face, his eyes wild with glee.

"Start the motor, let's boogie!"

As I roasted the tires and bounced off the curb into the street, I caught a glimpse of the man's outraged face in the doorway.

"Hoo-wee, wait until you see these shots!" Cody exclaimed. "He had her buns up kneelin', and he was wheelin' and dealin'. You should have been there."

"It was supposed to be a covert operation, Cody. The guy wasn't supposed to know he was being watched."

"It doesn't matter. It's a divorce case, right? These pictures cut to the bottom line. Your client is gonna love you for this."

After a few miles we pulled over at a neighborhood lounge near the airport. We sat in a booth and I checked out the photos Cody had taken. I had to admit he'd hit pay dirt. The expressions on the couple's faces as they tried unsuccessfully to hide their nakedness were comically distorted. One picture in particular was both graphic and hilarious, and despite my anger at Cody for his spur of the moment role in my investigation, I fell into a fit of punch-drunk laughter. Cody smiled and winked at me, holding up a tall glass.

"To the good times, Dirt, to road trips and road beers and loose women and bars and easy paychecks and no worries."

How could a man not drink to that?

• • •

The following afternoon, after a relatively mild night in Salt Lake, we drove back to Reno and then south to Carson City. I wanted to continue over the pass to South Lake Tahoe, but Cody suggested we stop at the library in Carson.

"His car hasn't left that garage, right?" he said.

"I'd have been sent an alert if it did."

"So he's probably still local. Let's go use the wireless hotspot at the library. I want to check a couple things."

"All right," I said. "I'll type up my case report and e-mail it to the lawyer while we're there."

Cody began working on one of the library PCs while I downloaded the photos from my camera onto my computer. A few minutes later he interrupted me.

"Guess what? Jimmy Homestead is logged onto an e-mail account right now."

"Where?"

"The IP address has a longitude and latitude in Reno. My hacker buddy is dialing in the exact location. In ten minutes he'll be sending me an address."

"I'll believe it when I see it."

"Always the skeptic," Cody smiled, slapping my back and drumming a quick cadence on the table with his knuckles.

35

IT WAS SUNDAY, AND Jimmy and John Homestead were lounging around, watching football and eating roast beef sandwiches, when John heard his cell ring. He hauled himself off the couch and retrieved it from the bedroom.

"John, it's Lou Calgaretti. Everything okay there?"

"Sure. All quiet. Why?"

"Just checking. I'm driving back to Tahoe from San Jose. Is your son there?"

"Yes."

"Why don't you put me on the speaker, and I'll give you an update."

John brought the phone to the living room and turned off the TV.

"I found nothing to support Sheila's claims she has any association or involvement with a Mexican drug dealing ring," Lou said.

"You're sure about this?" John said.

"I checked her phone records and tailed her for a few days. I even visited her for a haircut. If she has any connection, I could find no sign of it."

"It's like I figured," Jimmy said. "She's full of crap."

"Based on my findings, you're probably right. But I also spent some time watching Tony Sanzini. He *is* involved with a Mexican gang, and they are definitely not nice people."

"What about Sheila being connected to Sanzini?" John asked. "She told Jimmy that Sanzini had brought the Mexicans to her house, to offer Sheila the chance to get Jimmy to pay them off to resolve the stolen coke issue."

"Clearly Sheila had contact with Sanzini at one point," Lou said. "How else would she know him? But my suspicion is Sanzini contacted her back when Jimmy ripped him off, in an effort to find him. That could well be the extent of their connection."

"Meaning she's had no recent communication with him?" John said.

"None that I could uncover."

"So, what's the bottom line, Lou? Do I need to be worried about any of this?"

"Jimmy, I think the most likely scenario is your stepmother fabricated the story to trick you into paying her."

"What about the two guys with her?" John said.

"They could be hired muscle, but I haven't been able to turn up anything on them yet."

"Well, screw her, then," Jimmy said. "I got people to meet and places to be."

"Here's what I think would be best, gentlemen," Lou said. "I'll keep tabs on Sheila and Sanzini from my office for the next couple weeks. If I see anything to be concerned about I'll contact you. If you see or hear from Sheila again, call me. Or call 911 if need be."

"Cool," Jimmy said.

After Lou hung up, Jimmy looked at his dad. John Homestead had lost a few pounds but still looked flabby and out of shape. Jimmy was about to suggest he put down his greasy sandwich and hit the exercise room, but instead he went into the den to check his computer. His eyes lit up when he saw hot Debbie had sent him a message. She said she had a few days off work and proposed driving up to meet him! Jimmy e-mailed her his address, and Debbie wrote back saying to expect her tomorrow afternoon.

Jimmy paced around the room, grinning and pumping his fist. This chick was smokin' sexy, and she was chasing after *him.* It was like a blast from the past, to the days when he bedded the hottest babes in town. Back then, he used to practice his motto, *find 'em, feel 'em, fuck em, and forget 'em,'* every chance he got. And he'd done so many he lost count. Those were the days when he ruled, when he was on top of the world. He smoothed his hair back with one hand and grabbed his crotch with the other. Were his younger years as a womanizing cocksman really a thing of the past? Hell, no. The time had come to give the whores a rest and reclaim his position as a mainline stud.

He took his shirt off and looked in the mirror. Shit, the good life was starting to take its toll on his slim physique. He'd have to start riding the stationary bike and maybe pump some iron. No time like the present, he thought, feeling a burst of energy. He changed into shorts and tennis shoes, went into the mirrored room that served as a gym, and began pedaling. Soon he was breathing hard and sweating. He turned the resistance down and slowed his pace.

All he could think about was the upcoming date with Debbie—the suave, witty things he'd say, and how she would no doubt find him irresistible. It had been over ten years since he'd been on a real date, but he didn't feel the slightest trepidation. Rather, the anticipation of meeting her was like being high, like he'd just snorted a big rip of uncut Colombian rock. Hey, maybe he would score some coke, in case she wanted a toot. He remembered having some great romps in the hay with Bettys who were whacked on blow. But there was always the danger he'd get a case of coke dick, and going limp would be a disaster. The hell with it then, forget the blow. Instead, they could have a few drinks, maybe smoke some weed, and then let the humpathon begin. Not a bad agenda.

A half an hour later, Jimmy toweled off and found his father still watching sports in the living room.

"Hey, Pop, I've got a gal coming to visit me tomorrow."

"You do? Who is she?" John said.

"I met her on the Internet."

"Oh."

"Yeah, so I need you to make yourself scarce tomorrow, beginning around two. Probably best you spend the night somewhere. Maybe I can book you a room at the Atlantis or the Peppermill."

"Okay, no problem."

Jimmy sat down and they watched the Raiders get their asses kicked by the Broncos for a few minutes, until the game paused for a commercial. "You think we'll ever hear from Sheila again?" he said.

John leaned forward and put his chin on his fist. "I don't think we've heard the last of her," he said. "We should keep our guard up in case she tries something else."

Jimmy shrugged. "I'm not worried about her." He pointed the clicker at the TV and started changing channels.

"Look, we can order the new James Bond movie on pay per view. I just need to call Comcast and set up an account. I'm gonna turn my phone back on." When John started to protest, Jimmy shook his head. "Should be no problem, Pop, Lou said we got nothing to worry about." He dialed the cable service and gave them all the information they needed. When the flick started, Jimmy kicked his feet up, watching Bond defy death and still find time to get laid by sexy babes. Not too different from his own life, he thought.

36

AFTER NINE HOURS OF hard driving, Mort arrived in Tahoe Valley. As he neared the darkened town, he looked at his face in the rear-view mirror. His eyes were horribly bloodshot and burned as if soap were dripping from his brow into his pupils. At the first gas station in South Lake Tahoe, he pulled over and rubbed his eyes with his fists until the sting receded. He sat with his lids shut, and after a while he needed to relieve his bladder, but when he climbed from the car his back cramped so badly he could barely breathe. He finally wrenched himself straight and shuffled to the restroom, his teeth gritted, sweat beading on his forehead.

When he returned to the Toyota, he drove behind the building where it was dark and quiet. He reclined his seat and took shallow breaths until the spasms in his back subsided. Within a minute he was asleep, and his dreams came fast and vivid.

A faceless man walked beside him along a paved trail between rolling fields of freshly mowed grass and a sparkling lake. Paddling silently, a family of ducks swam near the shoreline, the parents leading a string of ducklings. It was a warm summer day, and families and young couples were picnicking under colorful umbrellas. The scent of charcoal and barbequed hamburgers wafted in the air. Dogs chased and leaped after Frisbees, and children played on swings, their faces bright and exuberant. The sun shined down on this idyllic setting, and Mort asked for a cold soda when they walked past a sidewalk vendor. The faceless man said no.

"Please?" Mort asked.

Then the scene shifted to a room, and Mort was punching the man bloody, until he was swinging his fists into a liquid maw. His anger unabated, he continued punching after the man was headless. His mother watched quietly from a corner. Every now and then, she would sneak a sip from a bottle she hid in her purse. Mort finally took the bottle from her and tossed it out the window.

It was past midnight when Mort woke. For a few minutes he was disoriented and unable to fully extract himself from the dream. He was desperately thirsty. After finding and gulping a bottle of water that had rolled under his seat, he sat hunched for a time. He was struck by a strange and powerful sense that he was detached from everything that was him, as if he occupied the body of a stranger whose background and motivations were unknown. Finally he snapped out of it, telling himself it must be exhaustion.

He dialed the number for Harrah's on his disposable, untraceable cell phone and asked for Jimmy Homestead. When the clerk said no one by that name was checked in, Mort was neither surprised nor frustrated. Instead, he felt an odd emptiness, as if he had been drained of all emotion. Crawling into the back of his little car, he wrapped himself in his jacket and slept until dawn. He woke shivering, walked into the mini-mart, and bought himself a coffee and a donut that left a coat of grease on the roof of his mouth. When he finished eating he drove off into the dark gloom of the morning, heading around the black lake toward Reno.

The fleabag he chose in Reno was among the sleaziest hotels in town. A pair of whores leaned against a car, eyeing him sullenly as he went into his room. After washing his clothes in the shower and hanging them to dry, he counted the remaining money stashed in his suitcase. Then he called the security firm in Reno and asked for Joe, the man who had originally traced Jimmy's cellular signal to Las Vegas. Joe agreed to meet with him but needed to wait until tomorrow.

Mort hung up and sat in the wooden chair in the hotel room and stared at the wall. A police car pulled into the parking lot, siren wailing. There was a commotion involving a guest and a prostitute, and the cops eventually sorted it out and took them both away in cuffs. Mort continued staring blankly. Hours later, when his clothes had dried, he dressed in his disguise and drove to an army surplus store, where he bought a survival knife and a sharpening stone. Back in his room, he sat holding the knife, weighing its presence in his hand. The furrows above his eyes eventually eased, and his jaw went slack. He began honing the blade, meticulously working it until it was razor sharp.

The next day he paid Joe $400, and drove back to his hotel to wait, after the initial attempt to connect to Jimmy's phone was unsuccessful. He tore pages from the phonebook and passed the time dangling the sheets from his fingertips, slowly slicing them to ribbons.

That evening Mort saw a dude riding a chopped Honda check into the hotel and take the neighboring room. Within a few minutes the volume from the TV next door was cranked up so high that Mort could hear every word. He pounded on the wall, and the man, who looked like white trash prison riffraff, pounded back. The TV continued to blare for the next hour. Mort held his knife, his hand trembling. It would be so easy to kick the door down and slit the man's throat. Instead, he settled for puncturing the Honda's tires in the wee hours of the morning.

He left at daybreak, found another discount hotel, and called Joe, who said it seemed that Jimmy's phone was turned off. Joe promised to continue calling until he could get a signal. Mort began exercising in his room, doing hundreds of pushups and sit ups. He wanted to be ready to take down Jimmy Homestead when the time came. The physical exertion made him feel focused and he felt his angst recede. So far, Jimmy had been very lucky. That was the only explanation Mort could fathom for him being so hard to track down. But Jimmy's good fortune was coming to an end. Mort could feel it in his bones.

• • •

When Garrett Rancour walked outside in the morning and saw his motorcycle's tires were flat, he turned in a slow 360, staring hard in every direction. The sun had just edged over the horizon, and the parking lot was still and empty of people. The signal light on the boulevard turned green, and trucks and busses went through their gears, filling the air with gritty fumes. A young black man stepped out of his room a few doors down and lit a cigarette. He walked past Rancour, looking at the Honda.

"That's fucked up, man," he said.

"You see who did this?"

The brother shrugged, and a shit-eating grin formed on his face, as if Rancour's misfortune had brightened his day. He continued walking down the street to the bus stop.

Rancour sat on the pavement and inspected his front tire. He hoped someone had simply let the air out of the valve. But the chrome stem cap was still in place. He looked closer, his stomach sinking, and saw the sidewall had been punctured. His eyes clouded in despair when he saw the rear tire had suffered the same fate. Both tires would need to be replaced.

He had intended on having a big breakfast at the Denny's out near the freeway. Now he would have to deal with buying new tires and finding a shop to install them. He went back to his room to look through the phone book for the closest motorcycle repair shop. But he stopped when he noticed the empty parking space next to his bike. Last night a shit-box silver Toyota Corolla had been parked there. It probably belonged to the asshole next door who pounded on the wall.

Rancour knocked on the door of the room next to his. No answer. He knocked again and put his ear to the window. Then he went to the hotel office. A fat, unshaven man with bad breath sat behind the counter.

"I need the name of whoever was staying in 108," Rancour said.

"You do, huh?"

Rancour slid a ten-dollar bill across the counter. The man glanced at it and smirked. "Not much I can do with that."

Rancour placed two fives on top of the ten. The man took the bills and flipped open the registration book. "John Smith," he said with a chuckle.

Rancour leaned over the counter and grabbed the book. He saw that license plate numbers were recorded next to each guest's name, including his own. He copied down the plate number next to John Smith, then tossed the book onto the lap of the fat man.

"My tires were slashed outside my room last night. Don't you got any security at this roach pit?"

The man rolled his eyes. "Yeah, Reno PD. You got a problem, take it up with them."

Half an hour later, Rancour was pushing his motorcycle down the street. He'd underestimated the effort it would take to push the bike with two flats. He made it a quarter mile before stopping to rest, the repair shop still a mile away. His pits were soaked through, and he'd stripped to his T-shirt even though the temperature hadn't yet hit fifty. By the time he made it a half mile, he was swearing out loud and had to rest for ten minutes before the burn in his shoulders and legs faded. He sat on the curb, smoking a Marlboro 100, wondering who rat-fucked his ride, and why. He knew there were uppity bikers out there who considered his Honda a joke. He even beat the shit out of a smartass yuppie once, for referring to his bike as a chopped moped. But most likely he felt it was John Smith who screwed him over—whoever that chickenshit bastard was. Maybe the prick was pissed about the TV being turned up too loud. But slashing his tires was a pretty extreme reaction.

Until today, Rancour had been enjoying his stay in Nevada. The last seventy-two hours had been especially pleasant, since he had a pocketful of cash, and there wasn't much to do since his security agency buddy claimed he needed to lay low for a bit. Without any input to help him locate Jimmy Homestead, Rancour was content to chill and wait. He was in no hurry, and he found the small casinos and strip clubs in Reno to his liking.

He started down the street again, and decided to definitely find John Smith and beat him to a pulp. With the license plate number, locating him might not be too tough. Ripping off Jimmy Homestead was still his first priority, but he would find time for Smith too—let there be no mistake about it. He would do so as a bonus to himself.

37

DRESSED IN LEATHER PANTS, snakeskin boots, and a button-down designer shirt, Jimmy watched the street from his upstairs window. His new shirt has cost $185, and was embroidered with a trippy purple and green pattern. He felt the shirt conveyed his cool and edgy persona, and he wore it outside his jeans and unbuttoned halfway down his chest. The watch he'd bought along with the shirt read 2:30. When Jimmy looked again, three minutes had passed. He went downstairs and double-checked his bedroom and bathroom. Shit, he wished he'd had time to hire a maid.

The doorbell rang, and Jimmy bolted to his feet, then stopped and took a deep breath. He walked to the door and slowly opened it, his lips parted. The female standing in the doorway wore tight bell-bottom jeans low on her hips and a short, orange top showing off her tanned midriff.

"Hey, Debbie, babe," Jimmy said, eyeing her up and down.

"And you must be Jimmy."

"None other." She walked in and gave Jimmy a little hug, pushing her boobs against his chest while closing the door herself. She made sure it was unlocked, just the way Eric told her.

"Nice pad," she said. "Are you gonna show me around?"

"Sure, Deb. How about a drink first?"

Heather was glad he asked. The five-hour drive to Reno with her husband had been hell. Eric made her repeat every order he gave her on the operation. When he was finally satisfied that she'd memorized his instructions, he turned on the music and ignored her. When she asked what his plans were for the money they planned to coerce from Jimmy, he told her that information was only available on a "need-to-know" basis. "I'll give you an allowance, don't worry," he said.

Jimmy gave Heather a tour of the house, getting behind her every chance he got to check out her magnificently curvy ass and the tattoo on her lower back. They went out on the deck overlooking the swimming pool, but it was too chilly for a swim. When he asked if she wanted to burn a joint, she declined, and instead asked for another Vodka Collins.

As they walked around the house, Heather's nerves calmed. Clearly Jimmy didn't recognize her from that regrettable one-nighter when they were in high school. She barely recognized *him*, all wrinkly and looking like a middle-aged man trying to cling to his youth. The fact that he didn't remember her meant he must have really cooked his brain on alcohol and drugs, because she *knew* she hadn't changed that much in the last seventeen years.

They took a seat on the couch and listened to music, mostly annoying classic rock, while Jimmy talked about himself. Heather let him blather on, and at exactly 3:30, she touched his leg.

"You haven't showed me the bedroom yet."

Jimmy gave her a knowing leer. "Ah, yes, my *boudoir* is right this way." He led her down the hall, his heart beginning to thump in anticipation.

The master bedroom was large and spacious. Jimmy sat on the king-sized bed, leaning back on his elbows. She asked him to put some music on, then came to him and began performing a lap dance. Jimmy pawed her ass and rubbed his face in her bosom, and she pulled her top up so he wouldn't cover it in slobber. She told herself to relax, and that she'd done it a thousand times, but she was repulsed by the man who had given her warts when she was a teenager. She let him squeeze her breasts through her bra while she checked her watch. Three more minutes, then Eric would be here.

Almost on cue, Jimmy reached down, unzipped his pants, and freed himself.

"Just needed to give the big guy some room," he said.

Heather backed away, dancing and killing time. After a minute she reached down and pulled his leather pants down to his ankles, carefully avoiding his hairy rod, which was at full attention. Where the hell was Eric?

"Come on, Deb, let me check out your hot ass."

Heather toyed with the buttons on her jeans and pushed them partially down her hips.

"Oh yeah," Jimmy said. "Man, you're teasing me. Come here, baby."

With Jimmy's pants bunched around his ankles, Heather thought she'd be safe, as long as she kept out of his reach. She danced around him, watching him squirm. Then Jimmy kicked his boots off, and his pants were next, and in a second he was up and lunging toward her.

"Hey!" she yelled, squirming, trying to avoid his stiffened member. He got behind her and pushed her pants down and she felt his cock hard against the flesh of her ass. She was beginning to panic when Eric burst in the bedroom door.

"Get your hands off her, slimeball!" he yelled.

"Rape! He tried to rape me!"

"You scumbag piece of shit," Eric said, rushing forward and hitting Jimmy with a tremendous uppercut to the gut. Jimmy collapsed to the ground, his wind gone, his mouth wide in a futile effort to catch his breath.

"Oh my god, he's turning blue," Heather said.

"He's gonna wish he was dead when I get through with him," Eric said. He lifted Jimmy by the hair and pinned the bare-assed man against the wall. "Say your prayers, asswipe."

Jimmy's eyes were round with shock and fear. He couldn't breathe, but finally his diaphragm relaxed, and he gulped air and then projectile vomited his lunch onto the bedspread. Eric deftly stepped aside to avoid a direct hit.

"Jesus Christ, what a pussy. You don't deserve to live. I'm gonna snap your freaking neck."

"Wait, don't kill him!" Heather said. "Let's just call the police and send him to jail. Then he can get raped and see what it's like."

"It's a nice thought, but I don't think so," Eric said, and reared back his fist.

"No, please," Jimmy moaned.

Eric shot a punch at Jimmy's face, but pulled his fist back at the last instant. "Ah, fuck it. You're not worth skinning my knuckles, you piece of shit." He tossed his mobile phone to Heather. "Call 911. And you," he said, turning back to Jimmy, "put your pants on. I'm tired of looking at your scrawny ass. You're going to prison. Your ass will be real popular there. It will be the size of the Holland Tunnel in no time at all, with at least as much traffic. Count on it."

"But I didn't try to rape her!" Jimmy cried.

"It's your word against ours. Good luck on that one."

"Why?" Jimmy stammered. "Why are you doing this to me?"

"Because you're a spoiled little homo, trying to prove he's a real man. Which you ain't."

"But, who are you? What did I ever do to you?"

"Sit down and stop cringing," Eric said. "You're pathetic."

Jimmy yanked his pants on and sat on the edge of the bed, trying to calm his breathing and compose himself.

"You want out of this mess, you got one chance, right here, right now. We drive out to your bank, just the three of us. You withdraw three million in cash. Then I'll drop you off somewhere, maybe a little inconvenient, but you'll live."

Jimmy's eyes shaded for a moment, a gesture that did not escape Eric. "You don't like this deal, just say so. Then I'll decide whether to call the cops or maybe just put you in a wheelchair for life."

Jimmy took a deep breath and risked a brief glare at Debbie and Eric. Did this muscle-bound moron and his fake-titted cohort really think he could walk into a bank and withdraw $3 million in cash? When Jimmy was in a bank last, in South Lake Tahoe, he tried to take out fifty grand and was told only thirty thousand in hundred dollar bills was available. If these two were stupid enough to think ripping him off for three mil was so simple, maybe the best answer was to get into a public situation at the bank, and wait for the police to arrive.

"Okay, let's go," he said.

Eric let Jimmy brush his teeth and put on his boots. Then they headed downstairs and opened the front door to a late afternoon warmed by a sun low in the blue and cloudless sky. It had been overcast for days, and the clear weather was a welcome change, but there was a slight problem. Standing in the doorway were four men who shouldn't have been there. And one was pointing an ugly little automatic at Eric's gut.

38

"IT WILL TAKE ME about an hour to finish my report," I told Cody. "Why don't you relax and read a good book?"

Cody looked at me as if my suggestion was the silliest thing he'd ever heard, and wandered back to the computer he'd been using. In fifteen minutes he was back by my side. He slid a sheet of paper over my keyboard.

"Here's the address where Jimmy's logged on. It's a residential neighborhood about twenty minutes from here."

"Are you sure?"

"Finish your report later. Let's roll."

I raised my head. "I need to do this now, if I want to get paid in time for my mortgage. Why don't you wait until I'm done?"

"No guarantees how long he'll be there, Dirt. Let me borrow your rig, then."

I sighed and pulled the keys from my pocket. "Don't stop at any bars."

"Hey," he replied, his large paw outstretched. "Maybe I'll come back with your ten grand."

"That would be nice," I muttered, but my interest in Cody's scheme had waned. I needed to prioritize my time on work that would definitely result in a payday. "Call me and let me know how it goes," I said, dropping the keys in his palm and turning back to my report.

I raised my head again when I heard tires squealing and the blare of horns. I looked out the window and saw Cody pull away from the curb, cutting off an elderly lady driving a '70s Plymouth sedan. She jammed the horn and shot her middle finger out the window. I could see Cody grinning as he stabbed the accelerator and drove away.

• • •

When Hector Escobar saw the scowling hulk of a body builder appear in the doorway, it took him no longer than a second to decide what to do. Escobar pulled the trigger of his .32-caliber Kel-Tec pistol, the three-inch barrel bucked, and a small red hole appeared in Eric's shirt. Then Escobar raised his arm and fired a round through Eric's forehead. Eric fell back into the hallway, dead before he hit the ground, his stunned eyes locked open as if he'd just learned that all he ever believed in was illusory, and his true role was that of a bit player and a dupe.

Heather and Jimmy stared down at Eric in mute horror, watching the pool of blood spread across the marble tile. Then they simultaneously looked up, as if their heads were attached to a puppeteer's string. Three Latinos and one white man stood before them. The Latino with the gun was clearly in charge—the other men stood back and seemed to await his instruction. He was almost six feet tall and rail lean. Tattoos covered most of his exposed skin, including his unusually narrow face. His eyes were dark and set deep in his skull, his lips thin as blades, his sharp, angular jaw highlighted by a pointed goatee. Looking very out of place, his nose was broad and flat, like a boxer's nose.

"Inside," he said. Jimmy and Heather, stunned and speechless, backed in as the men crowded into the foyer, stepping around Eric's body. One of the group, a stocky Mexican wearing a red bandana, gave Heather's ass a long squeeze as he went by. "*Hola, chola,*" he said. The third Latino, an older, mustachioed fellow who looked like a migrant farm worker, stared at Heather with a lusty smile, his teeth brown and disgusting.

The fourth man was Tony Sanzini.

• • •

"It's too bad about your friend out there," Escobar said, once they were assembled in the kitchen. "I guess it just wasn't his day."

From where Heather stood, she could see Eric's arm and the trickling path his blood had taken to the edge of the tiles. She felt nauseated and lightheaded and thought she might be in shock. The only thing that held her together was a tiny, happy thought in the back of her mind: Eric was dead, and she would no longer have to fear him. But when she took account of the men holding her captive, she realized she might have bigger problems to deal with. They were all leering at her, except for the beefy white man.

"You owe me two grand, shit for brains," Sanzini said, stepping toward Jimmy. "Plus interest and late fees. Call it twenty grand even. You got the cash?"

Before Jimmy could respond, Escobar cut his eyes to his associate and said, "Santiago." The one with the bad dental situation reached out and smacked Sanzini with a sharp backhand across the face. "You were told to keep your mouth shut, white boy," Escobar said. Sanzini froze, touching the blood on his lip. Jimmy glanced at Sanzini and looked away quickly when he saw the murderous glare in his eyes.

"Tie them up," Escobar said.

"Hey, whoa," Jimmy said. "There's no need for any more violence, okay? Why don't you just tell me what you want, and I'm sure we can find a happy ending."

At that moment they heard the clunk of a car door shutting.

"Expecting company?" Escobar said to Jimmy. "Go see who it is, Octavio." The stocky *cholo* opened a leather bag, removed a few items, and went toward the front door.

"On your knees," Escobar ordered. "And keep your mouths shut."

• • •

Cody pulled up to the executive home in the posh South Reno neighborhood. Except for a gray Chevy Blazer out front, the house looked unlived in; no oil stains on the driveway, no potted plants, no knickknacks visible on the windowsills. He parked, finished a beer, and knocked on the front door. When it opened he caught a brief glimpse of a red bandana over a white shirt, then he was hit in the eyes with a blast of Mace.

"The fuck?" Cody said, staggering back, his eyes on fire. A fist struck his ear, and Cody threw a blind roundhouse, catching nothing but air. His eyes were burning and tearing heavily, and when he opened one eye he could make out only the faintest of colors and motion. He punched and flailed blindly at his attacker, taking a kick to the groin and another to the shin. One of his wild punches made contact, possibly a shot to his adversary's shoulder or chest. He tangled with the man and tripped, his weight crushing downward. A loud crack sounded, the snap of bone, then a voice cried out in Spanish. Cody scrambled to his feet but was knocked down by a sharp blow to the back of the head. Another blow, and after that, nothing.

Octavio Sanchez pushed himself up, his body shaking, his face contorted in pain. "He broke my arm!"

"We'll make you a sling," the man called Santiago said, a lead-filled sap dangling from his hand. "You're going to have to tough it out, *guerrero.*"

Sanzini came outside and helped Santiago drag Cody into the entryway, after they pushed Eric's blood-soaked body to the side. Escobar led

Jimmy and Heather, their hands bound behind their backs, to where Cody lay unconscious.

"Your friend?" Escobar said.

Jimmy stared at Cody in surprise, recognizing him as one of the two men he'd met when Sheila confronted him at the small town bar off 395. But Sheila had said he was working for a Mexican drug gang. Obviously that was not the case, at least not these Mexicans. Other than that, Jimmy had no idea who the huge, red-bearded man was, or what his motivations were. The events of the last hour had left him in a state of utter confusion. Who were all these crazy people messing with him?

"Yeah, he's my friend," Jimmy said, deciding it might somehow help his situation to portray the big dude as an ally.

Escobar ordered Santiago to pull the gray Blazer into the garage, and they bound Cody's wrists and wrestled his mass into the rear section of the vehicle. Octavio, his arm in a sling, sat in the front passenger seat. Heather, Jimmy, and Santiago crowded into the bench seat in the rear. Sanzini stood outside the SUV, looking at Escobar, who started the engine.

"There's no room for me. What do you want me to do?" Sanzini said.

"You wait here. Stuff that body in a closet and clean up the blood. We'll get you when we're ready."

Sanzini opened his mouth to protest, but when he looked into Escobar's eyes, he quickly decided otherwise.

• • •

About twenty minutes outside of Reno, the Blazer turned onto a dirt road. The road was rutted and the vehicle swayed and bounced hard off the furrows in the terrain. Escobar steered around a huge pothole and looked at his friend in the passenger seat. Octavio clenched his teeth, holding his arm by the elbow, trying to insulate it from the sharp pain he felt every time they hit a bump.

In the back, Santiago sat wedged between Jimmy and Heather, who were squirming uncomfortably, their hands tied behind them. Santiago put his arm around Heather and cupped her breast. She looked at his pitted face and jerked her body away from him. He snickered, pulled her close by the hair, and whispered in her ear.

Jimmy watched Heather's predicament, still feeling some leftover affection because she was so hot, but also fully aware she was part of a scheme to rip him off. Fine, then. Let the bitch be raped. She was the enemy. Maybe she and her partner, or boyfriend, or whatever he was, made a career out of scamming Lotto winners. But now the boyfriend was dead, and she'd have to fend for herself. Jimmy would be too busy looking out for himself to worry about what she would have to endure.

The pieces of the puzzle were starting to fit together for Jimmy. The Latinos had to be Sanzini's coke connection. Sanzini probably told them Jimmy would be an easy mark, once Sanzini found out he'd won the lottery. As weird as it seemed, maybe there was some truth to Sheila's story. The arrival of the red-bearded tough guy probably meant Sheila was still lurking somewhere in the background.

The Blazer slowed and made a sharp turn down a steep path that was little more than a trail overgrown with brush. They crept along the narrow passage, shadowed by a canyon wall rising some forty feet. At the end of the wall the terrain gave way to a shallow desert valley. Bare rolling hills lined the small basin on either side. A decrepit structure, perhaps twelve feet square and built of ancient barn planks and adobe, stood at the base of one hillside. A ways out, a section of barbed-wire fencing began and ended with no seeming purpose. In the middle of the area, a half dozen six-foot fence posts had been set, as if a brief attempt to develop the land had been made and then reconsidered.

Escobar hit the brakes and the vehicle rumbled to a stop. Santiago shoved Jimmy out the door. Santiago followed him and reached in and pulled Heather, struggling, out into the darkening afternoon. Octavio Sanchez climbed gingerly from the vehicle, his brown face pale. He walked to the building and sat against the wall, clutching a bottle of tequila.

It took ten minutes to tie Heather, Jimmy, and Cody to the fence posts. The three sat with their backs against the wood, tightly bound and unable to stand. Cody was only half conscious. His chin lay on his chest, and every now and again his head would loll from side to side. Escobar and Santiago stood watching them. Then Escobar reached back and snapped his arm forward, the bullwhip in his hand hissing through the air. The string popper tip cracked on Cody's forehead, and blood spilled down his face. Santiago grinned and spoke to Escobar in Spanish. Escobar moved to where Jimmy sat.

"I gave your friend a small idea of what is to come," he said. "But your girlfriend there—she is so pretty, it would be a shame to give her a taste of the whip, don't you think?"

"Hey, slow down there," Jimmy said. "I already told you I'm easy, man. Just tell me what you want and let's take care of it. You don't have to hurt anyone."

Escobar squatted down next to Jimmy, grabbed his hair, and leaned into his face.

"That's a good start. Now, we're going to take a drive, you and me. If you behave and it all goes smooth, we'll end up back here, and your friends will still be alive."

"Okay, then. Where are we going?"

"Your bank."

39

The Blazer bounced off the dirt track and onto the two-lane highway. The only sign of civilization other than the paved strip was a line of telephone poles that grew tiny in the distance. Jimmy sat in the passenger seat, glancing at Escobar, considering the outcome of the next few hours. He knew his life depended on how he played it. Although he was being held captive by a man who had just murdered a person in cold blood, Jimmy felt oddly calm. Part of the reason for that was the tattooed Hispanic had actually saved him from a very ugly situation. As concerned as Jimmy was about his current predicament, he still felt a sense of gratification for being rescued from the violent, muscle-bound motherfucker, who Escobar shot dead with no more hesitation than if he was swatting a fly.

"Listen, you just want money, right?" Jimmy said.

Escobar eyed Jimmy and gave a brief nod.

"Right. And all I want is to be let go unhurt, and the same for my friends, okay?" Jimmy thought that was a clever move; let the Mexican think he gave a shit about Debbie and the big dude. "So how about untying me? My wrists feel like someone took sandpaper to them."

Escobar didn't respond, but when the freeway entrance appeared a few miles further, he abruptly hit the brakes and pulled to the shoulder.

"Here's how this is going to work," Escobar said, his *cholo* accent thick and his black eyes boring into Jimmy. "There's a Wells Fargo branch in

Reno that keeps large amounts of cash on hand to support the casinos. They're expecting you today and have one million in cash prepared. I'm going with you into the bank. They'll ask you questions, but nothing you shouldn't be able to answer. Understand? They will have an armed guard that will escort us back to the car. As long as you keep your mouth shut, he shouldn't be a problem. If you mess this up, I'll shoot you dead on the spot, and then I'll kill your friend and rape your bitch."

Escobar leveled his pistol at Jimmy and handed him a cell phone.

"Call them now and tell them you're on the way."

"They're expecting me?"

"That's right. It's all been arranged."

"Wow, you're really organized, huh?"

"Shut up, *pendajo,* and make the call."

"What happens after you have the cash?"

"If it goes smoothly, I'll drive you back to your friends, and then you can go."

Jimmy looked at the gun pointed at his face and swallowed. At that moment, he knew Escobar planned to kill him. The only question was when.

• • •

The Wells Fargo in downtown Reno was a brick building adjacent to a Safeway and a long strip of small restaurants and stores. It was four-thirty in the afternoon, half an hour before closing. Jimmy watched the steady flow of people in and out of the bank as Escobar cut the ropes binding his wrists. The parking lot was crowded with shoppers, forcing Escobar to park a few rows from the bank. The Latino put on a Sacramento Kings cap, hiding the ugly tattoos on his forehead. Then he handed Jimmy a black leather satchel, and they left the Blazer and began walking.

A Reno PD cruiser pulled out of a Starbucks and drove within shouting distance.

"Don't even think about it," Escobar said. "I'll shoot you dead."

Inside the bank, Jimmy took a deep breath and surveyed the scene. A small line of customers waited for three tellers handling transactions behind the counter. To the side, another four bank employees worked at desks. From one of the desks rose a gray-suited Asian woman, her hair in a bun, her smile professional and polite. She introduced herself as the bank manager and escorted them to her short-walled cubicle. She started talking, but Jimmy didn't hear a word she said.

Forms appeared for Jimmy to sign. While scrawling his signature, he kept looking up, hoping to spot an opportunity, any sign that might embolden him. What if he just bolted from his chair to the front door? Or suppose he simply announced he'd changed his mind and didn't want to make the withdrawal? How would Escobar react to that—would he risk shooting him in public? Jimmy's stomach started to tighten in panic. He knew he was running out of time, but he couldn't bring himself to act.

A few minutes later, a security guard handed Jimmy Escobar's leather satchel, packed heavy with paper money. "We never recommend cash transactions this large for security reasons," the bank manager said. "Unless an armored car is involved, one million is the most we can do." The guard, a white-haired man wearing a sidearm on his hip, stood waiting. Jimmy mumbled a thank you and proceeded toward the exit, followed by Escobar and the guard.

Once in the parking lot, the three men walked silently, Escobar's gun hand deep in his jacket pocket. When they reached the Blazer, Escobar opened the passenger door and motioned for Jimmy to get in.

"Here, take the money," Jimmy said, shoving the bag at Escobar, who took his hand from his pocket to grasp it. Then Jimmy darted around the

Blazer and scurried behind a row of cars, hunched low. He ran to the next row, then toward the Safeway.

"What the..." the guard said.

Escobar almost pulled his pistol, but in a second realized he'd lost control of the situation, and would need to change plans. Ignoring the guard, he got in the Blazer, wheeled out to the street, and hit the gas.

40

I WORKED METICULOUSLY ON my report, trying for a more professional tone than my usual style, and I certainly didn't include any mention of Cody's antics. It took a little over an hour to finish and e-mail it to the lady attorney. I stood and stretched and dialed Cody's cell. When he didn't pick up, I waited a few minutes and tried again. No answer. I tried him continuously for ten minutes without success. Shaking my head, I pulled from my pocket the sheet of paper with the address where Cody said he could find Jimmy Homestead.

"Well, goddamn it," I said. Then I went out to the street and flagged down a cab.

Fifteen minutes later the taxi dropped me off and drove away, leaving me staring at my Nissan truck, which was parked in the driveway of a ritzy home on a huge hilltop lot. The house was at least two hundred feet from its nearest neighbor, and the afternoon was quiet. I walked around my truck and saw nothing unusual. I dialed Cody once more, and when he didn't answer, I started toward the front door of the house. My fist was poised to knock when I noticed a badly trampled row of flowers next to the porch. I stared at the boot prints in the soil and the crushed petals, then went back to my truck. A spare key was in a magnetized case under the bumper, and I found it and unlocked the steel box welded to the bed. I removed my Beretta .40-cal automatic, checked to make sure a round was in the chamber, and stuck it in my coat pocket.

The front door was unlocked. Opening it slowly, I slid into the entryway. The first thing I saw was a reddish stain along the edge of the tan carpeting next to the tiled floor. I looked more closely and also saw a faint red smear on the tile. I pulled my piece from my pocket and crept forward into the kitchen. It was empty. So was the adjoining living room, but when I moved into the hallway, I heard the swish of clothing. I ducked just as a large iron skillet swung past my head. It grazed my shoulder and crashed into my hand, sending my pistol clattering to the hardwood floor. I dived after it, but the weight of the man who jumped on my back slammed me to the ground.

The hallway was narrow, putting me at a disadvantage. Whoever tackled me was heavy and strong, and was trying to punch me into submission. I took a shot to the back of the head that probably hurt him more than me, then I felt his fist raze my ear, but that just made me mad. Without room to maneuver laterally, I shot three quick elbows to his ribs. The man grunted and tried to crawl over me toward my gun. I landed another solid elbow to his midsection and felt him move back, which allowed me to rise to my knees. He tried to take me down again, and I hit him with a snap punch, hoping to break his nose, but I just bruised my knuckles on his forehead. Then he catapulted himself forward, his hand nearly reaching my piece. Before he could grasp it, I jumped on him, got my arm under his neck, and jerked him into a choke hold. He bucked his head and flailed, but I had him firmly, and he was out cold in ten seconds.

Breathing hard, I stepped over his prone body and recovered my gun. My hand was throbbing. I made a fist, checking if the blow from the heavy pan had broken anything. I didn't think so, but it still hurt like hell.

When the man came to a few seconds later, I grabbed his hair and stuck my pistol in his face. It was only then I recognized him as Sanzini, the dumb-ass biker I'd fought a couple of weeks back, out in front of the cathouse. His dulled eyes stared into mine.

"Where's Cody Gibbons?" I said.

"Who?"

"The big guy with the beard."

Sanzini hesitated for a long moment. "I don't know who you're talking about."

"Multiple choice question time, asshole. Tell me where he is, or I'll give you three choices where to take a bullet: The hand, which will make it useless if the doctors don't amputate it, the foot, meaning you'll limp for life, or the nuts, and hopefully you can figure that one out on your own."

"You ain't gonna shoot me."

"Yeah, you're right," I said, and kicked him in the chin hard enough to knock him out again. Then I dragged his dead weight out the front door and left him on the driveway. He lay there while I took a pair of handcuffs and my stun baton from my truck. I cuffed him and shoved his inert body into the front seat, then looped a length of chain around the cuffs and padlocked the chain to a steel D-ring protruding from the floor of my passenger seat.

Sanzini's eyes fluttered open after I waved a stick of smelling salts in front of his nose.

"Let's try this again. My friend—where is he?"

Sanzini eyed me and shook his head. "I think you broke my jaw," he said.

"That was nothing," I said, and jolted him with a medium volt stun blast. His face blanched and his wavy hair straightened. When his body stopped shaking, a string of drool fell from his lips onto his chin. "Fuck! Don't do that!"

"That was only level five. It goes up to ten."

"Oh, man." He closed his eyes tightly.

"Ready for round two?" I said.

"No! All right, they took him, along with some bimbo."

"Who's 'they'?"

"The freakin' beaners, man."

I turned the baton to six and zapped him again. He screamed, and tears coursed down his grainy face.

"I want details. Now. Who, when, and where."

"The Mexicans," he blubbered. "They're the Locos 14 gang. They kidnapped Jimmy Homestead for his money. But they also took this girl and a guy who knocked on the door."

"Where did they take them?"

"Out to the desert, man, I'm telling you these spics are serious shit, they killed a dude already, and—

"Killed who?"

"This steroid freak who was with Homestead and the bimbo. Escobar just looked at him and blew him away."

"Here?"

"Yeah, about an hour ago. Then he took off with Homestead, the big dude, and the girl."

"How many Mexicans?"

"Three."

"You better know where they went," I said, poking him with the baton.

"I do. Just keep that freaking thing away from me."

We drove out to the freeway. Sanzini sat hunched forward, his arms extended between his legs, the short length of chain preventing him from sitting upright.

"Listen, man, I got nothing to do with your friend. He just showed up out of nowhere. Escobar thinks he's one of Homestead's buddies."

"What's your interest in Homestead?"

"Asshole ripped off an ounce of my stash, man. I've been hoping to run into him for three years. When I found out he won the Lotto, I figured it was time to collect."

"How did the Mexicans get involved?" When he didn't answer I tapped his head with the baton.

He squeezed his eyes shut, then sighed. "When I couldn't find Homestead on my own, I went to them and said, hey, there's this rich dude I need to settle a score with, and I just want like twenty grand out of the deal, but if they get involved they can take him for millions."

"Did you ever talk to Sheila, Jimmy's stepmom?"

"No," Sanzini said, too quickly. "No, I never heard of her. Take this exit. The dirt road is a couple miles ahead."

I drove down a straight two-lane at ninety until Sanzini told me to slow, then he pointed at a lone tree, a dead bristlecone pine near a break in the barbed wire. The squat trunk was twisted and stripped of bark, the branches bone white. There was no signage marking the unpaved track, just the tree. I pulled over and strapped on my flak jacket and grabbed an extra ten-bullet clip.

"When we get where we're going, I recommend you keep your head down," I said.

41

JIMMY BOBBED AND WEAVED through the parking lot, zigzagging and sprinting, expecting at any moment to hear the report of Escobar's pistol and feel a bullet pierce his flesh. But when he stopped, crouched behind a car, he spotted the gray Blazer accelerating toward the exit. He stood in surprise, adrenaline pumping through his veins. Was it that easy? Had he done it? Yes! He had escaped from the cold-blooded, murdering son of a bitch!

"Nine-one-one, nine-one-one!" Jimmy yelled, running around the lot and gesturing wildly. He dodged a minivan and ran up to a lady pushing a cart full of groceries. "Let me use your cell phone—I've just been ripped off for a million dollars!"

"Get away from me, you psycho," she said.

Jimmy spun around and spotted a sheriff's cruiser on the far side of the lot. He ran as fast as he could toward the cop, who pulled away obliviously.

"Help! I've been ripped off!"

Passersby and shoppers stared at him. A group of teens laughed and one said, "Get a life."

Jimmy finally ran back to the bank, where the elderly security guard waved him down.

"What the hell is going on?"

"That man with me had a gun, and was going to kill me. Fucking Christ, gramps, call the cops!"

Within five minutes a flood of police cars raced into the bank parking lot. Surrounded by patrolmen, Jimmy blurted out his story. It took a few minutes, but once he convinced them that hostages were being held, a policeman opened his car door for Jimmy, hit the siren, and, tires squealing, led a group of squad cars out to the freeway.

• • •

Escobar pushed the Blazer down the rutted trail as fast as he dared, bottoming out the suspension, careening violently and raising a cloud of dust. He was forced to slow when he turned onto the narrow section, to avoid slamming the steep hillside or sliding over the drop. When he reached the entrance to the valley, he pegged the throttle and slid to a stop near the old shack.

Octavio sat against the building, feet splayed, his broken arm propped against his chest. The bottle of tequila in his hand was half empty, and he was passed out drunk. Escobar slapped him hard across the face. "*Despierte, stupido.*"

Octavio groaned and blinked. Escobar slapped him again and went through the rickety door. The damp interior was cold and lit by a single battery-powered lantern. A solitary piece of furniture, a raw wooden table, stood in the middle of the room. On the table lay Heather Sanderson. A shaft of daylight from the open door fell across her body. She was stripped naked and spread-eagled, her wrists and ankles tied to the table's legs, her face battered and swollen. She raised her head, then lowered it in despair.

"Put your pants on," Escobar shouted at Santiago. "I've got the money, but the police are coming."

Escobar rushed out and began replacing the plates on the Blazer, then stopped abruptly. Cody sat tied to the fence post, his face coated with dried blood, his eyes alert and glowering. He was about sixty feet from the Blazer. Escobar opened the back hatch, grabbed his Tec-9 machine pistol, and snapped in a thirty-round clip. He jogged to where Cody was trying to dig his heels into the earth and push back on the post in a futile effort to break it.

"Only a chickenshit pussy would shoot a defenseless man," Cody said.

Escobar clicked the safety off and leveled the machine gun at Cody. His black eyes were empty, his face expressionless—until he heard the very real sound of a motor revving and rocks spitting from under tires.

• • •

When I came power sliding around the final corner to the small valley where Sanzini told me Cody was being held, the first thing I saw was a dusty gray Chevy Blazer parked next to a small, decrepit structure. To my left I caught a brief glimpse of Cody sitting, his body still as a statue, his great bearded mug staring at me. A man stood near him, a short-barreled machine pistol in his hands. A second later, a burst of automatic fire spider-webbed my windshield. I ducked low, straining to see out of a small section of undamaged glass, and pushed the pedal to the floorboards, accelerating toward the shooting figure. Bullets whirled overhead, ripping holes in the seats and punching through the roof. Glass rained down, and I heard the distinct sound of steam hissing as a series of slugs pounded into my radiator. Then the clatter of the weapon stopped, and the man froze for an instant before he dropped it and ran for the Blazer. But he wasn't quick enough. I turned and hit him at almost forty miles an hour. His body folded under my bumper, and I felt the bump as my rear tire ran him over.

I scrambled out of the truck and aimed my pistol at the shack. A faint female voice yelled for help from behind the walls. I ran toward the Blazer, and saw a disheveled gangbanger wearing a red bandana stagger from around the building, pointing an automatic. He held the gun sideways, palm down, arm extended. It may have been a trendy gangster style, and I'm sure he thought it looked cool, but it is not an effective way to aim in a combat situation. His shot went wide, and I slid to a knee and returned fire, hitting him in the chest. There is no mistaking the outcome when a man is shot in the torso from twenty feet with a hollow-point .40-cal round. The man fell forward, a fist-sized hole in his back. He shuddered briefly and died.

Sanzini said there were three, and I assumed the third man was in the shack with the girl. He would either come out on his own or come out holding her hostage. Regardless, Cody was in an extremely vulnerable position. Keeping my eyes on the shack, I ran back to my truck for a knife, then reached behind the driver's seat and took my back-up piece from its hiding place. It was a Glock 9mm, a weapon I considered inferior to the Beretta, but no less deadly. Sanzini was crouched as low as he could get in the passenger's seat.

"You hit?" I asked.

"No," he rasped.

"Stay down."

I sprinted the twenty yards to where Cody was tied.

"Having fun yet?" I said, cutting the ropes around his wrists.

"Give me that piece. There's one still in there with a rifle." Cody pushed himself to his feet, his eyebrows creased low over his eyes, blood caked and scaled on his face.

"You go left," he said, running behind my bullet-riddled truck, the Glock trained at the shack. I took position behind the rear of the Blazer. We were no sooner in place when the door opened and a Hispanic man in his forties stepped out holding a large hunting rifle, probably a 30-06, to the head of a naked blond woman. Even though she had been roughed up some, the natural beauty of her face was striking. So was her curvaceous, tanned body, which could have only belonged to a stripper. I wondered if he had raped her yet.

"Drop the gun, gringo," he said. I didn't think he could see Cody crouched behind my truck from his angle.

"Okay, don't hurt her," I said, dangling my gun from the trigger guard. He lowered the rifle and pointed it at me, and that was all the room Cody needed. The girl jumped as a blast split the air, and the Latino's head exploded, his hair, teeth, brains, and gore painting the wood slats behind him. His body collapsed in a blood-soaked mess.

"Oh, my fucking god!" the woman screamed, and puked on his corpse.

I walked to my truck and found a blanket. Cody was inspecting the Glock as if amazed. "Nice shooting," I said. He nodded as I brought the lady the blanket and draped it over her bare shoulders. She stood shivering for a moment, until she remembered her clothes were still in the shack.

While she dressed, Cody picked up a half-full bottle of Herradura someone had left on the porch. We walked away from the carnage and sat on my tailgate and took a few pulls. The sun was going down, and a single dark rain cloud stood against the clear sky. Columns of light spilled from the cloud, striping the barren hills in sunlight and shadow.

"He's still alive," Cody said, pointing to the body of the man I'd run over.

His legs were twisted at wrong angles, and he had lost an eye. I could see the tread marks where my tire had crushed his ribs. Blood gurgled from his mouth with each wheezing breath, and his remaining eye twitched madly, as if it was still trying to understand what happened to him.

"Should I offer him a shot?" Cody said, gesturing with the bottle.

I knelt down to the man. "Where's Jimmy Homestead?"

His eye stopped twitching, and he turned his head to look at me. His lips started moving, blood flowing down his chin.

"Chinga tu madre," he whispered, then he gasped and died.

"Nice last words," I said. I pulled my cell phone and started dialing just as we heard the first whine of the sirens. I put the phone away and took the Glock from Cody and secured it and the Berretta in the lock box behind my cab. Then the girl came out of the shack, her hair tangled, her face dark with bruises. She teetered across the dirt in form-fitting jeans and high heels and managed a small smile before she sat between us on the tailgate. I offered her a hit off the bottle, and we sat there waiting for the cops to arrive.

42

IT WOULD BE INADEQUATE to describe what happened next as simply chaotic; a more apt description would be to say it was like a rowdy acid trip. A pair of military-grade SWAT vehicles rumbled around the corner and bore down on us, followed by four Reno PD squad cars. A dozen fully outfitted SWAT commandos spilled out, and in seconds we were staring down a phalanx of AR-15 assault rifles. The uniformed cops dispersed and scrambled about, and in the confusion, they actually tried to interrogate one of the dead men. Jimmy Homestead jumped out of a squad car, only to be wrestled to the ground and cuffed. Amid the yelling, a coyote trotted by a little ways out, and one of the Reno cops drew his service revolver and took a pot shot. The SWAT team freaked and one heaved a stun grenade at the perplexed patrolman.

Cody lit a smoke and handed me his pack. We sat on the tailgate until eventually the cops were satisfied the crime scene was secured. The SWAT teams left, leaving the local police to conduct interviews, gather evidence, and otherwise sort things out. I gave my keys to Gordon DeHart, a cop I knew from a run-in I had with the Carson City police last winter.

"Aren't you out of your jurisdiction, Lieutenant?" I said.

The portly, balding officer freed Sanzini from my truck and shook his head. "Reno, even if you're innocent of any wrongdoing, which I doubt, do you have any idea how much paper work this is going to take? You're on my shit list, buddy."

"Another member of your fan club, I see," Cody said.

They separated the four of us to take our statements. Within a few minutes, Sanzini was again cuffed and escorted to the rear seat of a squad car. Two young patrolmen fawned over the blonde, whom I overheard crediting Cody and me for saving her from being sexually assaulted.

"You might as well start at the beginning," DeHart said. "But do me a favor and try to make it quick."

I looked at my watch. "Yeah, I know, it's damn near happy hour."

"Get on with it, Reno."

I took a deep breath. "Jimmy Homestead's stepmother hired my partner and me to find Jimmy after he won the California lottery a few months back. We found him, but she stiffed us on our fee. So Cody went to talk to Jimmy to see if he'd be willing to pay us in return for our disclosure of what we knew about his stepmom."

"Which was?"

"Not much, really. Anyway, Cody borrowed my truck to drive to where he thought Jimmy was staying. When he didn't answer his cell, I took a cab out there. Here's the address." I pulled the folded sheet of paper from my pocket.

"And?"

"Sanzini was the only one at the house. He tried to take me down, but I subdued him, and then he admitted his associates kidnapped Homestead, the babe, and Cody. He also said one of the Mexicans shot and killed a man earlier at the house."

"Another dead body? This just keeps getting better."

"Yeah, no shit. So I convinced Sanzini to tell me where the Mexicans were, and when I came here, one of them opened up on me with a machine pistol." I pointed to my truck. "You think insurance will cover that?"

"I doubt it," DeHart said.

"That's okay, I think I have a skateboard somewhere. Anyway, I ran over the dude, and another one shot at me with a pistol, and I returned fire, hitting him in the chest."

"What about the third guy? Looks like his head was in the wrong place at the wrong time."

"He came out of the shack holding a rifle on the woman, who was naked, obviously not by choice."

"And?"

"Cody shot him."

"With what, a bazooka?"

"No, a Glock nine shooting hollow points."

DeHart sighed. "What do you like on your pizza?"

"I'm kind of in the mood for pepperoni. Why?"

"You and me, and the rest of this merry band," he said, waving his hand at the police and civilians alike, "we're all going back to the station, and maybe if I get lucky I'll get to go home tonight."

"What about me?"

"You'll get a nice cot, until I talk to the DA in the morning."

"I guess stopping at a bar on the way to the station is out of the question?"

DeHart didn't answer, but his expression said he wished he could.

• • •

The interview room at the Reno precinct station was drab and poorly heated. I sat at a metal table, facing DeHart and a younger black officer who was clearly playing the role of the bad cop.

"So let me get this straight," the black cop said, leaning over the table, supporting his weight on his hands. "You walk into a home, uninvited, looking for your buddy."

"That's right."

"Then you claim to be attacked by a man who you choke unconscious, chain to a D-ring in your truck, and torture with a stun gun until he tells you what happened to your partner."

"Yeah. I was in a hurry, and the stun baton usually brings pretty quick results."

"Wow. You sound like quite the expert. So, first we got trespassing, and now let's add assault, battery, and kidnapping to the list. And we haven't even got to the best part yet."

"You mean the gorgeous nude woman and the bottle of tequila, right?"

"Reno," DeHart said from where he was sitting in the corner. He shook his head, and looked down in an effort to hide his expression.

"I'm glad you think this is so funny," the black cop said to me. "Actually, I was referring to the two men you killed."

"They were both shooting at me. I killed them in self-defense. So what's the point here?"

"The point is, instead of calling the police, you took it upon yourself. And now three people are dead."

"I got there just in time to save the life of my best friend, and also to prevent the rape and probable murder of an innocent woman. There was no time to wait for the police."

"All right," DeHart said, rising from his chair. "Let's go back to how these people are connected. Tell me again what Sanzini said to you."

"He said the three Mexicans were gangbangers who wanted to rip off Jimmy Homestead."

"And the connection between Sanzini and the Mexicans?"

"All Sanzini said was Homestead had heisted some coke from him, and when Sanzini heard he'd won the Lotto, he tried to find him to get payback. When he had trouble finding him, Sanzini called the Mexicans for help."

Both cops were silent. We'd been in the room for over an hour, and I'd repeated the same answers to their questions more times than I could count.

"Owens, is the pizza here yet?" DeHart said.

"I don't know."

"Well, go out and check, would you? I'm starving, and I'm sure Mr. Reno is too."

The man blew his breath through his teeth and stomped out the door.

"They took your friend Gibbons to the hospital," DeHart said.

"They did? How is he?"

"He had two huge knots on the back of his head and complained of a headache. Probably has a concussion."

"Shit."

"They'll most likely keep him overnight for observation. He's down the street at Reno General."

"You still planning on keeping me here tonight?"

"No," DeHart sighed. "But don't make me regret it. You know the routine—don't leave town, and make yourself available if I call."

"No problemo."

"One more question, Reno. Jimmy Homestead claims he knows you. Said you went to the same high school."

"That's true."

"So what's the connection?"

"Connection? I haven't seen or spoken to him in over fifteen years. Other than his stepmother hiring me to find him, there is no connection."

"I don't like coincidences."

"Well, if it's really bugging you, I suggest you contact Sheila Majorie."

"Maybe I'll do that."

"If you do, tell her she owes me about thirteen grand. And if my insurance doesn't cover the damage to my truck, I'll send her the repair bill for that too."

43

I WALKED OUT TO the small lobby of the precinct, eating a slice of pizza and wondering how I'd get home. Sitting on a bench against the wall, her hands in her lap, was the blond woman. Her makeup was tear-streaked, and when she looked up, her expression made me think of someone lost at sea.

"Hi," she said weakly.

"Hello. It's cold out. You don't have a coat?"

"No."

I looked out the plate-glass windows into the black night. "Where you headed?"

"My car's parked at Jimmy Homestead's house. But my keys are in my purse, and my purse is locked in the car."

"The cops didn't offer you a ride?"

"One did, but I didn't like the way he looked at me."

I stuck my hands in my pockets. "It shouldn't be too tough getting your car open," I said. "We could take a cab over there."

"Really? That'd be great. I'm Heather, by the way."

"Dan Reno," I said, taking her hand. "Listen, I know you've been through a lot, and I don't want to impose. But my truck's ruined, and I need to get to South Lake Tahoe tonight. It's about forty-five minutes away."

"Is that where you're staying?"

"It's where I live."

"Oh. You're asking for a ride, in return for you getting my car open?"

"You don't have to."

"Do you think you could find me a hotel there?"

"Sure."

She nodded, and I took off my jacket and fitted it over her shoulders. "I want to check on my buddy at the hospital first, for a minute. Then I'll call us a taxi."

We walked down the block toward the medical center. "I want to thank you, and your friend, for being there," Heather said. "That man was ready to rape me."

"I'm glad we were able to stop him."

"Yeah, you sure did stop him." We walked in silence, then she said, "Did you kill the other two?"

"Yes."

"Does it...bother you?"

"No. They tried to kill me."

"It was just so, well, violent, you know what I mean?"

"I think so. You were probably shocked, right?"

"Yes, very much."

"It might bother you for a bit, but it will pass in time."

"They were bad men," she said, looking at me with teary eyes. "I'm glad they're dead."

It was almost nine P.M. when we got to the hospital. Heather waited in the hall while I went to Cody's room. He lay propped up, dozing in his bed. A nurse told me to go ahead and wake him.

"Can't a person get some shut-eye around this joint?" he grumbled.

"How's your melon, man?"

"Soft. Whoever coldcocked me wasn't playing around."

"Well, they're dead and you're alive, if that's any consolation."

"It'll have to do."

"What do the doctors say?"

"They're gonna take X-rays for a fractured skull and keep me overnight. I should be ready to split in the morning."

"Give me the keys to your truck and call me when you're ready. I'll come pick you up."

"They're on the nightstand."

"Get some rest," I said, then left so he could, after taking a metal coat hanger from a peg on the door.

Fifteen minutes later a cab dropped us off at Jimmy Homestead's house. A beat-to-shit Ford LTD was in the driveway, and it looked like every light in the house was on, as if someone were throwing a party. Heather's silver Camaro was parked across the street. I pushed the coat hanger through the molding between the window and frame, and worked it until the door lock popped open.

"That's pretty cool," she said, trying to smile despite her fat lip. She found her keys in her purse and asked me to drive. I turned on the heater and made a U-turn, staring at the Ford junker. I guessed it belonged to Jimmy's father. I couldn't imagine a car more opposite Jimmy's exotic ride.

I drove us out to the highway, southbound toward Tahoe. After the car became warm, she took off my coat and tucked her legs underneath her. I sensed she wanted to tell me something, but we drove on in silence.

The events of the day had left me emotionally numb. Now that the adrenalin of the battle was long spent, the violence felt unreal, and also random and pointless. But then I thought of Cody, tied to a fence post in that hidden desert basin, blood caked on his face, while Heather Sanderson was stripped naked, her face beaten, a rifle held to her head by her would-be rapist.

"What are you thinking?" Heather asked. She was staring at me.

"Things could have ended up a lot worse out there."

She touched my arm and nodded solemnly.

We crested the summit over Spooner Pass and I steered her Chevy through the sweeping curves leading down the grade to Tahoe Valley. The lights of the city etched the south shore of the lake, the body of water a black abyss against the dark sky.

"I guess I'm a widow now," Heather said.

"What?"

"My husband was shot and killed at Jimmy's house. He was killed by the man you ran over."

"Why?"

"No reason, really. We were leaving Jimmy's house and when we opened the door, they were standing there. It was the skinny one. He didn't say a word, just pointed his gun and shot."

I didn't say anything for a minute. Whatever Heather's involvement with Jimmy Homestead was about, I didn't care at the moment. But I also didn't believe her husband was murdered for no reason.

"I'm sorry," I said finally.

"We were getting a divorce anyway. He was bad news."

"Oh. But still...were you and your husband friends with Jimmy?"

"Yes. He invited us to visit. We were just leaving when all hell broke loose."

We came off the pass and drove around the lake, past the casinos, and crossed the state line into California. I pointed out a few hotels.

"My place is just a couple miles up the road," I said. When we pulled into my driveway, I shut off the motor and looked at her. "Hey, you're welcome to stay in my guest room. You should probably get some ice on that eye."

"That's kind of you. I'm not working now, so money is sort of tight."

"I hear you."

We went inside, and I threw some logs in the stove while she showered. When she came out to my living room she was wearing a loose cotton sweat suit. Her hair was still wet, and she had combed it straight. "Here," I said, handing her a bag of frozen peas. "Fifteen minutes on your eye, then fifteen on your lip." She sat curled on the couch, watching me stoke the fire.

"How did you get involved in all this?" she asked.

I closed the stove door and stood. "Are you hungry?"

"Yeah," she said shyly. "What do you have?" She followed me into the kitchen.

"A couple cans of soup. Some bread. Cheese. Eggs. Cold cuts."

"I'll cook," she said, but I made her go back to the couch. I heated her some soup and made a grilled-cheese sandwich.

"Do you have any booze?" she asked.

"Sure." She sat at my kitchen table, and I brought her food and a vodka cocktail. I had originally thought she was about twenty-five, but without makeup and under bright lighting, it was clear she was in her thirties. Her nose was on the small side, and her blue eyes looked quite large and doe like. It was her eyes that made her face look so young.

"Thank you, this is very good," she said.

"You're welcome."

She took a bite from her sandwich. "So, what is it you do?"

"I'm a private investigator. Jimmy Homestead's stepmother hired me to find him, after he won the Lotto."

"Oh. Do you always carry a gun around?"

"Not always."

"I'm sure glad you did today. It seemed like you knew those cops who showed up. Did you?"

"Yeah, one of them. There was some trouble here last year, and I got caught in the middle of it. I helped uncover some crimes committed by a county sheriff."

"Does that mean the police like you?"

"Not exactly. But they'll cut me some slack at times."

"I imagine that's convenient in your line of work."

"Can be," I said, mixing a drink. "Are you planning to drive home tomorrow?"

Heather stared at her glass and took a long swig. "Yes, I suppose I will. We have an apartment in San Jose—I mean, I have one, and…oh." She tried to speak but her voice cracked, then she bowed her head and began crying. After a couple of minutes, she looked up and tried again to speak, but she was sobbing and her words were incoherent. She pounded her fists on the table and bawled until I thought she probably had no more tears left in her. It became awkward sitting there, so I went and started straightening up the kitchen.

"I'm sorry," she said, sniffling. "I was hoping I wouldn't do that, but it's been a really bad day."

"Do you want to talk about it?" I said.

"I don't want to bore you with the details of my crummy life."

"I'm a good listener. And no one's life is perfect, believe me."

She looked up at me with her vulnerable face, and I knew men could easily be smitten by her. Her eyes were her most alluring feature, but what really got me was how her heart-shaped lips moved when she talked, her teeth flashing white the few times I'd seen her smile. It was a face to kill for. As for her body—her outrageous curviness and the trimmed patch of blond hair between her legs—it could tempt and torment a man until his life was a complete shambles. I squeezed my eyes shut and actually wished I'd not seen her naked.

I chased the lustful thoughts with the remains of my drink. She had been beaten and almost raped, and this after her husband was murdered before her eyes. I felt like a creep for even thinking of trying to seduce her.

We moved to the couch, the heat from my stove warming the room, the flames dancing behind the glass.

"I like your place," she said. "It's cozy."

"I like it too. I moved here about a year ago, from San Jose."

"Really? That's where I live. I've been there almost my whole life. I lived with my parents, then I lived with girl roommates, and then I met Eric. This will probably sound really stupid, but you know why I married him? The main reason was because of his looks. He just fit the mold of what I always imagined my husband would look like—tall, strong, blond, and handsome. I figured everything else would just fall into place."

"Everything else?"

"Yes, well, financially I mean. He told me he had plans to be a real estate agent, and we'd have plenty of money. I just figured the money would be a given, I guess. Things had always worked out for me. I was very popular in high school, head of the cheerleading squad, homecoming queen. Even after high school, life came easy. My college teachers, the men anyway, gave me good grades even when I didn't turn in assignments. I worked as a receptionist, and it was easy and fun and the pay was fine. But it all started going bad after I got married."

"How so?"

"Eric turned out to be different than I thought. He liked to talk big, but he had issues with his temper and struggled career-wise. Every time he got a job, he would screw it up. Then he started taking steroids and things got worse—his personality got more extreme. He was always wound up, and he just had so much anger. He scared me."

"Did he ever hurt you?"

"Not physically, no. But I knew eventually he would. After he lost his last job, I started working at a strip joint because we needed the money. But I got tired of men drooling after me, you know? All my life I've been attractive, and men chased me. But being a stripper meant taking advantage of my looks for money. After a while it made me feel sleazy, like I was a whore. So I quit. And Eric went crazy. I knew then I had to get away from him."

"Sounds like he was a bad guy."

"You're damn right he was. You know how I feel now that he's dead? I feel relieved. That's it. No grief or sorrow. Just relief. I know that might make me seem like a real cold-hearted bitch, but it's the truth."

"I think your feelings are justified."

"Thanks. I mean, thanks for understanding."

"What are you going to do now?"

"Actually, I see this as a turning point for me. I'm going to get a real job and find a real man. Someone calm and level-headed and nice, someone who makes a solid, consistent living."

"That sound like a good plan, Heather," I said, stoically aware that my lack of a steady income precluded me from her vision of a real man.

She smiled and wiped a little tear from her eye. "My life may be upside down now, but I'm looking forward to getting things straightened out."

"I have a question for you," I said. "What were you and Eric really doing at Jimmy's house?"

She paused, and I saw a tiny shift in her expression. "Why do you want to know?"

"Do you know Sheila Majorie, Jimmy's mother?"

"No. Should I?"

"No."

"I don't get where you're going with this," she said. "What does she have to do with anything?"

"She hired me to do some investigative work involving Jimmy. I have reason to believe she was somehow involved with the men who killed your husband and abducted you."

"Wow. That's interesting. But I have no idea who Jimmy's mom is."

"That's good," I said, more to myself than to her.

"I'm pretty tired," she said. "I better get some sleep."

She said good night and went to the guest bedroom. I sat for a minute and considered her life and where it was going. I had the same questions about my own. After turning the lights off, I thought about mixing a final drink, but I was exhausted. I felt sure Heather's visit to Jimmy Homestead was more than an innocent social call, but I reminded myself that my interest in the case had expired, save for whatever effort, most likely futile, I would expend to get paid by Sheila. I walked to my room like a zombie, wondering what I'd do now that my truck was out of commission and would probably cost thousands of dollars to repair. Pine needles rattled against my window, and when I looked outside, tiny snow flurries were blowing in all directions, as if the laws of gravity no longer applied, and each flake was left to find its own way.

44

FROM THE BACK SEAT of the cruiser, Jimmy watched the cops sort out the mess. They covered the dead bodies, took pictures, strung yellow crime-scene tape all over the place, and finally loaded the living into squad cars: Sanzini in one, Debbie in another, and the two dudes who were Sheila's hired muscle into a third.

Jimmy stared hard at the second man, who had mysteriously shown up. Was he responsible for the death of the three men who kidnapped him? It appeared he was. The longer Jimmy looked at his face, the more he felt sure he recognized him from some time in his distant past. He could actually hear a crackling sound as the neurons in his brain kicked into overdrive, trying to dredge up a clue from who knows how many years ago. But he finally conceded he'd cooked too many brain cells.

He shifted uncomfortably in his seat, trying to keep the cuffs from digging into his wrists. Why the asshole cop had cuffed him, Jimmy didn't know. He leaned forward and his eyes settled dully on the carpet below him. And then, in a quiet and brief moment of revelation, it hit him: the guy's name was Dan Reno.

Jimmy remembered him from high school, or maybe shortly afterward. His father was a crackpot who had changed the family name from Reynolds to Reno. Someone had teased Dan Reno about it—once. Jimmy remembered Reno as a tough but reasonable type, someone you'd want on your side, if possible.

But what in Kelsey's nuts was Reno doing here now, and whose side was he on? What was he doing with Sheila? Why had a man Jimmy casually knew fifteen years ago reappeared at this juncture, shortly after Jimmy won the Lotto? Jesus Christ, what a mind fuck. Jimmy shook his head and wished he was drinking highballs somewhere. His day just kept getting stranger.

• • •

Things didn't get any less weird at the station. Jimmy expected the cops to quickly realize that he was a victim, and his escape in the parking lot was a heroic act. Jimmy liked the sound of that. It was true—he was a freaking hero. But the Reno PD brought in a couple of detectives who apparently felt the events of the day just didn't add up. They sat him in an interview room and questioned him relentlessly about his past relationship with Sanzini, and tried to insinuate that he had some illicit dealings with the Latinos who kidnapped and almost killed him. Then they shifted gears to Debbie and her husband. Jimmy told them the pair was running a scam on him, but the detectives had other ideas.

"We think you lured Heather Sanderson to your house to assault her."

"Heather? She told me her name was Debbie. I met her on an Internet dating site, and she visited me for a date. She was giving me a lap dance when this big motherfucker invaded my house and hit me so hard in the stomach I probably have internal bleeding."

"And next thing you know, the 'big motherfucker' ends up dead. How convenient." The cop standing over Jimmy had close-set eyes and a receding hair line.

"Yeah, it was real convenient getting my ass kicked, then being forced at gunpoint to withdraw money from my bank."

"And then, you scamper away, just like that."

"Like I said, I distracted him, and before he could pull his gun, I darted behind a car and ran away. I thought he'd come after me, but there was a security guard there, and he already had my money."

"Let's get back to Heather and her husband. Had you ever met Eric Sanderson before?"

"Her husband? I had no idea the bitch was married."

The detectives looked at each other, and Jimmy stood. "Just so you know, right now I'm probably the richest person in Reno. I was thinking of settling down here, but if this is how you treat your residents, the hell with this place."

"The chamber of commerce will be heartbroken," the balding detective said.

They let Jimmy go after that, but it took another hour for him to recover the leather bag stuffed with cash. At first the cops wanted to hold it as evidence, but they finally relented after the portly senior detective said there was no need. Before leaving the police station, Jimmy called his father and asked to be picked up. John began asking questions, but Jimmy told him to just calm down and come get him pronto. Holding the black satchel, Jimmy stood in the precinct lobby and waited for the LTD to arrive. At least the cops gave him his money. Other than that, he thought they were the biggest group of dipshits he'd ever met.

• • •

Sitting at a table in the Peppermill Casino lounge, John organized the brochures he'd picked up from the local auto dealerships. He had narrowed his choices to a Cadillac, a BMW, or a Lexus. They were all big, comfortable cars. Though he felt the BMW and Lexus had some advantages, the Cadillac really captivated him. When John was a young man, owning a Caddy was a huge status symbol, back before the Japanese and German cars became commonplace. He sipped his cup of coffee and wondered what color would be best.

After a while he went to his room and tossed the glossy pamphlets on his bed, then headed to the hotel gym. Pedaling the stationary bike, he worked up a light sweat and let his mind wander. Meeting Jimmy was turning out to be exactly what he had hoped for. But now that he felt cautiously optimistic about the financial end of things, he knew he had to take care of his health as well. Being a fat slob didn't jive with his image of himself for the future. A slim, toned physique would be more like it. That, and a nice car, a comfortable condo, and then who knows? Anything was possible. Maybe he could even attract a desirable woman and have a sex life again. He pedaled faster, watching the drops of sweat fall off his nose.

Despite all the good things happening, John still didn't feel comfortable with Lou Calgaretti's conclusions on Sheila. The woman had gone as far as hiring two thugs to try to convince Jimmy to pay her off. She had obviously invested quite a bit of time and money in her scheme. Would she just give up? John didn't think so. The virulent words that spilled from her during their divorce were not something easily forgotten. If she still harbored that kind of hatred, who knows what she might do?

Later that night, over a low-carb dinner at the casino restaurant, John decided to talk to Jimmy about safe investments for his fortune—not as a money-making venture, but as a way to protect the money from conniving bitches like Sheila. No doubt there would also be others out there who would view Jimmy as a target. He worried that Jimmy's millions might evaporate quickly, either stolen by con artists or wasted by his own imprudent spending. Maybe he could help Jimmy put the majority of the money in certificates of deposit, or some kind of account where accessing it wouldn't be so easy. In the morning he would visit a bank and get educated on the options, John decided. Right after he bought his new car.

Confident all was in order in his world, John sat down to slay a few hours at a twenty-one table with a cute female dealer. He still had two crisp hundred-dollar bills in his wallet, left over from the $500 Jimmy gave him earlier in the day. He ordered a rum and diet cola, and was on a nice winning streak when his cell rang, and Jimmy asked to be picked up at the Reno police station.

45

THE LTD RATTLED TO a stop, and John watched Jimmy come out the glass doors, his hair uncombed, his clothes streaked with dirt.

"What in hell?" John said.

"Listen, Pop, I need a drink bad, okay?"

"You want to go to a bar?"

"No. Just take me home."

"I take it your date didn't go well?"

"That's an understatement."

John stopped at a traffic light and turned toward his son. "Were you arrested?"

"What?" Jimmy laughed briefly. "It was nothing like that. What happened to me today…" Jimmy paused and tried to find the right words. "A pack of greedy bastards tried to steal my money," he said finally.

When they got to the big house, it was dark and the front door was locked. John let them in, and Jimmy flipped on the light switch in the entryway. "See that?" he said, pointing to a darkened area where the tile met the carpet. "That's the blood of a man I saw murdered a few hours ago."

Jimmy found a beer glass and mixed himself a stiff vodka. He walked through the house with his dad, turning on every light. He looked in the closet where the cops told him Eric Sanderson's body had been stuffed.

Apparently, cleaning up the blood was not part of the "serve and protect" deal.

After a few minutes they sat in the living room, and Jimmy gave a detailed recounting of the day. At first John was incredulous. It sounded like two separate schemes had collided at the house. First, Internet date Debbie and her now-dead husband, and then Sanzini and his Mexican drug dealing pals. When John got over his shock, he carefully considered all the details. There was one main issue he kept coming back to: the presence of the big dude and Dan Reno was a clear sign Sheila was still working some kind of scam.

"Son, the most important thing is you weren't seriously hurt."

"Yeah, I guess. Although I was freaking humiliated."

"It could have been a lot worse. I think you need to start thinking what you can do to protect yourself from this kind of thing in the future."

"I'm down with that. But how?"

"Let's start by talking to Lou Calgaretti," John said. He poked at his cell phone, and Lou picked up right away.

"Lou, John Homestead. Listen, the shit's really hit the fan over here."

John put his phone on speaker, and Jimmy talked for ten minutes before Lou began asking questions.

"Have you pressed charges against Heather Sanderson?"

"No. I figured she'd been through enough already," Jimmy said. In the back of his mind, he thought he might call her and arrange a few sex sessions in return for him not pursuing legal action.

"Apparently the police don't plan on charging her either. Do you think she could be a threat to you moving forward?"

"I doubt it. Not with her husband out of the picture."

"What about Sanzini?" Lou said. "He's still being held, right?"

"Yeah, that's what I heard. I'm not sure what they're going to charge him with."

"A number of things, I'm sure. Accessory to kidnapping and robbery, for a start."

"Sounds like he's in deep shit."

"I'd say that's an accurate assessment."

"What about Dan Reno?" John said. "I think my ex-wife is still trying to find a way to get her hands on Jimmy's money. And she hired Reno."

"I know of Reno, but I don't know him personally," Lou said. "He's a private eye here in South Lake Tahoe."

"Can you find him and get him to tell you what Sheila's up to?"

Lou grunted. "Finding him should be easy. But I doubt he'll tell me anything useful."

"I see your point," John said. "Jimmy and I have discussed hiring professional body guards, at least until we feel comfortable he's no longer in danger. Can you recommend anyone?"

"I'll make a few calls and get back to you. Give me until tomorrow."

Afterward, they settled in to watch a movie, a comedy about horny frat house boys getting drunk and chasing college girls. Jimmy had finished the better part of a fifth of vodka and was sitting on the couch smoking a joint, his head lolled back on the cushion, his legs splayed, his body nearly horizontal. When John looked at him, he felt a surge of annoyance, followed by a creeping twinge of disappointment, not only in Jimmy, but also in his own parental ineptitude. Then he thought back to when Jimmy was a small boy, sitting on his lap. John looked away, stunned as a rush of paternal affection replaced the distress he'd felt only a moment before. His eyes moistened and he blinked rapidly. How strange that a parent could never let go of those early images and feelings. Even after not speaking to Jimmy for fifteen years, John Homestead still loved his son as if he were a child.

• • •

In the morning, John made coffee, then spent a half hour in the exercise room. He showered and dressed and at 9:30 went to check on Jimmy.

"You want coffee, son?"

Jimmy groused out of bed, gobbled some aspirin, and staggered out to the kitchen. "Next time let me sleep in, would you?" he said, but he cut his complaining short when his cell rang. He talked for a moment, then snapped the phone shut. "Hey, my car's ready," he said, his face brightening.

"I was going to head out to the Caddy dealership," John said. "I can drop you off."

"Let me wake up first," Jimmy said, pouring a second cup and scratching his balls.

John sat on one of the barstools at the kitchen counter. "I've got an idea," he said. "You said you used to know Dan Reno. And obviously he knows who you are. So why don't you call him and ask him what's up with Sheila? He might be more likely to talk to you than Lou."

Jimmy rubbed his eyes. "That's not a bad idea, I guess. Just give me until the caffeine kicks in. Then I'll call him."

46

THE SKIES WERE STILL dark when I woke. I rekindled my stove and drove Cody's truck to a convenience store and bought yogurt, fruit, and some pastries, hoping it would be to Heather's liking. If not, she could join me for toast, eggs, and bacon. But she was still asleep when I got home. I'd read the entire *Tahoe Daily Tribune* and finished my sixteen-ounce coffee by the time she finally came out of the guest room.

He eye and lip had swelled overnight, and she had traded her sweat shirt for a pink, short-sleeve top. She was braless, her breasts high and firm, and she didn't seem aware her nipples were neatly outlined against the material.

"Good morning," she said. I brought her coffee and told her the options for breakfast.

"You're a very nice man, do you know that?" Her smile looked crooked under her swollen lip.

"Thanks," I said, a little uncomfortable with the compliment.

"Well, thank you for letting me stay. The bed was very nice."

"Did you sleep well?"

"Yes. Well, no, actually. My head was full of thoughts, trying to figure out what I'm going to do."

"Did you reach any conclusions?"

"A couple, I think. First, I need to get a real career. I don't want to have to rely on a man to take care of me."

"You might find working fun."

"I always did before. But I don't want to do anything that has to do with my looks. I've got a good brain. It's time I made use of it."

"That's the spirit," I said, smiling at her enthusiasm.

She giggled. "When are you going to feed me?"

After we ate she went to dress, and I stood looking out the large window behind my desk. The sun had crept over the ridgeline to the east and rested in a narrow strip of blue sky under a layer of storm clouds. A pair of squirrels scurried from below my deck and sniffed at the air and poked around my yard before heading out to the meadow, leaving tiny tracks in the light dusting of snow from the night before.

My cell rang. I didn't recognize the number.

"Is this Dan Reno?"

"Yes, who's calling?"

"Hey, Dan, it's Jimmy Homestead."

"What's happening, Jimmy?" I said after a second.

"Too much, man. That was some pretty crazy shit that went down yesterday, huh?"

"Yeah, I'd say so."

"Well, I'm lucky to be alive."

"You ain't the only one," I said.

"I heard you killed two of those guys. Is that true?"

"Someone had to kill them."

"Huh? Oh yeah, I guess so."

"What can I do for you, Jimmy?"

"Well, first I want to say, that was a hell of a way for us to get reacquainted. What have you been up to all these years?"

"Just trying to make a living. How about yourself?"

"Shit, it's a long story. Look, I wanted to talk to you about something, if you got a minute."

"Go ahead."

"Right. So after everything that happened yesterday, I'm trying to sort things out. I'd like to ask you about a few questions, because I'm pretty confused."

"Why don't we start with you telling me your version of what happened yesterday," I said.

"My version? Okay, it's pretty simple. I put up an ad on an Internet dating site, and Heather, who actually said her name was Debbie, responded and drove to my house. We were ready to get it on when this big dude, who I'm told was her husband, comes into my room and roughs me up and demands three million in cash, or else he'll beat me to a pulp. Either that, or they'd call the cops and charge me with attempted rape."

I felt my stomach sink. "And then?"

"We were leaving when the Mexicans showed up and shot the dude."

I looked up and saw Heather walk from the guest room to the bathroom.

"What do you want to know, Jimmy?"

"It's about Sheila. You were with her at that bar near Mount Whitney, and you slapped my drink out of my hand."

"Sorry about that."

"Are you working for her?"

"Not anymore," I said.

"Well, I want to know if she was behind some of the shit that went down."

"Here's the deal, Jimmy. I was hired by Sheila, but she hasn't paid me, which means our contract is null and void. So I'm free to tell you all I know. I'm willing to do so if you'll pay what she owes me."

"How much is that?"

"About thirty grand. Plus whatever it takes to fix my truck."

"You mean the one shot to shit?"

"That's right."

"Thirty grand, huh? That's pretty steep. But I feel like I owe you for killing those assholes, so I don't mind. You want to come over to my place?"

"What time?"

"Make it in the afternoon."

• • •

Heather walked into my kitchen wearing fitted jeans and high heels. She had done her hair and applied makeup to her eye. Her shirt was the same pink number she wore earlier, but at least this time she'd put on a bra. Just the same, my breath caught in my throat, and I felt an electric buzz course through my groin.

"I guess I better get going," she said.

I carried her bag outside and set it in the back seat of her car.

"Here's my card. Call me and let me know how you're doing."

She smiled and thanked me and drove away. As I watched her car disappear, I told myself the person inside was flawed, and that she was nothing but trouble. That's what my mind said, but my body kept declaring otherwise. I went in my garage and did four sets of curls, hoping to reroute my blood flow. Then I gassed up Cody's Dodge, and began driving to Reno.

47

When Mort answered his cell, he could tell his connection at the security outfit in Reno was getting nervous.

"I finally got through to your number. But this is the last time," the man named Joe said. "I traced it to this address," he said, reading it to Mort. "Whatever you do, you didn't get it from me. Right?"

"Of course," Mort said, his eyes dilating as he scribbled down the address.

After unfolding a map and finding the street, he checked the shoebox he always kept near him. The lump of plastic explosive was still there, along with the rest of the components he'd assembled. A sense of calm came over Mort. These items were his tools, the necessary instruments to do a job efficiently, the result of a well-thought-out plan. Now, he just had to hope Jimmy was still at the address.

Hurrying, he dressed in his costume, sans the beard, which no longer fit convincingly. He put his survival knife in its leather sheath and looked in the mirror. The frustrations of the last few weeks were in the past. It was time to focus his energies on the present.

The noontime traffic was heavy, and he crawled down the main thoroughfare, hitting every light. The skies above Reno had turned gloomy again, after a brief clearing the day before. This morning a thin layer of snow coated the ground. Mort clenched his fist, looking at the cracked skin around his knuckles, brought on by the cold and the dry desert air.

He made it to the freeway and took the exit for 431, and within fifteen minutes turned into a newly built subdivision. The homes were large, and none were exactly alike, but they all shared the same color scheme. The subdued but classy designs reminded Mort of the house he used to own.

At the end of the subdivision, the street steepened and led to a house set apart from the others. It sat on a plateau overlooking rolling hills and, in the distance, the Reno cityscape. His pulse quickened when he saw the orange Lamborghini Diablo parked in the driveway.

Mort drove past the house slowly. Because it was built on top of a rise, there was no ideal spot for surveillance. He coasted down the hill a bit and parked where the road flattened, near a stand of white birch surrounded by heavy brush. A small trail led into the scrub, and when he was sure no one from the nearby houses was watching, he left his car for the trees and hiked a hundred yards down the trail.

From this vantage point, Mort could see the rear of the big house, the swimming pool, and the well-maintained lawn and landscaping. He was roughly 150 feet away and could barely make out a flicker of light through the sliding glass doors off the deck—most likely from a television, he thought. He crouched and waited thirty long minutes, hoping to confirm that Jimmy was there and was alone. A light blinked on and off from a small window, probably a bathroom. Mort returned to his car and drove back up the hill. He peered at the front of the house and regretted it was daylight. But he'd waited long enough for the opportunity and was not about to risk losing Jimmy again. He opened his shoebox and spilled the bottle of chloroform onto a hotel hand towel. Then he walked to the front door.

48

THE COST TO REPLACE and install two tires was double what Rancour expected. His wallet, comfortably fat the day before, was now reduced to at most another two days' living expenses.

"Fuck me," he said, riding away from the repair shop. It was early afternoon, and he'd not yet eaten. He stopped at a chain restaurant and powered down a chili cheeseburger with fries and onion rings, and washed it down with two beers. He leaned back and relaxed after he finished eating. Sanzini's black leather jacket lay next to him in the booth. The coat had served him well. Rancour figured he'd dispose of it when he got back to San Jose—which might be sooner rather than later, unless he was able to score some cash in a hurry.

From the pay phone out front, he dialed his buddy at the security agency.

"Hey man, I need to know where Jimmy Homestead is, or I'm gonna have to call this thing off."

"Like I told you, it's becoming a problem. How much you gonna guarantee me?"

"Minimum a thousand," Rancour said.

"Call me back in a half an hour."

Killing time, he cruised around downtown, checking out girls on the street, and he almost stopped at a strip joint. But he rode on and eventually found himself in a run-down apartment neighborhood. He watched a woman with droopy eyes and a cigarette dangling from her lips throw a bag of trash in a Dumpster. A man with a huge beer gut covered by a dirty white T-shirt yelled something at her, a cigar clenched between his teeth. Two grease-smeared black men wrenched on a junker next to the curb, while the cry of a baby sounded from a broken window bound with masking tape. A scattering of beer cans and a shattered whiskey bottle littered a nearby patch of lawn.

It all reminded Rancour of his childhood, a piecemeal blur of Tennessee foster homes. He'd run away from the last, after telling his foster parents he wished them dead. He eventually came to California, his wry grin in place no matter what life threw at him. He didn't ask for much—never had. A bedroll, the clothes on his back, and enough scratch for smokes, food, and a few brews. An odd job here or there, maybe snatch a purse or boost a car when the opportunity presented itself. If things got a little sketchy, he could always just move on, down the road to the next town.

But then he got popped and spent fifteen months in the can. Not a big deal, it was an occupational hazard. Except when he hit the streets, he was flat-ass broke, and his parole officer said he had to get a steady job and a permanent address. He went with the program at first, trying to fit the mold. Sure, his warehouse job had been a joke, and the rent money he paid each month was for a squalid boardinghouse room. He didn't mind it, though. He saw it all as temporary. If today was grim, there was always tomorrow. Such was life—an unstoppable chain of negative and positive events, mostly beyond his control or influence. Whoever thought up "shit happens" was right on the money.

He remembered a beautiful sixteen-year-old girl he banged on a blanket one night in a park. She still made his heart ache a bit, but he knew that nothing is permanent, so why sweat it? She was an opportunity, and there would be more. The good times would come again, when he'd ride victory laps with his dick hard, leaving his adversaries awestruck and bitter. His gut told him his time would be coming soon. And it would be in the way of a big cash score, courtesy of Lotto winner Jimmy Homestead.

He imagined the reaction from his dumb-ass roommates when he rolled back home, his pockets stuffed with cash. He'd throw his clothes in a bag and tell them they could keep the shabby furniture in his room, since he'd be upgrading. When they asked questions, he'd smile and wink and let them wonder. Maybe he'd piss all over Sanzini's jacket and leave it with them. Then, after heading south to San Diego or maybe Santa Fe, he'd call Sanzini and tell him he could go pick it up.

Rancour found a pay phone at a gas station on the outskirts of town, and his friend read him the address where Jimmy charged a cable movie. Bingo - it was that easy. When he hung up, Rancour looked out at the vast desert landscape. The sun rested high over a jagged collection of ridgelines, its heat stifled behind the heavy skies. Then the clouds parted and the shadows lifted into the heavens, and the surface of the land was bathed in warm light. Rancour stood watching for a long moment and swore he heard horns playing in the background.

49

SPORTING A NEW HERRINGBONE sport coat, pink shirt, and tasseled loafers, John stood outside the auto garage and listened to Jimmy rev the Lamborghini's motor. Jimmy dumped the clutch and left two black rows of rubber on the road as he roared away. John shook his head, trying to remember what it felt like to be an irresponsible, crazy teenager. Then he remembered Jimmy was in his mid-thirties.

When John pulled up to the Cadillac dealership, the LTD sputtered and coughed after he turned off the ignition, and the motor continued to run until it finally died with a loud bang. Two of the younger salesmen tried unsuccessfully to stifle their laughter. John ignored them and found the elderly, black manager he had spoken to before.

"How much will you give me for my trade in?" John said.

The man smiled. "I'll take her out back and shoot her and bury her, free of charge."

John laughed and they started in on the paperwork. Jimmy had called earlier to arrange for the dealer to accept his credit card. After signing forms for an hour, John took a break and removed his personal effects from the glove box of the LTD. A bottle of aspirin, a few stray diet pills, and his small, semiautomatic handgun. It had lain untouched since John had put it there, after Mort first called him. He dropped it inside the pocket of his blazer, the weight heavy on his chest, and went back into the dealership.

It was past lunch hour when he drove off in a brand-new, red, $65,000 Caddy sedan. It was a splendid car, with fat leather seats and a variety of fancy electronic features. The ride was so smooth John felt like he was sitting on his living room sofa. He took her for a spin, marveling at the feel, watching people check him out.

He stopped to eat after Jimmy didn't answer his cell. The restaurant he chose had tables set with wine glasses and fine silver. They seated him next to a window so he could look out at his car. The waitress was an attractive middle-aged brunette, and after bringing him a salad and a small steak, she stayed and chatted for a while. John flirted with her, his confidence soaring with every word. He felt like a million bucks. He grinned at the thought, and when he finished eating he went to the bar, ordered a gin, and shot the breeze with the waitress some more. He was feeling so good he actually asked her out. When he left the place with her phone number, his face was glowing.

He drove home and parked his car in the driveway next to Jimmy's Lamborghini. Side by side, the two cars looked like a glitzy testament to opposing lifestyles; the Lamborghini, wild and sexy, and the Cadillac, comfortable and elegant. And the battered old Ford John left for the car dealer to dispose of, what did that represent? An aging loser on his last legs, but that person had been reborn today, as a charming fifty-year-young man of sophistication and wealth. John walked to the front door, his step lively, his keys jingling in his pocket.

"Hey, Jimmy! Come check it out!" he said, walking into the empty living room. John took the clicker from the coffee table and turned off the television. "Jimmy!" He walked around the downstairs rooms, then went up the stairs, listening for the shower. But it was quiet.

"Jimmy?"

At the end of the hallway, the door to the master bedroom was closed. John knocked, then slowly pushed it open. "Son?"

In the corner of the room, Jimmy sat tied to a chair, his mouth duct-taped shut. His pants were bunched around his ankles, and more duct tape covered his crotch. Plastic restraints secured his limbs to the chair. His eyes were wild, and he jerked his head to the right.

A blur of motion from behind the door startled John, and he instinctively raised his arms. A man leapt toward him, jabbing with a knife. The blade caught John inside his coat, penetrating deeply into the flesh under his armpit. John staggered back, blood soaking his shirt. The man holding the knife was overweight and wearing glasses, but when John looked into his green eyes, he immediately recognized the brother he hadn't seen in years.

John stared at Mort, his lips struggling to form words. "You lousy…," he said finally, pulling the automatic from his coat pocket.

Mort lunged at John again with the knife. John dodged back, pointed the gun, and pulled the trigger. The bullet popped a small round hole in the plastic of the phony protruding gut that served as Mort's disguise. Mort froze, his eyes raging with shock and desperation, then he tried once more to stab John. The blade nicked John's shoulder as he fired a second time, hitting Mort in the upper chest. Mort's hands dropped, and John grappled with him and shoved him out the door.

The two men hit the railing to the staircase, the wood splintering under their weight. They fell hard onto the wooden stairs, and John rode Mort's body to the tile below. John pushed himself upright, dripping in blood. He clenched his arm tightly to his body, trying to stem the flow from the gash in his armpit. Mort lay on the floor, wheezing in pain, his fake glasses gone, the diagonal scar across his cheek glowing like an unhealed wound. Stumbling up, John searched his pockets for his cell phone, but it was gone. He limped out the front door, his car keys in his hand.

He fell into his Cadillac, his shirt sticking to his body like wet paint. Pools of blood began forming in the stitching of the leather seat. John knew he would bleed to death if he didn't get to a hospital. No cell phone. He needed a doctor. An ambulance. Someone who could help him.

He fumbled the key into the ignition and lurched down the driveway in reverse. He collided with something and heard a thump and the screech of metal twisting, and then a great, thunderous blast, the whoosh of air rocking the sedan on its shocks. When he looked in his rearview mirror, he saw a fuzzy tangle of color. His eyes fell shut, and his consciousness faded as the car bounced over a curb and rolled slowly away.

• • •

His body convulsing in pain, Mort knew he didn't have long. Images from his past flickered in his mind like a surreal slide show. The tenement apartment where he spent his years as a child. The failure of his company and the cell at Folsom. His father turning purple, his eyes pleading for mercy, before he jerked one final time and lay still. Mort summoned the last of his energy and rolled onto his side. He felt the button of the remote activator in his hip pocket compress, and a second later, the explosion blew out his eardrums. Burning debris from above rained down on him, but he felt nothing. You done good, boy, a strange voice said. For a brief moment he was happy, then he felt a strong, persistent sensation of downward momentum, as if gravity was pulling him into the floor. He opened his mouth in protest, but no words came.

50

The nurse at the hospital told me Cody was getting some tests done and wouldn't be checking out until later in the day. I drove back to the freeway, and after a few minutes took the exit to Route 431. The summit field of Mount Rose loomed ten miles ahead, covered in snow. I thought idly about the upcoming ski season, then considered my truck was totaled and my next mortgage payment would exhaust my bank account, unless Jimmy was actually willing to pay me as we'd discussed. I considered that far from a given.

When I came around the bend and over the small rise toward Jimmy's rental pad, I saw a motorcycle coming toward me. It was moving slowly, as if the rider was searching for an address. The bike had long forks, and the man on it wore a black leather jacket. It was Garrett Rancour.

I shook my head and sighed. Of all the screwy things. I assumed he was here to collect the money he claimed Jimmy owed him. But then he stopped next to a silver Toyota parked down the street. He seemed inordinately interested in the car, removing his helmet and staring as if perplexed. I pulled over and parked about fifty feet from Jimmy's curved, steep driveway. Over a short row of bushes, I could see the orange Lamborghini, and next to it a large, red sedan. My intention was to walk up the driveway while Rancour was distracted. I saw no benefit in conversing with the dude. But he spotted me, and pulled his helmet back on.

From the front of the house, I heard a car door close. Rancour fixed his eyes on me, juiced his throttle, and turned up the driveway while I was still on the street. What happened next transpired so quickly all I could do was watch in disbelief. The red sedan jetted down the driveway in reverse. Rancour had no time to avoid it. The rear bumper of the car hit him head on, snapping his forks and flipping him and his Honda over the trunk lid. The motorcycle smashed into the rear window, and Rancour bounced off the car's roof and was flung like a rag doll. His body slammed face down on the pavement.

The sedan continued in reverse, as if the driver was unaware he'd hit anything. I ran toward where Rancour lay. His head was cocked at an odd angle, his arm twisted behind his back. Just as I reached him, a huge blast from the house blew a chunk of the second-story roof into the sky. The concussion knocked me to the ground.

I pushed myself to my feet and saw the red car roll over the curb on the opposite side of the street. It went down a short hillside and stopped when it crashed into a backyard fence. I started toward the car, then stopped and went back to Rancour. No pulse. His neck was broken.

I looked up at the house. Smoke was billowing from the hole in the roof, and tongues of flame were lapping at the shingles. The front door was wide open. I ran inside and nearly tripped over a dead body at the base of the stairs. It stopped me in my tracks. The agony etched across the corpse's face was beyond anything I'd witnessed. The dead man's lips were twisted in a snarl, exposing yellowish teeth spotted with blood. An ear was burned to a stub, and while one eye was squeezed shut, the other was bulbous and staring, the eyelid and surrounding skin burnt away to reveal the entirety of the eyeball. A charred black stain outlined the body, as if he'd burned to death, but most of his flesh was intact.

I swallowed hard and went up the stairs to the smoke-filled room at the end of the hall. The walls were scorched and smoldering, and the king-size bed had been upended, the mattress leaning against a wall and feeding the flames. Scraps of kindling littered the floor, probably the remains of a large dresser or desk.

In the far corner of the room, propped upright on a collapsed chair, sat a figure unrecognizable save for the long blond hair falling almost daintily around what was left of his face. The smoke was thick and obscured the extent of his injuries, but when I stepped into the room my foot hit something. It was a severed leg.

A nightstand had somehow survived the explosion mostly intact. Its doors were open, and a black leather bag lay partially inside. Embers had burned a small hole at the end of the bag, revealing what looked like a stack of papers. Covering my mouth with my shirt, my eyes tearing and burning, I grabbed the bag, thinking to save whatever documents it contained from the fire.

Outside, I locked the satchel in the covered bed of Cody's truck and called 911. A crowd was gathering to watch the fire. It took the fire trucks only a couple of minutes to arrive, but by that time the upstairs was fully ablaze. Thick smoke poured from the roof and the windows, the wood crackling and popping, ash floating into the sky. A section of gutter broke free from the roofline and tumbled down, coming to rest across the hood of the Lamborghini.

The medics started for the front door. "Two bodies, one upstairs, one down. Both dead," I told them. They paused, then went in and pulled out the first man. The onlookers gasped, and the medics quickly covered the body. Soon enough the fire was under control, the house dripping with water, the downstairs flooded. A large portion of the second story had collapsed, leaving a gaping void in the structure. The room where the party ended for Jimmy Homestead no longer existed.

The driver of the red Cadillac was removed from his car and loaded into an ambulance. I went to get a look at him but was grabbed from behind.

"I can't wait to hear your story this time," Lieutenant Gordon DeHart said.

"I'm just an innocent bystander, Lieutenant. A good Samaritan."

"Is that the best you can come up with? You disappoint me."

"Life's full of disappointments."

"You don't know the half of it," he said, then cuffed my wrists and took me away.

51

THIS TIME DEHART KEPT me locked up at Reno Central for two days. When I asked what the charges were, he didn't answer directly, but muttered something about class-A felonies. Each morning he broke the monotony by bringing me to an interview room for questioning. He kept trying to figure out the relationships and connections between all the involved parties, be they living or dead. I wasn't much help to him. The only thing he accomplished was to reveal more to me than I otherwise would have known.

"John Homestead regained consciousness, and it looks like he's going to make it," DeHart said.

"What's he have to say?"

"Well, the body the paramedics pulled from the house was John's estranged brother, Mort. Supposedly he was trying to coerce Jimmy into paying him off. We assume he was the source of the plastic explosives."

"I doubt he knew what he was doing. He probably didn't mean to blow the house apart," I said.

"Who knows?" DeHart said, shrugging. "From all accounts, the guy was a whackjob."

"I assume John Homestead is first in line to inherit Jimmy's fortune," I said.

"Probably."

"What's Sanzini got to say?"

"Not much. When I told him Garrett Rancour died, he asked if he was wearing a black jacket. Said it belonged to him."

"It does. You should return it to him."

"Sure thing. I'll put that right at the top of my priority list."

"You know, Lieutenant, I get the feeling you don't intend to charge me with anything."

"I still consider you a person of interest, Reno. Don't make yourself scarce. I hope you enjoyed the free room and board?"

"Yes, it was splendid," I said, but instead of smiling, DeHart looked at me like he'd seen too much too recently, and was sick of it all.

• • •

A freezing rain was coming down when DeHart dropped me off at the impound yard where they stored Cody's truck while I was a guest of the city. Cody had stayed at my house since his release from the hospital, and he was there holding down the fort when I called.

"It's snowing here, Dirt. Take it easy coming over the pass."

"Did you drink all my booze yet?"

"Of course not! There's a shot or two left in your whiskey bottle."

"Well, I'm broke and I want to get drunk. How about my six-pack of beer?"

"I seem to have a vague recollection of seeing a six-pack. Budweisers, weren't they?"

"That's right."

"Yes, now I remember. They went down quite smoothly with the pizza in your freezer. I hope you weren't saving that for a special occasion?"

It was slow going over Spooner Summit. The late October storm shrouded the pass in a ghostly mist, obscuring the road and at times creating a near whiteout. I drove on slowly, alone in the elements. I'd had plenty of time for reflection during the empty hours in the Reno jail, but I'd drawn few hard conclusions. Regarding Jimmy Homestead and his demise, I didn't know whose side to take, or even if there was a side to take. I didn't fault Sanzini for his motivations, although by involving the Mexican gang, he unwittingly perpetuated their deaths and his own demise. He would pay the price for his stupidity in the Nevada prison system. As for Garrett Rancour, I thought of him as a petty crook looking for a big score. Although he put himself in the wrong place at the wrong time, he probably didn't deserve to die. He just had bad luck.

I felt more sympathy for Heather Sanderson, though my thoughts were no doubt skewed by images of her naked body. Lustful issues aside, I believed Heather was an example of a decent person dragged down to the level of her bad husband. If in some way her actions predicated his death, it was probably justified in the cosmic scheme of things. Actually, she may have been one of the few to benefit from the events surrounding Jimmy's downfall. With her husband gone, she could begin life anew.

Whatever angles John Homestead and his brother Mort were playing, it was clear their end games were the same—to take Jimmy's money. The plight of the two desperate brothers seemed sad and pathetic. From what DeHart told me of Mort Homestead, he would not be missed. On the other hand, John Homestead, after nearly bleeding to death, would probably soon have new friends coming out of the woodwork, since he was first in line to inherit Jimmy's fortune. I had no idea if he was deserving or not, and frankly, I didn't care. I had my own problems to deal with.

The snowplows hadn't yet cleared the main drag in South Lake Tahoe. I drove past the casinos slowly, the bright lights flickering and promising good times and easy money. A group of tourists walked the boulevard in shirtsleeves, seemingly oblivious to the weather. As I crossed the state line into California, the sun peeked out from a break in the clouds and quickly retreated. It started snowing harder.

My truck was parked in front of my home. A tire was flat, and snow had fallen through the caved-in windshield, coating the interior. When I walked inside, Cody hauled himself off my couch and gave me a once-over.

"You look like you lost a few pounds," he said.

"I didn't find the baloney sandwiches and mashed potatoes all that appetizing."

"Here," he said, pitching me a can of beer. "Welcome back to the land of the free."

I drank the beer while showering the jailhouse funk off my body, then threw on clean clothes and went to my fridge to grab another.

"I got to head back to San Jose tomorrow, Dirt."

"I may be joining you," I said. "I think I'll put the place up for sale next month."

"That bad, huh?"

"Yeah." I sat on the kitchen counter and finished my beer, then reached over and grabbed the fifth of bourbon next to the oven. Contrary to Cody's claim, it was empty.

"Hey," he said. "Let's head over to Whiskey Dick's. I'm buying."

"All right," I said, and hopped off the counter. "Give me a minute, though." I went out front, unlocked Cody's bed cover, and reached in and pulled out the leather bag I'd rescued from the fire in Jimmy's room.

"What's that?" Cody said when I walked back inside, dusting snowflakes off my shoulders.

"This was sitting near Jimmy's body. The place was burning down, so I grabbed it." I set it on the couch and unzipped the bag. Cody and I stood looking at the contents. It became very quiet. I tentatively reached inside and grasped a packet of hundred-dollar bills.

"Ten grand," I said. I held the bills up to the light for a long moment. Then I dumped the bag, and we began counting.

After a minute we looked up and our eyes locked. "Fuckin-A," Cody said.

"Almost a million dollars," I said.

Cody broke the seal on one of the bundles and tossed the bills in the air. "Happy days are here again!" he shouted.

I blinked and stared at the cash scattered about my coffee table and floor.

"Jimmy Homestead has no more need for it, Dirt," Cody said, his hand squeezing my shoulder.

"It rightfully belongs to John Homestead."

"Screw that. It's the spoils of war. We both put our lives on the line. We earned it."

I couldn't argue with his logic and didn't try. We split the money down the middle and headed out on the town, the new high rollers on the block. It took a few stiff drinks before my shock faded and I settled into the realization that I could keep my home and buy a new truck. Cody sat next to me, his face flushed with alcohol. He winked and toasted me, the expression on his mug confident and serene, as if he knew all along how things would turn out. I thought back to everything that had happened over the last four weeks and shook my head. Christ, what a way to make a living.

EPILOGUE

BY THANKSGIVING THE MOUNTAINS surrounding Lake Tahoe were covered with a record early season snowfall. The curvy, dark-haired woman I'd met when Cody and I were in Elko called, inquiring about the ski conditions. She showed up the next day, snowboard in hand, and after we got reacquainted, I took her to South Lake Tahoe's ski resort. It was a midweek blue-sky day, the slopes choked with fresh powder. We came off the summit chair at ten thousand feet and stopped a little way down the trail.

"My god, look at the view," she said. From our vantage point, we could see a wide panorama of Lake Tahoe and the surrounding Sierra Nevada mountain range. The sky was cloudless and azure above the snowcapped peaks. Highway 50 was clearly visible, the casinos at the state line dwarfed by the immensity of the landscape. She threw a handful of powder at me, and I followed her along the ridge until we came around a bend to where the mountainside fell away. Three thousand feet below us lay the Great Basin Desert, which extended for four hundred lonely, windswept miles across Nevada to Salt Lake City. The desert floor was brown and empty, as if from another world.

• • •

The next day my cell rang with a number I didn't recognize.

"Mr. Reno, this is Lou Calgaretti. You may not know me—I'm a private investigator in South Lake Tahoe."

"I've heard of you," I said.

"And me of you. Here's why I'm calling. I've been retained by John Homestead to follow up on a few details pertaining to his son's death. I'm aware you were at one time employed by Sheila Majorie."

"That's correct."

"Well, as you may be aware, Mr. Homestead claims to be the sole heir to Jimmy Homestead's estate. If you don't mind, I have a few questions for you about Sheila."

"Shoot."

"Will you tell me for what purpose she hired you?"

"I don't see why not. She asked me to arrange a meeting with Jimmy. During the process it became clear she hoped to convince Jimmy to share his Lotto winnings with her. As far as I know, he never agreed to do so."

"And I'm under the same impression. I have a more specific question for you, though. Do you have any knowledge of Sheila being associated with Tony Sanzini or the Locos 14 gang?"

"I don't. Did you ask Sanzini?"

"He refuses to be interviewed."

"How about the members of Locos 14?" I said.

"As you might imagine, they are not being cooperative."

"I don't know what I can tell you, then."

The phone went silent for a moment, and when Lou Calgaretti spoke again, his voice sounded somewhat more formal. "John Homestead is willing to pay you, Mr. Reno, for disclosing legitimate evidence as to Sheila Majorie's involvement with any of the individuals linked to Jimmy's kidnapping or murder."

It was my turn to pause. "Why?" I asked.

"Sheila has petitioned the court, claiming inheritance rights."

"Based on what?"

"As it turns out, her divorce from John Homestead was never officially completed. Somehow the final paperwork was not signed and filed. She's found an attorney who I believe she's seduced, and..."

I started laughing.

• • •

I wished I could have helped Lou Calgaretti, but there was nothing I could reveal about Sheila he didn't already know. She had held her cards close to her chest, apparently for good reason. I believed she may have tried to orchestrate the death of her stepson, but I would never know the extent of her actions. Whatever she did, I doubted she'd be found accountable. Quite possibly she'd walk away with a healthy portion of Jimmy's money.

I hung Christmas lights on my house and stood on my deck looking out over the snow-covered meadow behind my backyard. A breeze whispered through the pines, and a plume of snowflakes drifted away with the wind. I invested myself in the moment and tried not to ruminate on a world where money was the measuring stick for success, and men lusted insatiably after nubile women until the last of their desire faded with age. As for my own moral code, it was pretty simple: I stayed loyal to my friends and treated others with respect unless they dictated otherwise. Whenever possible, I lived within the law and sought out the ethical high road. My conscience was clear, and I woke each morning looking forward to the promise of the day. I knew better than to ask for more.

ABOUT THE AUTHOR

BORN IN DETROIT, MICHIGAN, in 1960, Dave Stanton moved to Northern California in 1961. He attended San Jose State University and received a BA in journalism in 1983. Over the years, he worked as a bartender, newspaper advertising salesman, furniture mover, pizza cook, debt collector, and technology salesman. He has two children, Austin and Haley. He and his wife, Heidi, live in San Jose, California.

Stanton is the author of five novels, all featuring private investigator Dan Reno and his ex-cop buddy, Cody Gibbons.

To learn more, visit the author's website at **DanRenoNovels.com**

If you enjoyed *Dying for the Highlife*, please don't hesitate to leave a review on Amazon.com:

http://bit.ly/AmazonHighlife

To contact Dave Stanton or subscribe to his newsletter, go to:

http://danrenonovels.com/contact/

More Dan Reno Novels:

STATELINE

Cancel the wedding–the groom is dead.

When a tycoon's son is murdered the night before his wedding, the enraged and grief-stricken father offers investigator Dan Reno (that's *Reno,* as in *no problemo),* a life-changing bounty to find the killer. Reno, nearly broke, figures he's finally landed in the right place at the right time. It's a nice thought, but when a band of crooked cops get involved, Reno finds himself not only earning every penny of his paycheck, but also fighting for his life.

Who committed the murder, and why? And what of the dark sexual deviations that keep surfacing? Haunted by his murdered father and a violent, hard drinking past, Reno wants no more blood on his hands. But a man's got to make a living, and backing off is not in his DNA. Traversing the snowy alpine winter in the Sierras and the lonely deserts of Nevada, Reno must revert to his old ways to survive. Because the fat bounty won't do him much good if he's dead...

Speed Metal Blues

Bounty hunter Dan Reno never thought he'd be the prey.

It's a two-for-one deal when a pair of accused rapists from a New Jersey-based gang surface in South Lake Tahoe. The first is easy to catch, but the second, a Satanist suspected of a string of murders, is an adversary unlike any Reno has faced. After escaping Reno's clutches in the desert outside of

Carson City, the target vanishes. That is, until he makes it clear he intends to settle the score.

To make matters worse, the criminal takes an interest in a teenage boy and his talented sister, both friends of Reno's. Wading through a drug-dealing turf war and a deadly feud between mobsters running a local casino, Reno can't figure out how his target fits in with the new outlaws in town. He only knows he's hunting for a ghost-like adversary calling all the shots.

The more Reno learns more about his target, the more he's convinced that mayhem is inevitable unless he can capture him quickly. He'd prefer to do it clean, without further bloodshed. But sometimes that ain't in the cards, especially when Reno's partner Cody Gibbons decides it's time for payback.

Coming in 2015:

DARK ICE

HARD PREJUDICE

Made in United States
Orlando, FL
30 July 2022